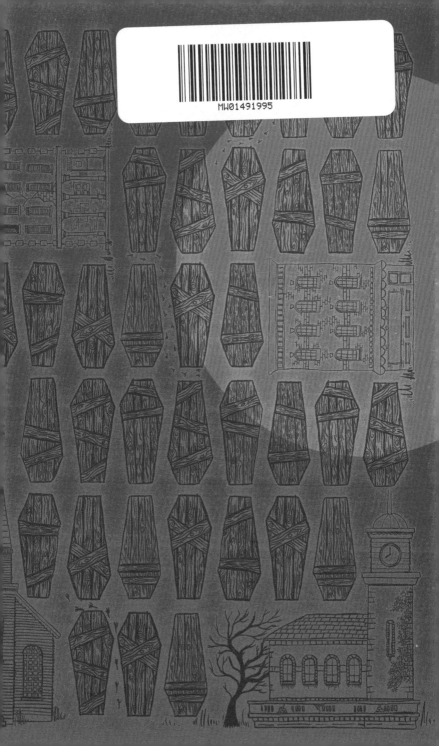

"Eric LaRocca is one of the best horror voices to emerge in the last few years. *We Are Always Tender with Our Dead* is his finest work to date, filled with relentless darkness, but beauty too. The story and characters will stay with you in your dreams long after you've finished it."

RICHARD KADREY, author of *The Pale House Devil* and the Sandman Slim series

"Blending the grotesque and the sublime, *We Are Always Tender with Our Dead* moves with the callous logic of a nightmare. LaRocca initiates us into his newest trilogy with a haunting meditation on affliction, grief, and the darkness that lurks beneath the bonds that tie—or trap—the residents of Burnt Sparrow to one another."

ELLE NASH, author of *Deliver Me* and *Gag Reflex*

"With *We Are Always Tender with Our Dead*, Eric LaRocca adds to his already remarkable body of work. Wielding his graceful prose with the deftness of a surgeon holding a scalpel, LaRocca cuts to the beating, bloody heart of a small New England town shocked by an act of unexpected brutality, then examines the network of consequences that results. In the process, he finds savagery, sorrow, beauty, and much, much more. The first in a trilogy, this novel signals an exciting new phase in Eric LaRocca's fiction. I can't wait for what comes next."

JOHN LANGAN, author of *Lost in the Dark and Other Excursions* and *The Fisherman*

"LaRocca is a maestro of the horrific, surreal, and uncanny, and his work never fails to illuminate the dark epicenter of the human condition while offering the suggestion of hope— maybe. Every tale is one that will leave you shaking and breathless, yet like a car wreck, you're helpless to look away."

RONALD MALFI, author of *Senseless* and *Come With Me*

*D*ear kindhearted reader,

    When I first approached Titan Books with the formal proposal of We Are Always Tender with Our Dead (Burnt Sparrow Book 1), I assured my editor that I would handle the very graphic subject matter I had planned to write with the utmost delicateness and sensitivity.

    I regret to inform you, dear reader, that I have failed miserably.

    However, I'm afraid I was always destined to fail in such a way when conveying these brutal and unpleasant subjects. There is nothing tasteful about incest, violence, and rape. These are truths of our existence—unpleasant matters that remain ubiquitous to our collective suffering as a species. Anyone who says they can write about such things with sensitivity and care is lying. These transgressions are not tasteful by their very nature. Of course, you may disagree; however, that's how I feel as an artist, as an author of horror fiction.

    Therefore, it's my unfortunate task to warn you that the book you are about to read is profoundly distasteful. It's certainly not a book that can (or even should) be enjoyed. At least not in the traditional sense. This novel contains graphic depictions of body horror, incest, sexual assault, animal cruelty, gun violence, murder, necrophilia, child sexual abuse, violent death of an infant, domestic abuse, torture, and bereavement.

    I have been encouraged by my very thoughtful editor to warn readers early on in case they might like to avoid such nastiness. If these things disturb enough to give you pause, I highly encourage you to seek entertainment elsewhere. This novel is not intended to entertain. I never set out to amuse or enthrall with my fiction. Instead, I hope to provoke, to elicit a reaction from my audience.

    If you are willing to join me, I thank you for your time and I sincerely look forward to greeting you on the other side.

ERIC LAROCCA
Newmarket, NH
November 2024

ERIC LaROCCA
BURNT SPARROW

We are always tender with our dead

TITAN BOOKS

Burnt Sparrow: We Are Always Tender with Our Dead
Hardback edition ISBN: 9781803368672
Signed Hardback edition ISBN: 9781835415764
Broken Binding edition ISBN: 9781835416679
Abominable Book Club edition ISBN: 9781835416686
E-book edition ISBN: 9781803368689

Published by Titan Books
A division of Titan Publishing Group Ltd
144 Southwark Street, London SE1 0UP
www.titanbooks.com

First edition: September 2025
10 9 8 7 6 5 4 3 2 1

This is a work of fiction. All of the characters, organizations,
and events portrayed in this novel are either products
of the author's imagination or are used fictitiously. Any
resemblance to actual persons, living or dead (except
for satirical purposes), is entirely coincidental.

A CIP catalogue record for this title is
available from the British Library.

EU RP (for authorities only)
eucomply OÜ, Pärnu mnt. 139b-14, 11317 Tallinn, Estonia
hello@eucompliancepartner.com, +3375690241

Set in Adobe Garamond by Richard Mason.

Printed and bound by CPI Group (UK) Ltd, Croydon CR0 4YY.

For Brian Evenson
A mentor, an inspiration, a dear friend

The threshold is the place to pause.

—GOETHE

TWO BURNT SPARROW RESIDENTS DIE IN HOUSE FIRE ON SWAMPSCOTT ROAD

Published March 3, 2004, in *The Burnt Sparrow Gazette*
Written by George McDowell, News Staff Reporter

Torch Darling (34) and Ruskin Cave (29) are reported to have perished in a house fire on Swampscott Road in the early hours of the morning on Tuesday, February 24. Both men were Burnt Sparrow residents.

The victims were found unconscious, kneeling together in the first-floor parlor when firefighters entered the house at about 2:45 a.m., officials said. At that time, Cave was declared dead on the scene. However, it's reported that Darling had a slight pulse when they inspected him. He was immediately rushed to a nearby hospital where he later died.

No cause of the fire has been determined yet. Autopsies will be performed on both men to determine the exact cause of death, said Fire Marshall Peter Blackwell.

The house belonged to Darling's grandfather named Henley Darling, who had passed away a few months prior to last Tuesday's house fire.

Torch Darling lived in the house by himself and hadn't worked in a long time, according to neighbors. He was also almost completely blind, they said, and seemed to have psychological problems.

Officials are investigating whether there was a third victim present at the time of the house fire.

"There are traces of a possible third party involved," Blackwell said. "Whether they started the fire and then fled the scene is uncertain. We're still investigating the area."

Blackwell also reports that his crew has uncovered a very peculiar imprint of a large bird seared into the remnants of the house.

Neighbors report that before his passing, Henley Darling purchased a rare bird from an exotic pet shop in the Boston area. Although the bird's remains have not yet been recovered, it's presumed that the creature perished in the fire as well.

Diary Entry Written By
RUPERT CROMWELL

March 26, 2004

I don't wish to confess anything to you. A confession implies that there's a semblance of guilt to be felt, a pang of humiliation to be tolerated for the sake of proper contrition. It implies I should crave to be absolved, to be forgiven for what I am, all I've done. I'm here to tell you there's nothing in this world that deserves my shame, my reflection, or my disgrace.

Perhaps once I might have deceived you and told you that I felt such embarrassment for how I've been perceived by others. Yes, even by people who claimed that they loved me. I might have told you how I owed them an explanation for my strangeness. I might have told you how I would give anything to bring them the honor they so rightfully deserve, the integrity that only a young man can offer his family. But such a statement would be utter trickery.

3

I cannot bring myself to tell you those things and make you think that I believe I'm at fault, that I'm some lowly, reprehensible thing, undeserving of the grace of a gentler person's forgiveness. I have spent so many years attempting to be tender in a world that will never understand softer languages like quietness, compassion. Perhaps once the world might have indulged in those kinds of whims, but it utterly refuses them now. Probably because soft things are easy to break. Moreover, soft things are so pleasing to break. It makes you feel like a stronger, more powerful person. That's how everyone wants to feel, especially when things seem so uncontrollable. We all want to feel as though we have the upper hand, that we have somehow evaded the callous, careless deity presiding over human affairs and have instead found meaning or purpose in all this exquisite pointlessness.

I regret to tell you there's nothing really to be found there. It's an empty sacrifice. There's nothing in this world that has meaning or shares any value. I've already been taught that human life holds no significance. It's sad to think how a corpse is very often worth more than a living thing. At least there's some value left in a dead body, however little, however insignificant. But what becomes of us when even the dead have little meaning? Perhaps that's when the world finally and truly rots. Either way, I'd give anything to watch this godforsaken place burn to the ground.

RUPERT
CROMWELL

December 2003

It's early in the morning—the dim whisper of a bloodshot sunrise leaking through the closed shutters like dark red smoke—two days after Christmas when Rupert Cromwell's father bursts into his bedroom and informs his son that "a backwards miracle has occurred."

At first, Rupert thinks he's dreaming.

His father never barges into his room, especially without the decency of knocking first.

Rupert stirs a little, pulling the bedsheets tighter and up over his head to block out some of the light leaking in from the hallway. But his father won't relent. Instead, he leans closer to him with a desperation that Rupert can sense, like when his father is caught in a lie. His father repeats himself once more. But Rupert doesn't answer. Instead, he's lost and unbound somewhere in the enchanted realm of twilight that bewitches the alert and conscious.

In his dream-like stupor, Rupert wonders what he was imagining that was too difficult to part with when his father first interrupted. Perhaps he was dreaming of the Christmas muffins they enjoyed, lathered with butter. Maybe he was imagining the gifts he had asked for from his father that he knew wouldn't appear beneath their tiny Christmas tree. Or perhaps, more likely, Rupert was dreaming of those magical Christmases he had spent with his mother, what now feels like eons ago—the hot chocolate they had warmed on the stove, the gingerbread homes they had gleefully built, the carols they had sung even though Rupert's father wouldn't join in the fun.

Although Rupert had tried to keep her spirit alive during the Christmas after she died, he knew he was incapable of completely resurrecting her delight, her liveliness, her essence. Now, several years after her passing, he doesn't even bother to make the effort. Much of the Christmas he endured this year was spent reclining in bed, and nursing an awful head cold which seemed to poison him completely and rob him of his remaining hopefulness for a cheery holiday season.

He sniffles a little, clearing some of the snot from his nose and scowling when he tastes it in the back of his throat. Even with his eyes firmly closed, he can still feel his father's presence lingering near the foot of the bed. He listens to the floorboards screech like newborn bluebirds while his father paces the small room, his weight shifting from one board to the next. He contemplates if his father were imagining the pleasure of prying up some of the wooden planks and cramming Rupert's body beneath them.

Although he knows in his heart that his father would never

intentionally hurt him, there's a distrustful part of him that doesn't know how to act around him. When they talk to one another, it feels as though they're speaking different languages. Rupert hasn't trusted anyone since his mother passed away three years ago. Although his father attempts to make an effort from time to time, Rupert has already closed away so many parts of himself to tenderness, sympathy, and affection. He's been told he's especially difficult for a seventeen-year-old boy, but he refuses to pay attention to any criticism considering all he's endured in such a short time span.

Rupert wonders if his father is making some sort of gesture—some absurd, almost comical signal—to bond with him. Rupert can't be too certain while he's buried in blankets and drifting in and out of sleep. But he wonders if this surprise morning visit is some kind of new ritual for father and son. Even if it is a feeble attempt from his father to crawl further into Rupert's mind, Rupert wants no part in the spectacle, especially before the arrival of daylight.

"Didn't you hear me?" his father asks him, leaning close enough so that Rupert can taste the warmth, the rancor of his fetid breath. "Something's happened…"

But what does Rupert care? He knows his Christmas has been wasted thanks to his sudden illness. While he's on the mend, he's still groggy and feverish. He hasn't been eating much lately either. His father knows all of this. *So, why does he insist on bothering me?*

Before Rupert can grab the bedsheets and pull them tighter, his father snatches the blankets from him and hauls them off the bed until they're crumpled in a heap on the floor. Rupert senses himself becoming more and more alert. For a moment, he stirs there, wondering if his father had really done that. His father is usually never so forceful, so unrestrained with him. There had been times when Rupert had imagined his father might have enjoyed the prospect of manhandling him so that Rupert would obey; however, it seems so ludicrous to happen now, after all these years. When Rupert realizes he's not going back to sleep anytime soon, he shoots up from dozing and stares at his father, begging him for an answer.

"Quick," his father says. "Get dressed."

Rupert glances at the alarm clock on the nightstand. 5:34 a.m.

He groans, slamming himself against the mattress and rolling over on his side until he's facing away.

"It's not even six o'clock yet," Rupert whines, his throat itching and burning. "I'm still sick."

But his father's already at the room's threshold, flicking on the switch. Light floods the small bedroom and Rupert winces, shielding his eyes.

"Ten minutes," his father says. "We'll be late."

"Late for what?" Rupert asks, straightening once more.

However, it's no use. His father has already moved out of the room and is hurrying down the narrow corridor, summoned by some soundless whistle.

Rupert sits in silence for a while, going over the possible scenarios in his mind, wondering what he could possibly do or say to get out of this. It's not that he doesn't want to be around his father. He would at the very least be honest with himself and confess that truth if it were accurate. But it's not. The truth is that Rupert plans to leave home when he turns eighteen and he doesn't want to feel homesick for a place he never truly connected with anyway. He's afraid of the surprise of a tender moment between father and son. He dreads the possibility of his father showing him that he's kind and gentle and giving—all the things his beloved mother was before she died. How unfair would it be for Rupert and his father to become close and bonded just before Rupert finally left town?

He doesn't want to indulge that thought. It upsets him too much. He's keeping his father at a distance for the foreseeable future. Any attachment, any connection could make it difficult for him to move on. Just like the connection he felt for his mother. He has already spent the last three years undoing that particular invisible thread, and he'll be damned before he allows another one to be fastened in its place.

With so much reluctance, Rupert slides off the bed and ambles toward the dresser situated in the corner of the room. He clears some of the phlegm in his throat—burning when he swallows—and he comes upon a small, framed photograph of him and his mother at the church rummage sale the summer before she passed away. In the photo, she's kneeling in front of an old vehicle that looks like it belongs in a silent movie. Rupert is at her side, making a goofy face to the unseen photographer and pointing at the car's headlights, which look like the eyes of some prehistoric insect.

As he gazes at the photo, he senses the firmer, more guarded parts of himself beginning to thaw. However, before his guard melts completely, he pushes the photograph behind some small bottles of cologne until it's partially hidden. His mother's face—her warm, inviting smile—obscured for now and ready to be admired again when he's ready, when he's feeling a little less vulnerable and prone to weepiness.

He certainly doesn't want to cry today. Or any day, for that matter. He's closed himself off for so long, he wonders if he'd even be able to cry if he wanted to. Rupert thinks of indulging in his misery for a moment, but he knows he can't with his father waiting for him. He slips on a shirt and a pair of pants, sliding into black socks. His father never told him exactly how to dress or what to expect, so Rupert certainly hopes he doesn't anticipate anything overly formal. His finger suddenly loops through a giant hole in the bottom hem of his shirt that he hasn't noticed before. He sighs, realizing it's probably time to buy some new clothes. Everything he owns is so tattered and worn—gifts from his mother so many years ago. He grimaces, wondering if throwing out the shirt she had once bought for him might be an insult to her memory.

When he's finished dressing, he stares at himself in the floor-length mirror beside the door. He's a little thinner than he'd like to be, the lines of his ribcage visible through the thinness of his skin when he poses a certain way. Some of the kids used to make fun of him at school for the crooked shape of his nose and how it curves like the beak of some bird, but they don't comment much more on his appearance ever since his mother passed away. Rupert figures that his classmates concede he's already suffered enough. He laughs, amused at the thought that even high schoolers are able to realize "enough is enough."

He wishes he had less body hair. So much of the hair on his chest and underneath his arms is completely unmanageable and makes him feel like a wild animal. He's tried to shave himself a few times, but the discomfort is not worth the price of momentarily accepting himself. Not to mention his hair seems to grow back darker and thicker than before, almost like his body were attempting to tell him that it's been insulted, besmirched.

Sometimes he stands in front of the mirror for hours and picks apart his naked reflection—from the scrawniness of his arms to his spotty-looking face to the smallness of his genitals. He often wishes he were someone else. Moreover, he often wishes he were somewhere else.

Anywhere but here: the dreadful town of Burnt Sparrow.

———

Rupert hesitates slightly, slowing as he shrugs himself into a plain black T-shirt. He lifts his bedroom window, cold air blasting him in the face. It's just then that Rupert comes to the peculiar realization that he can no longer smell the fetid stench of sulfur lingering in the air. He clears his nose with a tissue and smells the air once more. For the first time in what feels like an eternity, the scent is completely absent—those three-hundred-year-old contaminated spirits once dwelling at the abandoned town mill now completely and utterly gone. *But to where?*

The town of Burnt Sparrow has been clouded by the odor of sulfur for as long as he can remember. It seems so curious for the air not to hang heavy with that poisonous scent, not to churn with that loathsome, unbearable stink. He can't recall a moment from his childhood when he didn't have to plug his nose at the God-awful smell—the very scent of the town's failure: a large paper factory that's been abandoned for as long as he's been alive.

He always thinks of his father whenever the town's ancient paper factory creeps into his mind. He recalls how his father used to entertain him with gruesome tales of incidents he had witnessed while working at the factory before it finally closed. There was one story in particular that has always haunted Rupert—a story about one of the mill workers who had his arm seized and caught in one of the large printing machines. His father had told him how several line men rushed to the poor man's rescue while he thrashed there, screeching until hoarse as his arm slid further and further into the mouth of the machine before his bone finally snapped apart. Rupert grimaces whenever he reflects on how his father described the miserable sight of the poor, wretched thing—his empty, tattered sleeve dangling there and leaking dark blood all over the concrete floor.

Burnt Sparrow seems to be a place where the awful and the inevitable occur—a dreadful, haunted place. Rupert often laments and wonders if his very presence has somehow upset the balance of the community throughout the time that he's been a resident. His father is always so eager to remind him how the paper factory shuttered the very same week he was born. Rupert often wonders if the town has always been a dark, evil place, or if it's rather the sum of its miserable inhabitants.

He questions if perhaps his father, too, recognizes the very same absent smell of sulfur. He wonders if his mother might have noticed the absent smell as well. She was always so quick to complain about the lingering stench of rot that surrounded the town. She often told Rupert tales of how the scent of sulfur lingered in Burnt Sparrow long before the mill was first built in the late 1800s. Although Rupert's father openly detested it, his mother was always so keen to tell stories—to share folk tales that had been passed down through her family.

Rupert's mother had told him time and time again that Rupert was a natural born storyteller. Rupert wanted to believe this. He had dabbled with writing at school and had written several short stories for class contests that he regrettably did not win. From time to time, Rupert thinks about sitting at the desk in his bedroom and forcing himself to write a story he's been considering for quite some time—a tale about two people in love who continue to hurt one another again and again and again. He thinks of how he'd start the story—the careful way in which he'd construct the narrative. But inspiration never makes its presence known. He wants so desperately to honor his mother and tell a proper story, the way she often told him tales at bedtime. Rupert often worries he's not been endowed with the gift of storytelling as his mother once was.

Regardless, his beloved mother was always assuring him that he possessed the natural gift of a venerated scribe like Faulkner or Beckett. In the few months following her demise, Rupert had tried to write. He tried to tell stories that he thought his mother might once have enjoyed. But nothing seemed possible. It was as though a spigot had been fastened shut inside his mind—a doorway, a kind of threshold that could never be crossed again.

Rupert knows everything about thresholds. Standing at them and not going anywhere, that is. He often feels as though he's permanently fixed at a precipice, smelling the sweet scent of freedom drifting from elsewhere but never able to actually partake. If only he were brave enough to take that first step—to cross the line, to go across the boundary and make his way in the world. Regardless, the only thing that seems to matter in the present is the very noticeable absent smell of sulfur in the air. Where could it have gone? Is this an omen of things to come?

Rupert closes his bedroom window and makes his way over to the mirror near the closet door. He looks at himself in the reflection and thinks about how he's never once and truly felt like a man.

He already knows there's no music, no poetry in the male existence. Instead, it's a sort of void, a terrible kind of vacuum. Although there are indisputably brief moments when manhood seems obtainable to him—fleeting instances when he notices his natural coarseness, his rawness—becoming the true definition of a man seems like some impossible act, an awkward magic trick or an excessive kind of performance art.

Rupert often feels out of place around other men, almost like they possess a certain skillset he's never quite mastered, as though they speak an ancient language that he could never learn. Rupert frequently observes the way men are together and he tries to mimic what he sees. He admires the boorish way they address one another—their noticeable crassness, their indelicate way of presenting who they are like canines at some outdoor dog park. Not all men are like this. It's a gross generalization to argue that all men possess the very same unrefined, improper manner of behavior.

However, it's glaringly obvious that he does not fit in when he's around them. Rupert makes every attempt to match their crudity, their unevenness. But he knows his attempts are always brittle and hollow. They are pathetic imitations of true manhood, almost like he is some alien species that could never possibly translate the complexities of human behavior. Rupert has wanted to tell this to his father. He yearns to tell him how he doesn't ever feel like a man. But he knows that this kind of confession would destroy his poor father. It's not worth the heartache.

Early in the morning, Rupert often stands naked in front of the bathroom mirror, and admires the curve of his erection when he's fully hard. His penis feels heavy and firm when he holds it with his hand. Sometimes it feels like the only thing about his body that won't break apart. His stomach is flat and hairy. His muscles are somewhat defined, even though he doesn't exercise as much as he promised himself he would.

Rupert even tried growing facial hair at one point, wondering if it might make him feel more masculine, more permanently rooted in a brotherhood that undoubtedly exists only in his mind. To anyone passing him on the street, Rupert probably looks like a very commonplace and ordinary young boy—unremarkable in every way, but familiar all the same. There's something he loathes about that kind of familiarity. Something that's immediately distrustful when he recognizes it in other people. To a select few that truly comprehend, Rupert probably looks suspicious. He resembles something that appears almost like a man but is not quite altogether what he promises to be. Indeed, if someone thinks this when they pass him, they are correct. He is not a man. Not a boy. Nothing. Instead, he uncomfortably exists in some kind of liminal space between the two. He's a horrible fraud—a replica of something he once saw in a black-and-white movie, a crude mimicry of all the supposedly most perfect elements of true manhood, a soulless impersonation.

———

After he's finished dressing and whispering horrible things to himself in the mirror, Rupert moves out of his bedroom and creeps down the stairwell. Most of the house is still dark. The vague glimmer of dawn starting to break has already begun to bleed through the living room windows and fill the room with a muted glow like the light from a distant bonfire.

Rupert narrowly avoids tripping over some of his father's clothing strewn across the floor and his mud-covered black boots piled near the bottom of the staircase. Rupert shudders slightly as he passes over takeout cartons and fully drained beer bottles. He's always been embarrassed of his home, and, for that reason, he never invites friends over to his house. That means he must always be prepared with some legitimate excuse as to why his friends cannot come over, but thankfully the opportunities for such invitations are few and far between.

Rupert reaches the kitchen, where he finds his father seated at the table and struggling to pull on his boots. Rupert stares at him for a while, watching while he grunts and works his foot deeper and deeper into the leather boot. He flinches when his father's eyes dart to him.

"Wear shoes you don't care about getting dirty," his father tells him.

What could those possibly be? Rupert wonders to himself.

He has different pairs of shoes for different occasions. But he doesn't necessarily have a pair that he would mind if they got dirty. Perhaps he's accompanying his father on some sort of job assignment. It's been several months since his father has worked, and they've been living off rations and the benevolence of Rupert's grandmother in Boston. But surely she must be growing weary of taking care of Rupert and his father. It must be a loathsome reminder for the poor old woman as well—to continually donate money to her deceased daughter's husband. Rupert's father has mentioned the possibility of her not returning his letters. However, like clockwork, she sends a check on the third of every month.

Thinking this might be some sort of work opportunity for his father, Rupert quiets some of his selfishness and tries to think of what's best for both of them. He'll find a way to make money once he leaves town and journeys to the closest city. However, his father is troubled in such a way that makes it almost impossible for him to hold down a proper job.

His father is a dedicated and diligent worker, but there's something about him that employers seem to be repelled by. Whether it's the rotted stench of grief shadowing him at all times, or whether it's because he's different, Rupert cannot be certain why his father struggles to keep a paying job. It's surprising that he and his father were never closer, especially considering how unique the two of them are. Rupert supposes they're unique in different ways and, therefore, unable to truly appreciate what the other is capable of offering.

After Rupert snatches an old, tattered pair of sneakers from beside the door leading to the laundry room, he slips them on and tells his father he's ready to go. His father is already at the doorway, fishing inside his pocket for car keys and then swiping the flashlight from the nearby counter.

Rupert and his father make their way out to the green station wagon parked in the snow-covered driveway. Rupert burrows deeper inside his winter coat as soon as a cold gust of wind slams against him and nearly knocks the air from his lungs. His father orders him to grab the brush in the back seat and knock off the few inches of snowfall from the windshield and roof. Rupert does, his fingers freezing from the cold, and when he's finished, he climbs into the car and sees his father struggle to slide the key into the ignition. The car thrums alive, the motor sputtering in almost exact harmony with Rupert's coughs as he covers his mouth with a tissue.

As they peel out of the driveway and down the tree-flanked lane, Rupert wishes he knew where they're headed. He's never been asked by his father to accompany him on one of his job assignments. With the local schools being shut down for the holiday, Rupert wonders if the remainder of his winter vacation will be spent doing whatever menial job his father has acquired. He can't be too upset at the thought of his father working. Rupert knows his father wants to provide for him. Moreover, he knows his father only feels complete when he's been assigned some sort of task or commission. At the end of the day, his father merely wants a purpose. That's why the last three years have been nearly insufferable with the both of them living in the same house—their purpose, the reason for their determination, had completely vanished.

Rupert thinks of saying something to his father.

But what to say?

There's probably too much to say. But Rupert secretly wants none of it. Once he might have basked in the joy of getting to know his father and bonding in the way that all fathers and sons are supposed to; however, he no longer feels that intense desire to please his father, or even to get to know him. *Things are going to end the way they're going to end*, he thinks to himself. Rupert has every intention of leaving the town of Burnt Sparrow once he turns eighteen, and doesn't exactly have any plan of visiting his father. To him, his father is a wretched reminder of his mother—all that he has lost. Why should he make attempts to bond with him? He's going to lose him eventually.

———

Drifting in and out of sleep as the car gently rocks him while they drive along, Rupert leans his head against the passenger window. The frosted glass feels cool against the side of his face. He listens to the *thrum, thrum, thrum* of the car's engine while it sputters along, the road disappearing yard by yard in front of him. Sometimes he glances out the windshield and imagines the car devouring the road ahead, leaving nothing behind them but flickers of soot and ash. Everything in this town eats away at everything else. The road bends and curves, empty roadway stretching out with dim headlights pointed ahead to slice through the infinite canopy of darkness. He observes while trees flicker by, different houses he's known for his entire existence flashing before him while his father seems to push his foot down harder on the accelerator. *Why could he possibly be driving so recklessly?* He's filled with the delirium of a head cold, but even Rupert knows they're driving too fast, too reckless for his own comfort. *Where is he taking us?*

Rupert's attention is eventually pulled out of the passenger window, and he notices the abandoned ruins of the large paper factory perched on the nearby hill like the dark silhouette of a strange, otherworldly castle. It feels grotesque to witness the horrid thing sometimes. All the poor, wretched souls trapped there forever because that's where they had perished while performing the toils of excruciating labor. Rupert feels a pang of pity for the poor things permanently imprisoned in the town of Burnt Sparrow—both the living and the dead. He can't quite imagine the torment of the spirits who probably wander the factory late at night—those moth-eaten, threadbare souls aching to depart and then ultimately being met with refusal time and time again. Every place in this world is a kind of trap, whether you realize it or not. Very often, you'll come to recognize the signs when it's too late.

Rupert rubs his nose, wondering why on earth he can't smell the familiar scent of the paper factory—the stench that's haunted this town for years. It feels as though some gigantic cosmic vacuum has sucked up the foul odor and then left nothing in its place. He chuckles a little, amused at the thought of things being taken away from Burnt Sparrow bit by bit, day by day. A necessary penance for existing. A kind of natural atonement for the terrible sin of dwelling here and calling this awful place home. Rupert imagines some sort of invisible vampire draining the lifeblood from the town slowly but surely each day, without fail. There are some things in this world that only take and never give anything in return. As Rupert glances at the abandoned remnants of the paper factory three hundred yards or so from the main road, he wonders if *he's* similar to a vampire, some sort of nocturnal ghoul yearning to feed, to consume others. He fully recognizes how he takes more than he's given from time to time. He had done that to his mother. Whether she gave willingly or not was beside the point. Perhaps that's why he's uncomfortable around his father. Maybe it's because his father knows that Rupert is eager to take things that don't belong to him—a consumer, a being that feeds without reserve in order to survive.

As they continue to drive, Rupert thinks of how he ventured into the paper factory once when he was a few years younger. One of the kids in his class, a young boy named James Grott, had dared Rupert to spend thirty seconds inside the factory after dark. James and his cronies would time Rupert after he made the trek across the factory's threshold—a large door that had previously been boarded shut but had been opened by vagrants and other kinds of trespassers. Rupert recalls how he stood at the threshold leading into the abandoned factory, the noxious odor of the sulfur passing through his very skin. He stood there, whistling slightly to calm some of his nerves and to provide some of the much-needed resolve to enter the area. Rupert had urged himself to take the first step across the entryway, but his feet would not obey. He remained frozen, unable to move. His stomach curls when he thinks about what he thought he saw in that darkness—the bent, snarled faces of those who had perished long ago, those who had reluctantly sacrificed themselves for the sake of industry. He idled at the threshold for minutes until James and his friends' teasing became nearly unbearable. Rupert shudders a little, shifting uncomfortably in the passenger seat, when he thinks of how he recoiled from the threshold and then darted away from the factory until he could no longer hear the sounds of the other children cackling mercilessly at him—taunting him, jeering at him, shouting terrible names. He thinks back on that night with such shame, such disgrace for not crossing the threshold and not proving to them that he was worthy of being in their friend group. Instead, he was thought of as a coward. Rupert knows he cannot control the perceptions of others; however, it's impossible to avoid being defined by them. Perhaps one day he will cross that threshold. Yes, one day he will easily issue those steps toward becoming a true man. But today is not that day.

Another ten minutes or so pass and Rupert makes the sudden realization that they've been driving toward town—the narrow lane ahead of them veering to the left and winding through a small thicket before they finally arrive at the entrance to Main Street. But for some strange reason, they can't take Hatchet Street to the town center as they usually do. It's been blocked off by local authorities, police cars idling in the center of the lane with their lights flashing red and blue.

"We can't go that way?" Rupert asks his father.

But his father doesn't answer. Instead, he grips the wheel a little tighter and merges with the lane that feeds into the roadway where the local church is located. They arrive at the church and park near the recreation hall. Rupert continually looks to his father for an explanation, but his father will not meet his gaze and divulge his secret, no matter what.

"Grab the flashlights in the back seat," his father orders.

Rupert obeys without much prodding, snatching the flashlights before he and his father begin to move away from the church and toward Main Street. He feels as though he's merely going through the motions, obeying without much thought. But Rupert doesn't want to be a soulless thing, capable only of obeying his father's every bizarre command. He feels a dull ache in the pit of his stomach—a hunger to be his own man, a desire to walk away from all this senselessness. But he cannot. He winces, feeling an invisible weight piled on him like it's the giant finger of some deity hell-bent on keeping him stuck here. Everything in this world seems to want to prevent him from leaving Burnt Sparrow. *I'll probably die here before I have the chance to leave*, and then his shoulders drop with such defeat.

He notices more police cars blocking the main intersection in Burnt Sparrow, their cars idling and flashing bright red and blue lights.

Rupert and his father draw closer, and it's then that Rupert notices random dark shapes littering the empty roadway. From a distance, they look like sleeping animals—small creatures which have crawled out from the nearby underbrush and decided to doze in a public intersection. But there's something strange about their placement across the roadway. Some of them are clumped together in large groups. Others are lying far away from the others.

As they move closer, Rupert squints and realizes that the dark shapes lying in the roadway are wearing clothes. Some of the clothing is tattered, torn, and—*is it possible?*—soaked black with blood. Rupert shakes his head in disbelief, wondering what exactly these dark shapes are. He's surprised when his father grabs hold of his arm, pulling him along further and insisting they move swiftly. Rupert is shocked by his roughness. His father never touches him, let alone grabs him with such strength as to force him to quicken his pace. Although he attempts to slip out of his father's grasp, he can't. His father's hold is much too tight.

It's when they finally come upon the police barricade that Rupert recognizes what the dark silhouettes littering the roadway are… they're human corpses.

—

Rupert's heart hammers away inside his chest, thumping like a brick being slammed against concrete again and again.

He's never seen a dead body before. Not even his mother's when she perished. His father was careful to keep her corpse hidden from Rupert's sight, and he was grateful for that.

He had been hunting with his father and had seen all types of wildlife in various states of decay—from fresh, stinking viscera to the kind of deterioration that leaves behind small, almost unnoticeable stains. On one occasion, they came upon a fawn that had been mauled by a pack of wolves and left to die near the foot of a tree. The poor thing was still alive, twitching helplessly, when Rupert and his father first came upon it. His father had matter-of-factly dragged the shotgun from over his shoulder, aimed the barrel at the dying fawn, and pulled the trigger with a mere click. At the time, Rupert wondered how his father could be so cool, so casual about ending the baby deer's life. But Rupert had figured there wasn't much to be done as he winced at the sight of the fawn's silky innards unspooling from the gaping hole in its half-eaten stomach, blood leaking out like a gentle stream of black honey.

How his father had behaved in the presence of the dying animal had puzzled poor Rupert. It bewilders him even to this day, while he stands at the end of the main drag of town, gazing out at the piles of lifeless bodies. *Why have they been left here? What is everybody waiting for?* Rupert itches a little, sensing the thrill, the anticipation of something approaching—something inexplicable, something that cannot quite be named at present.

Rupert waits for his father to offer further instructions, but finds himself becoming antsy as he peers across the police barricade and out at the stretch of roadway littered with fresh-looking cadavers. A large *"Merry Christmas"* banner hangs above the entryway to Main Street, illustrations of pine trees and gumdrops painted across the poster. The scent of warm apple cider still lingers in the air. The smell of freshly roasted chestnuts, too. It seems odd for such a cheery location to be monitored with such a grim and intimidating police presence.

Others are milling about beyond the barricade that's been arranged at the end of Main Street. Some of them are being briefed by various men in uniform, while others are weaving in between the piles of corpses strewn across the two-lane roadway.

An older gentleman—clearly one of the town elders because of the way he's dressed entirely in purple formal wear—approaches his father and pulls him aside, whispering something to him. The town elder is gaunt-faced and so thin that he appears ill, frail. Rupert is out of earshot, but he tries to lean closer and listen to their conversation. He hears the words "family" and "incarcerated."

Rupert's father's eyes snap to him, like he's caught him eavesdropping. Rupert shrinks away until he's backed into one of the members of law enforcement guarding the street. Rupert's father approaches him, the older gentleman dressed entirely in purple now flanking his father wherever he goes.

"I trust you'll be brave for us, dear boy," the town elder says to Rupert, his eyes narrowing to slits when he forces a hideous grin of amber teeth. "Shall we begin?"

Rupert looks to his father for a semblance of guidance, direction. Anything.

"Dad. What are we doing here?" he asks.

Rupert's father glances at the town elder, looking hopeful that the older gentleman will excuse Rupert's naiveté. "We're helping the community, Rupert. Surely you feel love for the town you've known your whole life. Certainly, you want to help your neighbors. Right—?"

Rupert's father looks at Rupert, expecting him to answer. But Rupert doesn't. Rupert's not quite sure how he feels about the town of Burnt Sparrow. It's not necessarily a place where he's felt welcome over the years. The town's become even more peculiar to him ever since his mother passed away. The town is built like a hunter's steel trap—the more you resist and struggle, the deeper its claws hook into you.

There are countless other towns in the state of New Hampshire with a similar sort of difficulty when it comes to permitting the youth the necessary freedom to grow. Customs are so antiquated, and have been preserved in such a way for centuries, that nobody dares question why they do a particular thing. When Rupert was younger, it was customary for the town elders to do rounds late at night and check in on the members of the community. Rupert thought nothing of the arrival of a certain town elder late each night—a somber and yet friendly-looking face greeting his parents at the threshold of their home, a few pleasantries exchanged, and simple questions answered, before the elder was on his way. Still, it was the same each and every night for quite some time, until a new town mayor was elected, and they abolished the nightly check-ins.

Burnt Sparrow is not necessarily a kind place to those who are different. Rupert knows this to be true ever since puberty arrived and awakened certain desires, certain longings inside him that he would prefer to ignore. He never had the chance to confide in his mother his attraction toward the same sex, and he'll never reveal those shameful feelings to his father. It might destroy him even more than the loss of his wife.

The truth is—Rupert doesn't quite know how he feels about his hometown of Burnt Sparrow. On one hand, it was a wondrous and magical place when he was growing up. But now that he's older he's noticed how the same enchantment he once felt has soured. Neighbors look at him with such disdain and such questioning, as though they're wondering why he's still here. They regard him like he's taking up precious space. Rupert figures that even in a town that acts as a type of snare trap for the unsuspecting, like Burnt Sparrow, there's an invisible expiration date for when it's fitting to go out on your own and start your new life. Rupert hopes for that. He yearns for that. He aches for a day when Burnt Sparrow is but a distant memory—a mere ink stain on a massive sheet of parchment scrawled with all the wonderful things he'll do and see. Still, there's something at root in the heart of this small town—and probably every other small town in this country— that prevents anyone from leaving, Rupert especially.

For the time being, he's trapped here. More precisely, he's at the police barricade with his father and one of the town elders. They seem content with his agreeableness for the moment and the town elder waves to one of the members of local law enforcement. The officer steps aside and allows them to pass through the barricade and out onto the roadway where the bodies are lying.

Rupert's father asks him to switch on the flashlight even though the lights from the nearby cruisers are bleeding across the pavement and lighting most of their way. Rupert flicks on the light and shines it at the first corpse they come upon—a middle-aged man, his coat tattered like it has been tossed through a woodchipper. The poor thing's exposed skin—pocked and leaking little trails. He lies face down in the center of the roadway, his hands up above his head like he was attempting to surrender to whatever was attacking him. It looks as though he's been shot multiple times by some sort of machine gun.

They continue to move down the lane, passing other elders dressed in purple who are milling about the bodies and being briefed by law enforcement on the number of fatalities. Rupert's attention shifts to another body they pass. Parts of the person's hands and face have been blown away—almost disintegrated—so it's very difficult to identify them completely. Rupert doesn't quite know how to feel. He wonders why he isn't becoming ill and excusing himself to vomit. So much of what he's seeing looks artificial, almost like it's been staged for his amusement, for some sort of spectacle—an exhibition of senseless brutality, of meaningless atrocity.

His feelings change when he comes upon another battered body—this time, the corpse is face up, her pitiful eyes staring heavenward and filled with such hope, such desperation to be saved. He recognizes the woman as the old lady who works the circulation desk at the town library. He can hardly believe he's staring at her corpse, watching the way the blood has pattered and pooled around her lifeless body and how the pavement is stained practically black. Rupert cowers a little, thinking about how the poor woman is now nothing more than some worthless artifact—a gruesome kind of relic, forever housed in this public museum of human carnage.

Rupert's father must sense Rupert's disturbance, because he pulls him close and hurries him along until they come to another old gentleman dressed in purple and wearing a wide-brimmed black hat.

"Edmond, I see that you brought your boy," the man in the hat says to Rupert's father.

His father nods and pushes Rupert forward, encouraging him to shake the old man's hand. Rupert obeys. He's perhaps seen some of these men before, around town. Whether it was at the local library or the supermarket, he's unsure. It's still dark out and some of their faces are obscured by shadows from the broadness of their wide-brimmed hats. Rupert squints, trying to assess whether he recognizes some of these strange-looking gentlemen. His insides heat with warmth when he recognizes the owner of the local pharmacy. He cannot recall his name at present, but he's certain that he knows him. The recognition disturbs him.

Prior to today, he's only seen the old man wearing normal clothing and going about his routine business the same way every other gentleman in town does. But there's something curious about him now. Rupert feels foolish for thinking he had actually known him previously. They weren't on first name terms. But he had smiled at Rupert before, and warmly said "Hello" whenever Rupert had to pick up a special prescription for his mother before she had passed. There's something unnerving about the man in the wide-brimmed hat now. Rupert feels as though he cannot trust anyone, anything. *Everyone is someone else*, and the hairs on the nape of his neck prickle a little.

"I take it you already heard the news," the elder says to Rupert's father. "Rather grim."

"Rupert and I would've been at the parade on Christmas Day if he weren't sick," Rupert's father tells the old man. "I suppose we were lucky."

The elder in the black hat flashes a grin at Rupert, so monstrous that Rupert curls inward.

"You're feeling a little better, dear boy?" the old man asks.

Rupert nods. That's all he can seem to do. Even though he's seventeen, he still feels out of place around his elders. He thinks adults might prefer him to obey the ancient, well-known adage—*children should be seen and not heard.* He's not exactly sure why he feels this way, especially since none of the adults in town have chastised him for speaking freely. Then again, he's never truly revealed how he feels inside. There's a valve fixed somewhere deep inside Rupert; a valve that will remain shut in the company of his elders. His peers, too. He feels foolish for not speaking up when he has the chance—forever on the precipice of something else, permanently unable to take that next step.

He's certain he'd be able to communicate well with his elders. He's read Steinbeck, Proust, Hemingway, and Hawthorn. Surely, he's encountered certain literary works that some of these adults haven't even savored yet. He should feel like their superior in many ways. But he doesn't. He wonders if he'll forever feel like a child as long as he remains here—a pathetic, miserable waif who's only worth something if he's being kept quiet or obeying some unreasonable command.

"Has your dad filled you in on any of this?" the elder asks him.

Rupert looks around for a moment, noticing more corpses stretching further down the roadway—an impossible mountain of human butchery.

"No," Rupert says. "He just told me to come with him."

The man in the black hat laughs a little.

"I'll spare you some of the gory details," he says. "You've seen enough of the aftermath. We suffered a monumental catastrophe a few days ago. You're now standing in the wreckage. The town has decided to preserve the scene as it was after the incident. You and your father will be acting as 'Preservers'—watchmen, caretakers to make certain the roadway and its new inhabitants stay exactly as they are now."

Rupert's father looks at the elder a little distrustfully. "You're not moving the bodies?"

The man in the black hat stares him down so aggressively that Rupert's father appears to immediately regret the brashness of his question.

"We've been instructed not to move the bodies for the foreseeable future," the town elder explains. "Is that clear?"

Both Rupert and his father nod their heads in agreement.

"We start this morning?" his father asks.

"You've already begun," the elder explains. "Take this section for now. You'll operate in shifts with the others who have been contacted and assigned duty."

Just as the town elders are about to move away from them, Rupert's father reaches out and pulls one of them aside.

"Oh," Rupert's father says. "The matter of payment? I was told on the phone—"

The man in the black hat and the gaunt-faced elder look at one another and smile at some soundless joke shared between the two of them.

"All in good time," the man in the black hat tells Rupert's father. "You'll be compensated fairly for your efforts, I assure you. All of us presiding on the town committee make that pledge to our Preservers."

But before Rupert's father can ask another question, the two elders glide away and are at the police barricade in a matter of seconds.

Rupert, once again, looks to his father for a semblance of

guidance, a modicum of familiarity. But his father has none to share, unfortunately for both of them.

Rupert's father swallows nervously, clearing the catch in his throat. "You take this side of the street? I'll take the other."

He doesn't even wait for Rupert to respond. He's crossing the roadway and weaving in between lifeless bodies in record time, shining the flashlight wherever he moves.

Rupert, breath becoming shallow, resigns himself to the fact that this is what's happening to him right now. He could fight it, but what good would that do? If he had a chance to question it, he might have. If he had an opportunity to ask about the incident and to know more about how all this transpired, he might have. But none of those things came to pass. He's been assigned a role as a 'Preserver' in the town of Burnt Sparrow. Those are merely the facts. Rupert feels like he's been placed on some kind of invisible conveyor belt, moving without question or difficulty and accepting whatever happens to him as part of the inevitability of his existence.

Rupert glances down and notices he's beside another dead body. This one—the corpse of an elderly woman, most of her face still intact. She looks like she's sleeping there. Peaceful, almost. She doesn't resemble something dead aside from the bits of frost that have already eaten away at her face like spots of lichen. Rupert squints, looking closer, and suddenly realizes that he recognizes this poor old woman wearing a fur coat and matching hat. The mole on her left cheek is unmistakable. Rupert has seen her working at the local post office, her hair often tied back in a bun and her sweater pinned with a small brooch in the shape of a bird.

Rupert has admired the brooch time and time again. His mother also loved birds. The two of them would sit on the porch late at night during the summer months and observe while they flitted around the house lights and then roosted on the nearby telephone poles. Rupert had often thought of approaching the old woman at the post office and telling her how much he admired her bird pin, but shyness had always gotten the better of him. Now, as he stands over her dead body, he feels a pang of pity, of indescribable sadness for never telling her. Rupert clears his throat and shrinks away from the body of the old woman, her dark blood spattered across the pavement near where she's lying. But Rupert's attention cannot be pulled away from her body, for some inexplicable reason. Instead, he keeps his eyes trained on her, wondering if she'll finally move, if she'll offer the slightest hint that she's somehow still alive. He waits and waits. The moment never arrives.

Just then, he notices a small mouse when it perches on one of the nearby bodies. *What could this thing possibly be doing during the wintertime?* He was certain most animals in New England hibernated during the cold winter months.

The tiny creature stirs there for a moment, twitches its legs slightly and then scampers off into the nearby underbrush. If only Rupert could follow. He's certain the damn thing is heading far away from Burnt Sparrow, far away from the lifeless bodies littering Main Street, and far away from the darkness that's already planted its black, cancerous roots inside the mottled heart of this sleepy little town…

—

For the next several days, Rupert and his father set their alarms for five a.m. and prepare to head into the center of town to relieve the night watchmen from their posts. At first, much of their routine seems exhilarating to Rupert. He had been wasting away during winter recess with his head cold. But now he feels as if he's been endowed with some greater purpose, some noble commitment.

He's surprised how normal everything seems even though so many friends, neighbors, and loved ones have perished so violently. He's especially unnerved by the fact that the town elders seem to be presiding over the carnage with surreptitious glee, delighting in their authority. Rupert knows he shouldn't be so shocked. Things run differently in the town of Burnt Sparrow. He knows that. His father knows that. His mother certainly knew that when she was alive.

Whenever they make the fifteen-minute ride into town just before dawn, Rupert thinks of asking his father for the details of the carnage. He's certain someone's told his father by now. They must have. But Rupert is too afraid to ask. He wonders why he's fearful of questioning. He knows that awful things happen in the world outside of Burnt Sparrow all the time.

Rupert can hardly understand how someone could leave such wreckage behind in their wake. As he drifts between the piles of corpses scattered across the roadway, he wonders how someone could rob so many innocent lives. It's evident there was more than one individual involved in causing the massacre. It makes sense, considering how the bodies have been piled in clusters like they were desperately fleeing and fell as they were struck.

Sometimes, as Rupert walks along the road while on duty, he can smell the metallic scent of gunfire wafting through the air—the very same smell that seems to have forever replaced the haunting scent of sulfur from the nearby shuttered mill. The town's ghosts have dissipated over the course of several days and now the noxious odor of warfare lingers in its place. That's exactly what the main street of Burnt Sparrow has become—a horrible war zone, a nightmarish landscape torn from the mind of some demented surrealist.

———

One night, Rupert finds his father preparing dinner in the kitchen. He kicks off his shoes, peels off his winter coat and tosses it on a nearby armchair. He wonders if his father will say anything. Perhaps he'll ask him to be more thoughtful, to put away his belongings. But his father doesn't. Instead, Rupert notices how his father keeps his head down while stirring the ground beef in the frying pan on the stovetop. Eventually, the food is ready, and Rupert's father calls him into the kitchen to grab a paper plate. They don't use the expensive silverware and plates that they had used when Rupert's mother was alive. It's too depressing to keep washing cutlery, his father would say. So, instead, they eat off paper plates and drink out of paper cups like prisoners, like convicted criminals.

After piling his plate with food, Rupert sits down at the table across from his father. It feels strange to be alone in his father's presence sometimes. Every time they interact, there's a horrible opportunity for a misunderstanding. Rupert supposes that's the truth for most people trapped in conversation. But it's especially true when he and his father occupy the same area.

"The night crew told me one of the bodies was almost dragged away by a fox the other evening," Rupert says, eyeing his father and hopeful for a grunt of acknowledgement.

"Which body?" his father asks, stuffing his mouth with beef and chewing forcefully.

"In sector twelve," Rupert responds. "Body identifier: 12BKT908."

Rupert's father shrugs, taking a sip from a bottle of beer. "Well, we've been worried that might happen for a bit now. Not surprised it finally has…"

Rupert swallows, unsure. It feels so callous, so undeservedly cruel to be discussing the lives that were taken so coolly, so casually. What has become of us? He feels like he's permanently sleepwalking, marching around foolishly with vision and the gift of speech but all the while still convinced that he's dreaming.

His father downs the rest of his beer. Rupert secretly wishes he could hide his father's stash and prevent him from drinking.

"How long are we going to do this?" Rupert asks his father.

His father's gaze rises and meets him head on. He squints, his voice hardening. "Do what?"

"Keep monitoring the bodies," Rupert says. "How long are we going to tend to them? Shouldn't their loved ones come to bury them?"

Rupert's father grunts, almost sounding as if he's amused by his son's stupidity.

"You're so eager for us to lose another job?" he asks.

Rupert shakes his head. "No... That's not what I'm saying..."

"We're supposed to care for them as long as they tell us to. You should be grateful you're working... and that it wasn't you there on Christmas Day..."

Rupert's mouth opens slightly, but all words seem to clog there in the shallow grave of his throat. What could he possibly say? He knows he's expected to follow orders, but he never anticipated he'd be asked to perform such a gruesome duty day after day, night after night. He feels as if he's rotting from the inside out. Perhaps he was one of the poor souls who was gunned down on Main Street on Christmas Day. Perhaps all of this is an illusion. Perhaps a finger could snap at any moment and deliver him to reality, to the horrible truth that he didn't survive.

Rupert's father eventually excuses himself from the table, throwing his half-empty paper plate in the nearby trash can. Rupert could chase after him and hound him with more questions. But what's the point? He'll never get a direct answer out of his father as long as he lives. Instead, Rupert sits at the kitchen table. He grabs hold of his wrist and bears down until he leaves a dark red mark. He pushes a finger into the palm of his hand and wishes to break the skin. He wants to feel something. Anything. He thinks about taking one of the knives from the cutlery drawer and stabbing himself. Just to know that he's capable of bleeding. Just to appreciate the simple fact that he's still alive.

New Year's Eve eventually arrives, and Rupert asks his father if they're expected to work tomorrow, considering it's New

Year's Day. His father tells him to expect to work. Moreover, he tells him to be grateful to work, that much of their livelihood now depends on the grace and benevolence of the town elders. Rupert feels foolish for asking. His father sounded indignant. There's a part of Rupert that wants to be liked by his father. There's a part of him that exists in some secret grotto deep inside him that thinks if he has his father's approval, he'll be happier in life. Rupert isn't sure if that's true, but he's willing to believe in it.

Days pass and eventually winter recess comes to an end. Rupert arrives at school on Monday morning and isn't necessarily surprised when he notices how some of the seats in his home room are empty, his classmates absent. His teacher, Mrs. Wilkerson, moves in front of the chalkboard and addresses the small crowd of glum-looking high schoolers.

"I'm sure many of you are feeling upset with everything going on," she says, her voice quivering a little and threatening to break apart. "Grief counselors are receiving students in the main office if you'd like to speak with someone. We're going to do our best during this difficult time."

One of Rupert's classmates—a young boy named Oliver, who won a special award for an art project he designed last year—lifting his glasses to wipe tears away. Oliver's usually quiet during home room and he's never really talked to Rupert before. But Rupert wonders if Oliver knows something, if he's aware of what transpired on Main Street on Christmas Day.

Rupert whispers to him: "Hey. Oliver."

Oliver turns slightly, sucking back some of the snot collecting in his nose until he swallows.

"Did you hear what happened?" Rupert asks. "My dad won't tell me a thing."

Oliver wipes more tears away with his sweater sleeve. "Some family—out-of-towners I think—came to the Christmas Day parade and started shooting everybody."

Rupert feels his stomach begin to churn. He had expected the news to be grim. But the fact that a family was responsible for this heartache, this despair?

"A family—?" he asks.

Oliver nods.

"Does anyone know why they did it?" Rupert asks him.

Oliver shakes his head. "My dad says they're being held in the cellar of the town hall. They have prison cells there."

Rupert winces. The very thought of the people who did something so monstrous being so nearby is enough to make him retch. He doesn't, thankfully. Rupert's about to ask Oliver another question, but Mrs. Wilkerson stares at him for a beat too long and he loses the nerve.

For the remainder of the class, Rupert occasionally glances at the empty seats where his classmates once sat. There's Sarah Chessler—a cheery-faced blonde girl with pigtails—in the third row. She was in his Honors English class. She loved reading *The Turn of the Screw* by Henry James, and much to the chagrin of her fellow students, would often ask for extra homework when they were reading Brontë or Steinbeck. Then there's Marcus O'Reilly who used to sit in the second row closest to the classroom window. He was typically very loud, even in the mornings. Rupert was loath to admit how many times he quietly hoped Marcus would stop talking so that he could concentrate on whatever Mrs. Wilkerson was saying. He feels guilty now, realizing he'll never have the privilege of hearing Marcus's voice in the morning ever again.

Finally, there's Justin Sanchez who usually sat in the row behind Rupert during home room. Rupert turns around and gazes at the empty seat staring back at him. Although he would never admit it to anyone, Rupert cared for Justin. It wasn't love, but it perhaps could have one day grown into something like love if given the chance. Justin had a girlfriend and the two of them had been going steady since they were both sophomores. Rupert had often envied Justin's girlfriend and all the happiness he suspected she possessed. Rupert imagines most of that happiness was snuffed out on Christmas Day last week.

In the cafeteria, Rupert typically sits alone while he eats his lunch. Sometimes he goes to the library to hide among the bookshelves and read old copies of Milton or Hemingway or Poe. But he doesn't feel like reading today. He wonders if he'll ever feel like reading again. One of the very last things he read while at the school library was a book about New England wildlife, specifically birds.

He recalls a particular passage that was especially gruesome and gave him indigestion for two days straight. He couldn't eat anything. Rupert reflects on what he had read—how certain kinds of ducks will sometimes devour the other ducklings in the nest. It's not entirely known why this occurs, but many researchers have speculated that the carnage stems from boredom. As Rupert sits at the lunch table, thinking about the passage he read about birds eating other birds, he can hardly comprehend something so ghoulish—the very act of cannibalism out of boredom.

Rupert slows, his appetite waning, as he imagines all the unbearable moments he's endured for the sake of total boredom. He thinks of a larger duck swallowing a duckling whole, the poor little thing's neck breaking in half when it's finally consumed. Rupert can't bear the awful thought. Why should he think of something so obscene? Is this what comes out of boredom? These terrifying intrusive thoughts?

Out of his peripheral vision, he notices a group of boys glaring at him. They're not eating. Instead, they're regarding him intently while he takes a sip from his carton of apple juice. Rupert wonders why they're staring. This particular group of boys hasn't given him any trouble before, even if they are aware he prefers the same sex. He wonders what he's done to deserve their cruelty today. His question is answered when one of them shouts: "Corpse watcher." Then another: "Ghoul." Finally, a third: "Hey, do they let you ass fuck the corpses when you're on duty?"

Rupert tries not to react. Instead, he takes another bite of his sandwich and washes it down with a gulp from his juice carton. But eventually the teasing becomes relentless. He swipes his lunchbox from the table and heads to the school library. Perhaps he feels like reading today, after all.

———

Even though his father told him he would pick him up after school, Rupert finds himself loitering outside the building's entrance for an hour before making the decision to begin the trek toward home—if you could even call it a *home*. He figures he could wait for his father to arrive, to pull onto the curb and whistle at him with a signal that he's prepared to care for him, to nurture him the same way his loving mother had. But that day would probably never come. Especially not today. Rupert feels the air churn with an invisible kind of threat, a warning that more hardship, more misery is about to make itself known in town. He shudders slightly, thinking how strange it feels to recognize the fact that his hometown has become a dumping ground for affliction, for heartache, for such despair. He wonders if some of this has been earned over the years. Certain people earn their sadness over time—whether it's from the vileness of their transgressions or the way in which they use others for their own satisfaction. Rupert wonders if it's possible for a place to earn a kind of disease, a sickness that threads itself into the very fabric of the community until all things around it eventually begin to rot and spoil.

While Rupert makes his way down the narrow lane toward his house, he thinks of peeling off from the roadway and heading into the woods. There's an adventurous part of him that has always wondered what he might find if he kept walking, if he left the town of Burnt Sparrow and kept marching toward infinity. He's convinced that the very ground beneath him would crumple and give away eventually, would break apart and send him crashing into some bottomless pit. Rupert pulls his collar tighter around him when he thinks of how he's been taught that all life begins and ends in the town of Burnt Sparrow. Is there anything beyond this? Is there anything, anyone else out there?

Just then, he feels the front of his pants tightening. It's been a while since he's masturbated and he senses himself tremor a little, feeling the urge to waste a few minutes indulging in the release. But where could he go? He could move away from the road and make a dash into the nearby thicket where he wouldn't be seen. He performed many similar rituals in the wooded area behind his house when he was a little younger and more impetuous. He would sneak away into the forest, locate a quiet place where he could relax, remove his clothing, and then begin to work himself to a frenzy. He would imagine all kinds of different scenarios while he pleasured himself— being spotted by a random passerby, a virile-looking older gentleman who might indulge in his whims and take him right there, fuck the life out of him until they both creamed in unison. Such things never transpired in the woods behind his parents' home. Instead, Rupert would pleasure himself until climax and then aim his cock at a nearby bush to paint every leaf with his seed. He'd pocket himself, pull up his pants, and then traipse away from his non-responsive victim who had been left to drip bits of him until a passing storm might arrive to wash the incriminating evidence away. There were times when Rupert shuddered, imagining if it might be possible for some woodland creature to happen upon the place where he masturbated—to somehow become impregnated with his fluid. He imagined horrible scenarios where he would be walking through a thicket of trees and would notice a small fawn in the distance with a human-looking face—the faint outline of Rupert's nose, the vaguest shape of his frowning mouth.

Rupert had imagined crumpling to his knees, begging for

the poor creature's forgiveness, to not tell anyone. In all his dreams, the fawn would regard him with such apathy, such disinterest, and then would trot away until the wretched thing disappeared into the nearby underbrush. He would imagine himself trying to pursue the gruesome-looking thing until the forest would not allow him to go any further, until the path beneath him became muted and practically invisible. He cringes, thinking of the uncertainty of those imaginings—those horrible dreams. That's all they are, he hopes to himself. That's all they'll ever be.

However, while Rupert makes his way along the empty lane, he gazes into the forest and half-expects to see that frightening recollection—that mirror-like appearance, that loathsome creature with a human head. He shoves his hands into his pockets and keeps walking. For the first time in a while, he no longer feels like pleasuring himself. He doesn't deserve it. Instead, he has earned only pain.

———

When Rupert returns home, he's eager to find his father and rebuke him for his neglect. Even if he can't come out and say exactly how mistreated he's been feeling, he can certainly play the role of the sullen, sarcastic brat. But when he enters the house, he's surprised to find the downstairs area is completely empty. Instead, he hears his father humming to himself upstairs in the bathroom. Rupert eases the door open without warning and his father lurches back at the surprise.

"You're heading out?" Rupert asks.

His father slides the straight razor up his throat, scraping off more of the shaving cream with a flick of his wrist.

"I've been asked to go to the town hall," he explains.

Rupert's ears perk at the words town hall. That's where the people who are responsible for the carnage on Main Street are being jailed. Rupert leans against the door frame.

"I don't suppose I could join you?" he asks his father.

Rupert's father looks at him queerly. "You want to come?"

Rupert tries to laugh it off. "You're surprised?"

His father finishes shaving, tossing the razor in the sink, and wiping the remaining threads of white lather from his face. Rupert has never seen his father shave before. There's something private, so intimate about the activity—something a man must do and do alone, without supervision. Moreover, there's something inherently erotic about the sight of a man shaving. Rupert feels guilty for admitting so. He had watched an adult movie once before, and in the film, a young student athlete was guided how to shave by an older, seductive-looking male coach wearing bright blue gym shorts that were impossibly revealing for the sake of his modesty. The young actor's lips had parted slightly while the older man in the film slid the edge of the razor along his throat, shaving cream flicking away bit by bit.

Then, after all the shaving cream had been cleared from the boy's face, the older man forced the boy against the nearby wall and mounted him, panting deep in his ear and begging the boy to let him fuck him. Rupert becomes firm again at the exciting memory that he's never shared with anyone. His father would be disgusted with him for thinking something so obscene in his presence. Rupert doesn't even quite know how to make sense of these thoughts when around his father. All he knows is that he feels an intense pang of shame. Rupert figures that his father would be okay with his sexuality as long as his queerness exists in theory as opposed to in practice. If Rupert truly and sincerely wanted his father's love, he'd probably have to live as a eunuch, a completely chaste man. Rupert swallows hard, not entirely sure if he's willing to deny himself what he wants, what he desires. But what are those desires exactly? Rupert still isn't sure.

"Yes. I guess I am a little surprised," his father says. "You never came before whenever there were other town meetings."

"Aren't you happy I'm taking an interest?" Rupert asks him.

His father peers at him, then shrugs and tosses a towel over his shoulder.

"You're welcome to join," he tells his son. "I'm glad you're coming."

Rupert is surprised by his father's admission, his vulnerability. His father has never been so expressive with him before. Perhaps being surrounded by death for the past few weeks has melted parts of him, thawed some of the ice there.

Rupert slips back into his winter coat and follows his father outside toward the old station wagon parked in their driveway. As he walks, he glances back at the small house nestled in a thicket of evergreens—the only home he's ever known. A frightened part of him worries that it's the only home he'll ever know. When he was a child, the house seemed so much larger, so much more monstrous. Now it feels like it's somehow shrinking, like it's thinning and doing everything it can to squeeze Rupert out like something that's been only partially digested.

He'll never forget how he once played in the backyard with his mother—how they built snowmen and made "snow angels" in the freshly fallen snow. It's then he realizes that so many of the good, pleasant memories in this house are of him and his mother. His father was never truly there for those moments. He was nearby. But he wasn't ever really there for each of those special, meaningful moments.

More and more each day, Rupert feels as though he's talking to a strange thing that's pretending to be his father—almost like his father has been completely hollowed out and then filled with some other element, the way an empty vessel can be reused and repurposed. There are moments when they connect, but they're few and far between. Maybe because they've been so irreparably wounded. Rupert sometimes worries about the two of them being left alone together for too long—how two wounded people will try to hurt one another because they're used to how it feels.

As they drive toward the town hall, Rupert thinks of saying something to his father—something to connect with him, something that will surprise or delight him. This shocks Rupert. He has made every effort to avoid establishing a connection with his father for fear that such a relationship would trap him here. He doesn't seem to care about that anymore. Regardless of his change of heart, he says nothing. His attention drifts out the passenger window and he contemplates the houses as they drift by—the terrifying little secrets they must harbor in their darkest recesses behind their locked doors.

———

The entryway to the town hall is jammed with people as they swarm the building, elbowing past the guardsmen stationed with weaponry at the front door and into the large conference room where a makeshift stage has been prepared by volunteers.

Rupert watches the chaos from a distance while he and his father slowly make their way toward the building. He's never cared for large crowds of people, and if he had known there was expected to be such an impressive turnout, he might not have begged his father to let him come.

As he and his father elbow their way into the seething throng of neighbors, Rupert spots a girl from one of his classes across the corridor. She's a year younger than him. Her hair is trimmed short in a pixie cut and she wears glasses that are impossibly large for the smallness of her face. He recalls her name is Bernadette. She danced with him once at a school dance, and when he was too fearful to kiss her, she told him it was okay for him not to want to kiss girls. She had confessed to Rupert that she had heard rumors about him—rumors about the other boys he lusted after in their grade. But she didn't care. He shouldn't be ashamed of who he is. Rupert softens a little when he first recognizes her standing there with her concerned-looking mother near the water fountain. He's about to wave to her, but instead he's pulled into the courtroom by his father.

His father forces him into an empty chair near the front row just as a group of town elders begins to take the stage.

It feels strange for Rupert to find his father participating in

49

these town rituals. His father has always seemed so far removed from their presentations, their formal customs. He had found work doing odd jobs in the neighboring communities until his wife passed away. Then work became more and more scarce. Rupert wondered if his father had maintained the same work ethic, or if her death had drained him of all his vigor, his spirit. His father was once a specimen of health, of such masculinity. But now he appears as though he's thinning more and more each day, dissolving slowly before his eyes until he's nothing more than a wet imprint on a stretch of sun-scorched pavement. Rupert glances at his father next to him and feels so strange in his presence. He's slowly come to the realization that his father is a queer man. He's strange in a more unspoken way, a secret way that's not revealed at once but rather exposed carefully over time. Rupert eyes his father, considering the many ways he will never truly know him.

Just then, one of the town elders—the man in the black hat who had spoken to Rupert and his father that first awful day—moves to the apron of the makeshift stage and clears his throat, preparing to address the crowd of impatient onlookers.

"Friends, we've organized this forum as a way to heal," he announces, his voice rotted-sounding like he has just swallowed a handful of dried weeds. "It is with great sadness that I tell you that our little town will not be the same for quite some time. We need time to recover. We need time to come to terms with the horrible misfortune that arrived on Christmas Day."

Whispers begin to filter throughout the large crowd, a murmur growing louder and louder. The elder seems to notice this and he holds up his gloved hand, begging them to be quiet. The onlookers obey with visible reluctance.

"Nobody could have predicted this misfortune... We certainly did not ask for any of this hardship," the town elder says. "Our friends, our neighbors, our children—some of them gone forever because a decision was made. A decision made not by us. But rather by someone else. It's because of this we are now in mourning."

There are whispers joining him in full agreement wafting throughout the crowd.

"The elders have met and have agreed to put the fate of those responsible for our mourning in your very capable hands," the town elder declares. "Let their suffering, their hardship belong to you."

With a flick of his wrist, the elder in the black hat motions to a guardsman stationed near the small doorway. The guardsman obeys, turning the handle and letting the door swing open.

There's a flicker of movement.

The crowd shifts in anticipation, people clamoring and trampling over one another to get a better look at who—what—is approaching.

Thinking quickly, Rupert climbs on his chair and peers over the bustling crowd. He finally sees the prisoners—a family of three: mother, father, and teenage son shuffling out from the darkness beyond the doorway. They amble into the room with their heads lowered while the massive chains securing their ankles and wrists clank back and forth. At first, there's silence in the large room. The crowd merely watches the family as they inch toward the platform and are assisted onto the stage by guardsmen carrying rifles. After several moments, some members of the crowd begin to shout insults at the imprisoned family—"Murderers," "Monsters," "Rot in Hell."

But the crowd begins to grow quiet again when all seem to take note of the family and their unusual appearances. Rupert gasps when he finally notices it—they have no eyes. No eyebrows or nose either. Instead, they are three blank slates—featureless, utterly unidentifiable, like faceless children's dolls. They each have a tiny pinhole where their mouth should be, presumably so that they can breathe and consume nutrients. If it weren't for their different clothing or the fact that the mother has long, dark hair that falls well past her shoulders, it would be almost impossible to tell them apart. The father and the teenager look relatively similar aside from the fact that the faceless father's hair is thinning and prematurely grey.

Rupert can hardly believe his eyes. He stares at the faceless family with such intensity, begging to understand them. Everything about their grotesque appearance seems to contradict their ability to survive as living things. Yet somehow, they do.

The faceless teenager scratches his wrist, the chains securing his hand probably too uncomfortable. A guardsman knocks him on the back of his head with the butt of his rifle. The faceless teenager falters for an instant, shuddering, before correcting himself and keeping perfectly still.

The elder in the black hat approaches the crowd of onlookers. "These are the… *things* responsible for our misery, our tribulation. It's our intent to make certain something like this never happens again. The only way to make certain something like this never happens again is punishment. That's what these monsters deserve—to be punished."

"Burn them alive," someone near the doorway shouts.

"Tie bricks to their feet and throw them in the river," another person suggests.

"I want something more permanent," the elder says. "Something that will last longer."

Before another form of torture can be added to the list of possibilities, a man's voice pierces the room and quiets all others.

"Wait," the voice says.

The crowd parts and reveals a middle-aged man dressed entirely in black. He's thin and too boyishly good-looking for someone in their forties or fifties. The most remarkable aspect of his appearance—his perfectly coiffed facial hair, and how most of his beard is black save for a single streak of white zigzagging across his flawlessly sculpted jaw. The man drifts through the crowd, commanding the room to obey his every whim as more residents part while he approaches the makeshift stage.

"What good would it do to kill them?" the man asks. "What exactly would that do for us? Would that take away our pain? Would that take away our suffering?"

The elder in the black hat leans forward. "You have an alternative to suggest, Mr. Esherwood?"

Mr. Esherwood grins, pocketing his leather gloves and admiring the faceless family on the stage as if they were prizes to be won at the local carnival. He turns, facing the crowd of onlookers.

"You know me," he says to the crowd. "You know my family are some of the oldest members of our community here in Burnt Sparrow. Five generations of Esherwoods have lived in my home."

Whispers filter throughout the large crowd, some of the onlookers seeming to nod along in agreement.

Others are less enthused, however.

The elder in the black hat seems impatient, tapping his foot. "What exactly do you suggest, Mr. Esherwood?"

Mr. Esherwood closes his eyes and draws in a labored breath like he's considering his next words with such carefulness, such precision.

"I propose we relocate the prisoners to my estate," Mr. Esherwood says. "They can be sequestered in a certain part of the house with guards on duty. Once there, they will suffer."

The elder in the black hat smears some of the snot dripping from his wrinkled nose. "And how exactly will they suffer, Mr. Esherwood? How does giving them over to you benefit our community?"

Mr. Esherwood simpers, delighted the old man has asked. "Because I will open my home to every person in Burnt Sparrow. These derelicts, these monsters will belong to all of us. They will be available for torture day and night. So long as they are kept alive. I don't suppose you can promise such a thing with your overzealous guardsmen. I imagine the boy and the woman have already been violated while under your care. No—?"

The elder in the black hat recoils, visibly shocked by Mr. Esherwood's impertinence. But he doesn't fight him on his assessment. Perhaps because he's correct for considering such a despicable thought.

The elder and Mr. Esherwood simply glare at one another —a horrible challenge of who will look away first, who will be defeated with a mere glance.

"Why should we let you take these prisoners from our jurisdiction?" the elder asks Mr. Esherwood.

"The town will not have to pay for the family and their survival," Mr. Esherwood explains. "I will see to it that they're cared for. In between the torture they endure from our friends and neighbors. I realize that community funds are tight. I highly doubt the town can afford to warehouse these criminals, especially if you're after a more permanent kind of punishment. You want them to live, don't you?"

The elder in the black hat grits his teeth and snarls at Mr. Esherwood like a rabid dog. "I want them to suffer. Just like they've made our poor town suffer."

Mr. Esherwood smiles. "Then let me take care of it. I'll see to it that they suffer…"

Mr. Esherwood holds out his hand for the elder to shake.

The elder in the black hat glances at the silent crowd of onlookers.

"Do we have a deal?" he asks the crowd.

There are shouts of agreement filtering throughout the space, mild applause scattering there as well.

Without hesitation, the town elder grabs hold of Mr. Esherwood's hand and shakes it with a firmness that seems to astonish Esherwood at first.

Then the elder pulls Mr. Esherwood closer and whispers something in his ear. Rupert tries to study the movement of his lips—the muted words passing between them—and decipher what the old man is saying, but he can't. The crowd begins to surge, applauding as Mr. Esherwood turns and makes his way toward the room's exit.

The guardsmen prod the faceless family like cattle until they're shuffling off the stage and back into the dark room from where they came. Rupert's eyes follow them until they vanish beyond the door. He wonders how a family of three could organize and execute something so monstrous, so evil. He's unnerved at the recollection of their facelessness and the small pinholes they breathed through. Rupert's not necessarily surprised that something so evil doesn't have a face. He had expected it. He thinks about that while he and his father make the drive back home, the country road zigzagging in front of them. When they pass people on the street, Rupert now has to do a double take to make sure that they still have faces.

———

Rupert thinks about a threshold—a small, cramped, and narrow space big enough for only one person to pass through at a time. Of easing his foot across the edge, savoring in the excitement of passing from one place to another, almost like he was a spirit wandering from this world unto the next. He thinks of his sweet, beloved mother and how she left him at such an impressionable and tender age. Perhaps life in Burnt Sparrow might not make much sense in general, but he's certain he'd be far more guarded, more prepared for the unexpected if she were still present.

He rolls over on his side while lying in bed and pulls open one of the drawers in his nightstand. He swipes the small, black tape recorder his mother gave to him when he was eleven or twelve. She had recorded several folk tales about the town of Burnt Sparrow. Whether they were stories she had invented herself or had been told to her by others, Rupert could never be certain. It doesn't matter at this point. Rupert merely wants to hold onto any recollection—however tenuous—before she slips away from the theater of his mind entirely.

Rupert rewinds the tape from the last time he listened and then presses "Play." There's a sharp, crackling sound. Then, as always, he's enchanted by the lilting pleasantness of his mother's sweet voice while she tells him a story. She speaks to him over the tape:

I curse myself, wondering what on earth possessed me to agree to a weekend in the country with Audrey. We've been together for nearly eighteen months now and a trip out of the city had seemed inevitable for so long; however, I still can't comprehend why I agreed to such an uncomfortable option—her parents' cabin in the wilds of New Hampshire. I know for a fact that her parents don't care much for me. It's not that they've gone out of their way to make me feel unwelcome at family dinners, or that they've made disparaging remarks about me, but rather it's because they seem to continue to regard me the way most people observe trans men—a sideshow attraction, something to be watched and scrutinized, but never worthy of being wholly understood.

I've never told Audrey how prickly they often make me, but I'm certain she suspects given how many times I excuse myself to use the restroom when we're dining in their presence. Thankfully, I know that her parents won't be at the cabin while we're staying here. But the very idea of indulging in nature and partaking in outdoor activities unsettles me terribly. I know those things should excite me the way they seem to excite other men. But, once again, I do not feel like a true man. Instead, I feel like some crude imitation—a soulless effigy without purpose or creed, something that so desperately wants to be loved and accepted but will never be. It's not Audrey's fault that I feel this way. I would feel like this even if I were vacationing with friends or my own parents. I would wear my shirt when we would go swimming in the lake, ashamed of the scars where my breasts once were. I would sleep with most of my clothing on as opposed to how I prefer to sleep—naked.

Part of me wonders if I'll ever feel like a man—an identity I try to impress upon others: the way I lower my voice when I speak, the precise, calculated movements I make when I walk. I look in the mirror and I realize that so much of it appears rehearsed or artificial. I feel like I'm forever trapped at the edge of a precipice, a threshold—the excruciating agony of becoming something impossible. Even though Audrey tells me that I please her and that I'm the most loving and generous man she's dated, I sense some dishonesty in her voice—as if she were telling me something that she knew I wanted to hear.

Rupert had forgotten just how much he had missed the sound of his mother's voice—the way she pronounces certain words, the gentle way she speaks:

As we park the car and climb out onto the driveway, I glance at the small cottage framed in the sprawling thicket of greenery. I find myself staring at the yellow netting on the cabin's front door—a flimsy, almost completely unreasonable excuse for defense against the stream of mosquitos and other insects already trickling through the meshwork. Even though Audrey has raved about the summers she spent here when she was a child and how some of her fondest memories were collected here, I wonder if she's pulling my leg. The cabin seems like it's well past its heyday— shingles peeling from the roof, several windows cracked, pipes deteriorating and rusted. As humans, we go back to the precious places we once loved, but so often find ourselves disappointed. It seems all too inevitable to eventually realize that things will never be the way they once were.

That could easily apply to almost anything—even me and Audrey. When we first met, things were beautiful and the world seemed so open to receiving us as two of the lucky ones who found love, who made a pact with one another to never be apart. But slowly, for the past several months, things have become stale and rotted. The world around us seemed to change—friends we once knew pulling away, family expressing their concerns. It has been more than obvious that our relationship has soured. Audrey still knows this. I think that's why she suggested coming here in the first place. But, to me, it seems so pointless to try to rekindle the flame of something now long gone at a beloved cabin from her childhood.

I sense my stomach churning and I wonder if I'll double over from the agony. There's something I need to tell Audrey— something I've been putting off for the past three months. It's the very reason so much of our love for one another has subsided. There's a part of me that wonders if she already knows. She must suspect that I've been going out late in the afternoon and early evening to meet up with someone else. She must know this, especially since our lovemaking has become so infrequent, so irregular. Once, we were unable to keep away from each other. Now it seems unlikely either one of us will petition the other for any kind of intimate moment. Although she may suspect the fact that I've been seeing someone else, I know for certain she won't expect to be told I've been seeing a man for the past three months. She might be open minded—perhaps even curious—if I told her I was seeing another woman. But I expect she'll be devastated to know that I've been sleeping with a man named Callum.

I've gone through the different scenarios of how I should tell her, and I can't come to a proper decision. It feels so vile, so wicked to go behind her back like this, to carry on with our simple life together while I'm on my knees most evenings, begging Callum to breed me and to unknot the very last bit of my resistance, my unappeasable ache. It's strange to admit but I feel more like a man when I'm with Callum. The sex is rough, but I feel as though I'm his equal. There's my poisonous habit of comparing myself to him and languishing in the fact that he's a perfect specimen of manhood—the very same man I wish I could be. But he's gentle and tender when he needs to be, and he often holds me after our lovemaking. Perhaps Audrey would understand this on some level. Perhaps she would accept the fact that I'm sleeping with Callum regularly because I'm comparing myself—my manhood—to him. I know it seems unlikely for her to completely admit, but it's always possible.

Audrey slams the car door shut and I'm wrenched from my daydream. I watch her as she circles the vehicle until she arrives at the rear. She seems to deflate when she pries open the trunk, revealing a bed filled with our luggage. I know for certain she hates unpacking as much as I do. Since I'm supposed to be "the man" in this scenario, I urge her to move aside and promise her that I'll carry the heavier items if she'll open the front door. I toss one of her bags over my shoulder and heave the other suitcase from the trunk. She observes me with such intent for the first time in what feels like forever. Audrey tells me how strong I am, and I accept the compliment, but the feeling of pride abandons me all at once. It feels so undeserved and hollow. It feels as if it were somehow designed to wound me, to unravel all my vitality, all my hope of one day coming to terms with myself.

"There's something I need to tell you," Audrey says, blocking me from moving any further up the porch steps.

I cringe, shuddering a little. I wonder what she could possibly have to tell me. She barely spoke to me during the two-hour car ride here, and I had wondered if I'd done something or said something that upset her when we were in Boston.

"It's nothing too serious," she tells me, obviously sensing how alarmed I've become. "It's a tradition we practice whenever my family visits."

I feel the weight of the luggage digging into me, the strap nearly suffocating me while I falter for an instant on the porch steps.

"We always walk through the doorway and whistle," she says. "It can be any tune. Porter. Gershwin. Berlin. Whatever you prefer. But we must whistle whenever we pass through a doorway."

I cock my head a little, bewildered by what she's saying. It seems so unlike Audrey to follow the practice of some ancient superstition. Audrey has a master's degree in physics from Boston University, after all. It seems so wildly out of character for her to subscribe to some peculiar belief about whistling when passing through doorways. I wonder if she's teasing me. But her voice has firmed and how her eyes have fixed upon me with such intensity—almost silently begging me to take part in her private ritual, begging me to simply accept and not question anything.

"The cabin won't fall apart if I don't whistle?" I ask her, joking and trying to lighten the mood.

But Audrey doesn't laugh. Instead, she draws closer to me, her breathing becoming ragged and shallow.

"It would really mean a lot to me if you did this, baby," she says, resting one of her hands on my shoulder. "Please. Won't you?"

How could I refuse her? My stomach is already performing acrobatics from the guilt of my trysts with Callum and the unease of being so deep in the countryside. I think I might come apart completely if I rejected her pleas. I couldn't bear to hurt her in such a way. It seems so ludicrous. I'm afraid of hurting my beloved Audrey and yet I'm continuously returning to the arms of someone else—that blond-haired young man named Callum, the one who smells like patchouli and lavender.

I realize I'm merely standing there on the front porch, not saying anything. I nod at Audrey, and she seems a little comforted by the fact I'm willing to oblige. To show her that I'm a man of my word, I take hold of the luggage and start whistling as I pass through the front doorway into the small cottage. Audrey seems pleased for the first time in a while, smiling as she follows me into the entryway and whistles her own tune. I pause for a moment and glance around the cabin—from the dust-covered armchairs arranged near the fireplace to the cobweb-gowned stairwell leading upstairs to the loft. It seems so abnormal for Audrey to speak so highly of a place and then find it's a den of *filth and squalor. Audrey's parents are rather wealthy, and it's so absurd to think they've allowed their New Hampshire cabin to languish in such a state of neglect.*

I set the luggage down near the sofa and I move toward the hearth, noticing a row of picture frames lining the mantle. Some of the photographs are black and white. Many of them are of Audrey and her parents. But some are of faces I do not recognize. I presume they must be distant family members who perished eons ago, given that most of these photos are faded and crumpled inside cheap picture frames.

"Who's this?" I ask, pointing to the photograph of a young girl with a strawberry-print dress and pigtails.

She appears no older than seventeen or eighteen. She smiles at the camera, her hand blurred as if caught in mid wave when the snapshot was taken.

"I don't know actually," Audrey tells me. "Some of this furniture was left over from previous owners. My parents don't visit much anymore."

I glance around, noticing how empty the place seems—how ill-disposed, how uninviting.

"Are you sure it's okay to stay here?" I ask her.

Part of me hopes she'll realize I don't want to be here. That she'll recognize my discomfort and we will get into the car and drive back to the city.

But she doesn't do any of those things. Instead, she tells me how we won't be in the cabin much anyway. We'll be spending time outdoors instead, as if that's intended to make me feel better about the whole ordeal. I agree, even though I feel completely out of place.

She tells me to help her unload some of the bags of groceries in the kitchen. As I lead the way, she calls out to me like she's pained herself.

"What's wrong?" I ask.

"You're not whistling," she says, pointing ahead of me at the doorway leading into the kitchen.

I inhale sharply and start to whistle, making my way into the kitchen and all the while wondering when I should tell her—when I should unravel her thoughts of love and instead sew a cancer there that will eventually threaten to poison us both.

Later, while I'm unpacking our luggage, I notice Audrey removing some of the photographs of the various people I don't recognize. I don't say anything to her, but she moves about with such precision and quietness that it unsettles me, almost like she's preparing for the arrival of someone or something.

We spend some of the afternoon walking along the narrow trails in the woods nearby. I embarrass myself only a handful of times and Audrey never laughs, thankfully. She's always been kind to me like that. Even though I know I'm less than most others—especially other men—Audrey has never made me feel inferior or like I'm unworthy of her love. If I do feel any of those things, it's from my own doing.

Later that evening, we make dinner and sit at the kitchen table. There are so many things I could say—so many things I could finally confess and relieve some of the burden from my conscience. But I choose not to for some inexplicable reason. It's not that there are no opportunities for me to speak. The whole cabin is quiet. Audrey seems entirely spent when it comes to polite, idle conversation, poking the roasted vegetables on her plate with her fork and occasionally sipping from her glass of red wine.

I think it's perhaps the most perfect moment for me to tell her, for me to finally confess what I've been fearing to reveal: that I'm not only in love with Callum, but that I'm carrying his child as well. Perhaps that's why I'll never feel like a true man. Because even though Callum has respected me and loved me in a way that Audrey never could, he told me during our lovemaking sessions that he wanted desperately to make a child with me. He wanted to know that he and I had created life together. Finally, we had. It's still inside me as I sit at the dinner table across from my beloved and forlorn-looking Audrey.

Just as I'm about to open my mouth to speak, Audrey sets down her silverware and her knife clatters against the plate. It's so loud that it startles me, and I sense my cheeks whitening. Audrey looks at me, seeming to realize that I've been shocked.

"You've been so jumpy lately," she tells me.

"I just—I can't seem to get comfortable here," I say to her, setting my knife and fork down and pushing my half-empty plate aside. "It's too… quiet all the time."

Audrey's shoulders drop a little, seeming to mourn the fact that she knows she's not a gifted conversationalist.

"It's not your fault," I tell her, hoping that bit of kindness might please her. "It's—the house, I suppose. It's always so eerily still."

Audrey smiles. "We could tell each other stories… My father told me plenty of tales when we visited here when I was a little girl. Some were pretty scary."

I wince a little. Audrey knows I'm not a fan of anything frightening. For God's sake, I can't even watch certain commercials on TV because they unsettle me. Then again, anything else might be preferable when compared to the awful silence—that dreadful, all-consuming stillness that seems to pursue us wherever we go.

"What kind of stories?" I ask her, immediately regretting my curiosity.

Audrey sits up straight in her chair, clearly pleased I've asked. "There was one in particular my father told me that I've thought about for quite some time... I don't know why. Maybe he told it to me in such a way. Maybe I was too young to hear it and it frightened me..."

I take a sip of water and clear my throat. "What's the story?"

Audrey looks puzzled at first, almost uncertain how to tell me, how to properly describe what's been told to her.

"It's about something that lives between places... Some... creature that exists at the threshold and only at the threshold..."

"What kind of threshold?"

"Any," she tells me. "Any doorway. Any entrance. Any opening that leads to another place. It lingers there and waits for you... Almost gleefully hoping that you might make a misstep, that you might become its prey."

I sense the room chilling, like a nearby window has been opened and a nighttime breeze is running between the two of us.

"How would that happen?" I ask her. "What kind of misstep?"

Audrey's attention settles on me, and her face hardens with a sort of sour look. "Like passing through a doorway and forgetting to whistle. These things are blind most of the time. They can only see you in the brief moment when you pass from one room to another. Through the doorway..."

66

"What do they look like?" I ask her.

"I don't know," she says, shaking her head. "My dad wouldn't tell me. But he said that if you ever pass through a doorway—especially here in this cabin—without whistling, they'll catch you."

I feel foolish even asking, humoring her. "How?"

"My dad said you'll feel a small prick on the heel of your foot. Then all the hair on your head will stand perfectly on end. That way, they can see you..."

I force a polite laugh. "I can see how that might frighten a child..."

"It became sort of an—uhm—inside joke between my dad and me whenever we stayed here," Audrey tells me. "That's why I asked you to whistle whenever you pass through a doorway here."

I can't pretend to hide my confusion anymore. "You were trying to include me in your inside joke?"

"No," Audrey says. "Not exactly. It just—means a lot to me. It's something my father told me before we came up here for the first time and it's second nature to me now whenever I visit. Surely, you must understand... I'm sure you do things that don't make perfect sense..."

Indeed, she's right. But can I tell her that? Can I confide in her my secrets, my shameless affair with Callum? It truly doesn't make sense when you attempt to rationalize the situation. If you ever saw Callum, you might question me and why on earth I would risk my love with Audrey for someone so venomous-looking and dangerous. But then again, perhaps therein lies the answer.

I sense what feels like a concrete weight pulling further and further down, sinking deeper into the furthest reaches of

67

my stomach, and eventually reaching my lower pelvis—a terrible reminder of my unborn child, the secret that will undo everything I've ever loved. It feels as though I'm standing at the edge of an impossible threshold—waiting to finally cross over, waiting to completely and utterly come undone.

It's late that same night when I begin to feel an intense pain in my lower abdomen—a dull ache that throbs like a dreadful reminder, the pain I'm about to cause. Audrey dozes beside me, snoring a little, but I've decided to stay up and read a book I've been trying to finish for the past three months. I pull myself out of bed and make my way toward the door. Remembering and especially cautious after dark, I whistle as I pass across the threshold and into the nearby bathroom. I flick on the lights and gaze at myself in the mirror.

I remove my shirt, staring at my chest and the breasts that are now forever gone. I notice how some patches of hair have grown, some hair sprouting around my nipples. But it's not much. My armpits are a little hairier too, ever since I stopped shaving, and I'm prideful of that minor accomplishment. I rub my stomach, turning to the side so that I can see my profile in the reflection. I flinch, imagining what I might look like with a distended gut—a child growing inside me. I presume I'll confuse many people on the street. I like to pretend that fact doesn't bother me. But privately it does. Even though I've grown patches of facial hair and have defined some of my muscles, I can't help but still feel like a cheap imitation of what I've been told all my life a man should be. I lower my head, realizing that I will never be one.

It's then that I make the final decision to wake Audrey and tell her what I've done. I already feel like so much of a phony. I can't bear the thought of her not knowing the truth, of her going on pretending that everything's fine when it's clearly not.

I pry open the bathroom door, whistling, and I pass into the bedroom. I come upon Audrey while she sleeps, and I shake her gently until she stirs. Her eyelids flutter open, and she sees me staring back at her. I watch her face thaw with visible warmth. She glances at the clock on the nightstand, and she rolls her eyes when she realizes how late it is.

"You're still up? Go to bed, baby."

Even though she turns over on her side, I pull at her and force her to look at me.

"There's something I need to tell you," I say. "Something I've been putting off for a long time. Something I've been afraid of telling you…"

Audrey turns, clearly a little unsettled. She straightens until she's sitting on the bed, gazing at me for an explanation.

"I want you to know how much I love you," I say to her. "How much I care about you. How much I would never want to hurt you…"

Audrey's eyes lower. She already seems to know. "You've been sleeping with someone else…"

I clear the catch in my throat, fearful of speaking at first.

"Yes," I say. "I've been seeing someone. His name's Callum."

Without warning, Audrey leaps off the bed and starts pacing the small room.

"How long?" she asks me.

I can't answer at first. All words seem impossible. But she barks at me once more and I feel myself unspooling bit by bit.

"For a few months," I tell her.

"I can't believe this."

"There's more," I say to her.

Audrey stops, eyes boring holes deep into me. "What else?"

I feel as though the thread between us is slowly coming apart stitch by stitch, a massive tear soon to arrive at any moment.

"I'm pregnant," I tell her.

Audrey rushes at me, fists slamming into my face and arms. She beats hard against me, screaming hoarse, and I push her away so forcefully that I'm surprised by my strength.

"Audrey, please," I beg her.

But she won't listen. She's yelling absurdities at me. She screams so powerfully that all the words she says after seem to blur together, almost like both our heads have been forced underwater. Just then, in slow motion, I watch as she moves toward the door leading to the stairwell. I'm about to call out to her, but I'm far too late. She's already passed over the threshold and is standing on the other side of the doorway.

"Audrey," I say to her in desperation.

She seems to realize her mistake almost instantly—her eyes widening with such unreserved fear, the skin on her face whitening.

Audrey flinches, standing there in the frame of the doorway. She cries out, looking down as though something has pricked the heel of her foot.

I watch as dark strands of her hair begin to straighten from the sides of her head, threads of hair unspooling and sticking upright like they had been bronzed there in place. Every hair on her head is standing vertical like a dark, wiry headdress framing her terrified face. Her eyes are shimmering wet and shiny. She *looks at me with a soundless plea for mercy, begging me to undo what she had so carelessly done—the misfortune she has invited, the terror her father warned her about when she was a mere child. I respond by reaching out to her, swiping at the air between us, and trying to pull her back into the safety of the bedroom.*

But it's too late. It cannot be undone now.

She screams only once, her body levitating in the air—limbs straightening and snapping like kindling—and then floating there for a brief moment. Before I can touch her hand and pull her back to me, she's yanked away—wrenched into oblivion, the dark place where light will not follow at the very end of the corridor.

I stand there, carefully observing the dark outside the bedroom doorway—the dim place where the lights will not reach. I wonder if she'll answer when I call to her. I try. But she doesn't reply. Instead, the unbearable silence returns, settling over the tiny cabin and lingering there until I peel myself from where I'm standing and make my way downstairs, whistling all the way.

It's been several weeks since Audrey was taken from me at the cabin—a moment I cannot make sense of no matter how fervently I make the attempt.

I filed a report with the local Burnt Sparrow police and told them a fabricated account of the events that had unfolded the very last night we were together. How at nine p.m., Audrey left the cabin to take a walk in the woods and then didn't return. How I went outside looking for her for a few hours before I eventually gave up and telephoned the police. They had appeared moderately satisfied with my story, but there had been suspicious glances directed at one another while I told them my version of what had happened that awful night.

Sometimes, I take drives from Boston to the small cabin hidden away in the New Hampshire hills. Audrey's parents have kindly allowed me to stay there from time to time, realizing that I so desperately want to remain close by in case she ever reappears, in case she ever wanders back home. I recognize that it's most likely absurd to consider something so foolish. I know what happened to her. I know why she was taken.

Part of me detests going to the small cabin. It's not only the foul stench of antiquity that turns me off visiting more frequently, but it's the indescribable feeling that I'm being watched by someone, something. I wish I could say that I feel this way only when I visit the cabin in New Hampshire, but I don't. I feel unnerved, unsettled in my apartment in the city, forever thinking that something is staring at me and can spy me whenever I pass across a threshold.

Some of my friends think I'm foolish when I whistle, passing through doorways. But I try not to pay much mind to them. I can't shake the feeling that something is permanently following me—watching me, hunting me, waiting for that moment when I finally lower my guard and pass through a doorway without whistling.

I find myself whistling all the time now, especially late at night after Callum has gone to sleep. My stomach is swollen and sometimes I rub myself, wondering what I'm carrying inside me—the precious thing that grows and grows, the thing that only seems content when I whistle.

There are moments when I feel sadness—the tedious aching pain of guilt—for what happened to Audrey. I can't help but reason that my affair with Callum caused her demise. If she hadn't been blindsided by my confession, she might have remembered what her father had told her when she passed through the bedroom doorway. I know that I must take some responsibility for what happened to her.

Sometimes I think I deserve the same agony she endured. I think of silently passing across the threshold of a room, sensing the tiny prick at the heel of my foot and then watching in my peripheral vision as my hair stands on end. I imagine what it might feel like—the misery I might call upon with such an invocation. Perhaps that would cleanse me. Perhaps that would make me feel the weight of becoming a true man.

I stand at the precipice of the cabin doorway, heavy luggage in both my hands. I hesitate for an instant—wondering if I should whistle, wondering if I can bear to exist in this state of purgatory for the rest of my life. I continue to idle there, eyeing the dark that waits for me on the other side of the door—the invisible eyes that watch me and wait for me with such purpose, such dedication. If I'm quiet enough, sometimes I can hear them chatter to one another, pondering if this time will be the time that they're close enough to finally touch me.

After a while, I pass through the open doorway, whistling a tune by Gershwin, and I sense something—dagger-like claws as soft as Venetian lace—blindly swat at me and then pull away like a discarded invitation, like a neglected proposal from one ghost to another.

The recording finally ends, the tape player shutting off with a soft "click." Rupert sits there, thinking of his mother and all the other stories she had once told him—the chilling tales they had once frequently bonded over. All of it seems lost, impossible to recover. He thinks of whistling and, sometimes, he wonders if he can hear the distant sound of his mother calling to him—her spirit loitering there at every threshold he contemplates crossing.

———

Several days pass, and most of the people residing in the town of Burnt Sparrow can talk only of the dreaded "relocation." More precisely, the transfer of the faceless family of three to the Esherwood estate—a place known as "End House"—situated on the outskirts of the town. It's all Rupert's father can talk about at the dinner table, one of the very few times when they're willingly together. While at school, Rupert overhears how several people are convinced that the faceless family is going to launch another attack during the process of their relocation. Why wouldn't they? It would be the perfect opportunity to level another devastating blow against the town.

Why do they hate us? Rupert wonders to himself as he scrapes food into the trash can. *Why did they choose to come here? Why us?*

These are questions that he doesn't expect to answer. They are certainly questions he knows he'll never find in the terror-filled faces of the helpless victims they gunned down in the middle of the street—their poor eyes forever fixed open, their hands trapped permanently in the awful moment they were clawing their way toward safety, freedom.

Rupert thought he might allow disgust or fear to creep into his mind as he strolls up and down the street, guarding the lifeless bodies from nocturnal scavengers who follow the scent of blood. But surprisingly he doesn't. Instead, Rupert feels nothing as he traipses up and down the narrow corridors of bodies where they have been piled for safekeeping. For some reason, it's difficult for him to imagine that these were once loved ones, friends, neighbors. To him, they are merely small pieces on an ornate chessboard. He's especially surprised with himself because he's been subjected to quite possibly the grimmest, most upsetting thing littering the roadway—the corpse of an infant in a blood-spattered, reindeer-covered onesie. Parts of the child's head are missing, tiny bits of the poor thing's skull lying nearby like specks of hard candy that have been scattered across the blood-soaked pavement.

Rupert thought he might tremor in disgust, turn away or even vomit. But he doesn't. Even his father was surprised with him at the time. Although it had proved to his father that he wasn't overly sensitive or incapable of toughening up, Rupert felt a pang of disgust for accepting the sight of the infant with such carelessness, such utter apathy.

Sometimes, he goes over to the section where the child has been left—even though he's not responsible for the bodies in that particular quadrant—and he tries to force himself to feel something when he regards the little corpse: the impossible, almost absurd-looking puzzle of its exploded face, the pearly bit of bone poking through that almost resembles a giant tooth. He gazes at the poor thing until one of the quadrant leaders in bright, clerical red comes over to him and asks him to move back to his section. The outcome is always the same: he feels nothing. He desperately wants to feel something and yet he cannot. Something inside him—some part of him he hasn't been aware of until now—keeps him from reacting. It tempers him perfectly and makes it so that he stares at the deceased child with a look of such indifference.

Rupert wonders how long this will last. Not only his frightening apathy but preserving the slaughtered victims in general. It's easy now in the winter months to preserve the corpses; however, the rot and the decay will set in early in May or June, depending on when exactly warm weather arrives at Burnt Sparrow. He asks his father what they plan to do or how the committee has decided to address the reality of decay when the time comes. His father merely shoos him away whenever he asks such things.

"You don't need to worry about that," his father says while they're seated at the dinner table one night. "The elders will take care of everything and will tell us how to serve."

Yes, to serve. That's exactly how it feels to live in the town of Burnt Sparrow. It feels like you must pay penance for your livelihood, for the privilege to remain here and, more importantly, remain useful here. Rupert twitches whenever he thinks of the town, and how so much of his childhood was spent volunteering with his mother at the library or the church rummage sale. Rupert knows it's ridiculous to even consider it, but sometimes it feels as though the town—the very soul, the essence of this community—drained his mother of all her energy.

Perhaps that's why she died at the age of forty-seven. For God's sake, the poor woman had no major health issues or concerns prior to the illness that eventually claimed her life. Rupert never really considered his mother's passing as something natural, especially when the circumstances surrounding her demise were so unnatural. He's thought about telling his father his suspicions, but in the end what would his father do? *What would Father say? What could he say?* It would most likely only upset him more and drive a wedge further between them until the connection they barely shared broke completely.

His father's mind is elsewhere whenever they're home. That much is always evident to Rupert, even in his teenage, pubescent haze. His father's absentmindedness has been even more alarming as of late, however. He doesn't spend much time downstairs in the living room as he once did. Instead, he often sneaks away to his bedroom and keeps the door locked until they have to get up early in the morning and perform their shift before Rupert heads to school. After a few days of this, Rupert decides to watch his father more closely, especially when they're guarding the corpses in the early hours of the morning.

Rupert fears that his father might notice his distrust. But thankfully he doesn't. He's much too caught up in other matters, as usual.

Gradually, Rupert notices his father routinely going back toward the corpse of a young blonde woman—no older than twenty-four or twenty-five. Rupert doesn't recognize her.

She's lying on her back, half of her face completely blown away and sleek, soft-looking tissue drooping from the crater that's been opened there. Despite the notable absence of much of her features, her youthfulness and beauty are still evident to anyone passing her, watching and monitoring her corpse.

Rupert observes, eyebrows furrowing, while his father drifts beside her body—his eyes, his attention fully captivated by the nameless woman lying on the ground in a puddle of her own blood. His father moves away after a while and circles some of the other corpses. But he doesn't keep away for too long. After a few minutes, he returns and weaves around her body like a curious predator. His father's face seems to soften as he regards the young woman sprawled on the ground at his feet—her winter coat in tatters, her shoes kicked off both feet. Rupert's father looks at her with curiosity mixed with such longing—a deep and pain-filled look of yearning for something that was and that will never be.

Rupert's stomach drops, little pangs of anguish filtering there and occasionally testing his comfort. He knows that look all too well. It's the same look his father had when they closed his wife's casket—the portal to her love and affection being sealed shut for all eternity.

The thing that really frightens Rupert is that the look his father has when he regards the corpse of the nameless woman lying in the street seems more earnest, more heartfelt than he's ever seen before. The intensity of the way in which his father gazes at the woman is alarming. Rupert wonders if others notice, if others are aware of his fixation, his intense attachment to the dead woman. Regardless, she seems to accept Rupert's father's infatuation with the very same apathy that Rupert has when he regards the butchered infant.

It troubles Rupert to see how his father seems to notice

her apathy, and how he appears frustrated, almost as if he were wishing there were something he could do to convince her, to sway her empty mind and force her to belong to him and him alone.

———

It's late in the afternoon on a weekend when Rupert decides to take a stroll in the woods behind his parents' house. He concedes that it's been unseasonably warm despite the time of year and figures he won't need a heavy jacket, especially if he's out for a short amount of time. He throws on a coat, slips into a pair of old winter boots, and then makes his way down the front steps and around the house until he arrives at the entrance of the narrow, tree-flanked pathway leading into a small grove of trees near the rear of the property. For a moment, he stands there at the edge of the path, gazing into the mouth of the forest and wondering if he spies something staring back at him. *Not every living thing in this world wants to hurt you*, he tries to remind himself. *Certain things are merely curious, cautious.* Still, he realizes that he's earned a modicum of wariness as well, loitering there and wondering if he should take the next step—to enter the small grove and surrender to anything that might be waiting there for him.

Eventually, his feet make the decision for him, and he moves swiftly through the maze of tall trees. Shadows pursue him— long, dark ones with spindle-thin fingers that seem eager to wrap around him and drag him screaming from the safety of daylight. While he paces back and forth inside the small grove, Rupert thinks of the woman lying lifeless on the main drag in town, and how his father regards her with such longing, such—*dare he say it?*—affection. His father has softened, as though something deep inside him has come undone. Rupert knows there are things that he will never comprehend about his father. Perhaps it's best for them to keep certain secrets from one another. Perhaps that's the only way love will be possible between a father and his son. All other forms of affection between loved ones feel like hollow mythologies, empty legends that are not truly believable. *Then again, aren't all legends supposed to be blatantly fictitious?* Rupert shakes his head, frustrated at the unbearable thought of never completely understanding his father.

He's about to slip away from the thicket of deeply nestled trees and return home when he hears what sounds like an infant sobbing. It's a shrill kind of whistle, a high-pitched shriek that seems to be coming from the underbrush beside one of the larger trees. Rupert recoils, the sound of the crying becoming louder and louder as he approaches. His stomach feels as though someone's punctured a hole in it. The unseen thing won't remain undiscovered for long. Not if Rupert can help it. He peels back some of the shrubbery and that's when he finally sees it—a small, black bird reclining in the dirt and stirring there gently. But there's something hideous about the poor creature's appearance. There are no black, bead-like eyes. There's no appearance of a beak or anything birdlike. Instead, the wretched thing appears to have been cursed with the face of a human infant—thin, elastic-band-looking lips that part slightly, narrow slits for eyes that haven't quite opened just yet, a small, gentle, and almost perfect-looking nose.

Rupert's breathing becomes shallower and shallower as he gazes at the vile creature and wonders how such a hideous thing ever came to be. He glances around the thicket, pondering if the damn thing's mother tucked it under the bush for safekeeping while she foraged for food. But the way the poor creature sobs, the way it seems to screech uncontrollably and with such horrible force, it's almost unmistakable that the miserable thing has been abandoned.

Rupert shudders a little, wondering if this is somehow his fault. Although he doesn't recognize himself in the face of the small creature, he muses whether his awful dreams have finally come true. He thinks of all the times he's shucked off his pants in this exact spot and sprayed the ground with his seed after a few moments of self-pleasure. He curses himself for the indulgence, the foolishness of performing such a stupid ritual time and time again. Look at what it's caused for him—the creation of a living thing, some horrible, hideous mutant. For a moment, he thinks of picking up a rock and bashing the wretched thing over the head until its face is crumpled and twisted. Once he'd finished killing it, he could dig a small hole nearby and then dump the mutilated remains inside so that nobody would ever know. But Rupert would always know. He'd be saddled with the memory of having created something and then having killed it, snuffed it out so that it couldn't suffer, couldn't divulge Rupert's awful secrets.

Rupert shakes his head. He can't live with the poor creature's death on his conscience. He knows that. He could leave the damn thing here to perish—for some predator to happen upon its nest and then snatch it up before snapping it in half like some kindling stick. But could he live with himself and the knowledge that he had played a part in the poor thing's demise? Rupert isn't wholly certain. He senses himself folding, crumpling a little under the realization that it's *his* fault that this loathsome thing is alive, enduring such agony in the first place. That's what he truly believes.

Before he talks himself out of it, he ladles the tiny bird from the ground. It's small enough to fit inside the palm of his hand. He gazes at it for a moment, wondering what's to be done. He could squeeze it tight inside his fist and then all of this would be over. He could pretend to be godlike for a moment, to decide the fate of another living thing. But Rupert has never held such cruel aspirations before. Why should he start now?

He dumps the small bird with the human face into his coat pocket and allows it to settle there for a moment. Its cries eventually weaken, and it seems to soften inside the warmth of the comfort-lined pouch. Rupert shivers a little, sensing the weight of the bird while it nestles there inside his pocket—a reminder that certain things can never be undone no matter how much you might will them to be gone, no matter how much you might wish them away. Eventually, he makes his way from the grove of trees and back toward the house.

His father tries to speak to him, to greet him at the threshold, but Rupert cannot be bothered with an awkward, loveless encounter right now. Instead, he sneaks upstairs and arrives at his bedroom with the horrible little secret he now knows he must hide away as long as he's alive—the stain that will mark him, the blemish that might be the inevitable thing that causes him to fully and completely come unspooled.

When he glances at his bed, he's unsure of what he's seeing at first. A small pile of fresh, new clothing folded neatly on the edge of the mattress—a few T-shirts, several pants, a few pairs of black socks. When he approaches the small heap of clothing—some articles with the tags still on—he begins to thaw, softening and thinking about his father. He hadn't expected his father to do something so kind, so selfless. It makes sense to Rupert that his father wouldn't offer the olive branch to him directly and would instead prefer to go about things anonymously, so that it's less awkward, less difficult. His father has always been so unsure of how to act around Rupert—uncertain how to present certain things to him, almost as if he were fearful the tenuous bond between them might snap at any moment. Rupert settles himself on the edge of the bed, sifting through the small pile of new clothing, and continues to think of his father. *Perhaps he's not so monstrous, after all.*

IN A LONELY PLACE: THE UNUSUAL HISTORY OF THE TOWN OF BURNT SPARROW, NEW HAMPSHIRE

Originally published online at *Mister Jakes's Menagerie of Curiosities* (exact domain name currently unavailable) on December 12, 2012, at 3:33 a.m.

If you ask the average resident in the state of New Hampshire what they know about the small town of Burnt Sparrow and the awful tragedy that disturbed their community many years ago, you will undoubtedly be met with a look of puzzlement that such a place could exist on any modern map. There are some who are familiar with the Christmas Day massacre that occurred in December 2003; however, much of the public recognition seems to disintegrate as you move further and further away from the actual place where it happened. When something truly terrible occurs in a small area, the response is almost always insulated and confined to that particular place. It's almost as if the darkness—the kernel of bad tidings—that was planted there can only reach so far. Roots that are healthy and strong can weave themselves deep into the fertile soil of the heart, but they eventually wither and recede if not tended to properly.

If it doesn't happen to you in your community, does it actually matter?

It's far too simple to argue that such things matter and that all human events are tethered by some imaginary cord that binds humanity like small tabs collected on a thin string of chicken wire. The truth of the matter is that what occurred in Burnt Sparrow only matters to those who were unfortunate enough to survive the catastrophe. However, the sheer fact that so many folks—even in the state of New Hampshire—are unaware of the town and its misfortune remains contemptible and unsavory, given the town's contributions to industrial advancement in the 1800s. So much of that seems forgotten now, especially with the shuttered paper factory looming there at the edge of the town like some uninvited wraith at a candlelit gathering.

To fully comprehend the severity of the misfortune that occurred on Christmas Day in 2003, one must become more acquainted with Burnt Sparrow's strange history and the reasons why it remains so undisturbed and unknown to outsiders even to this day. Burnt Sparrow was one of the first settlements to be established in the northern region of the state in the late 1600s, when many settlers hailing from Scandinavia arrived at the area's threshold in search of more welcoming, hospitable land. What they found suited them well enough and provided decent refuge. It's said, though not confirmed, that the town received its unusual name from one of the settlers—a young man named Ludovic Enrikson—who, upon first arrival at the remote glen where modern-day Burnt Sparrow exists, noticed a peculiar-looking bird—supposedly the size of a small wooden wagon—caught in the center of the forest pathway and pinned to the ground by an intricately woven set of ropes tethered to nearby wooden posts. Reports indicate—though credibility typically remains an issue when it comes to Burnt Sparrow town history—that when Enrikson attempted to free the creature from its prison of bondage, the bird's feathers turned blacker than a charnel pit and the poor thing dissolved to a thin curtain of ash before drifting away on a passing breeze.

From that moment, when the small family of Scandinavian settlers established themselves there, they were convinced that the land was marked by some kind of otherworldly supernatural force—a peculiar kind of power that was neither malignant nor benign. At least, that was what the settlers were said to have believed as they tethered themselves to the area now known as Burnt Sparrow. Unfortunately, so much of the town history is marked by an inevitable sense of misfortune or calamity that seems to hang over the community like some kind of transparent burial shroud. In many ways the town has already been entombed, quietly buried in the small, private glen where those settlers first discovered the richness and the peaceful serenity of the surrounding hills. Many of the few outsiders familiar with the town's sordid history might welcome the death of Burnt Sparrow—the annihilation of a place so indelibly touched by darkness, by the shadow of inequity.

A few might be aware of some of the unusual events that have plagued the town since it was first founded. It might be worth noting that so much of the misfortune and unhappiness polluting the village began to occur when the town's first and only mill was built in the late 1800s. Although the paper factory was hugely efficient and largely responsible for the town's financial enrichment, many still cite the mill as a major catalyst for the community's unending hardship. Perhaps one of the most un-nerving and troubling events that happened in Burnt Sparrow's history was the surprising discovery of a small, nameless infant in one of the closets located on the lower level of the factory. The most peculiar thing about the child was not its unnatural presence in such a location, but rather that the baby was completely devoid of any recognizable human features. Reports indicate that the child possessed no eyes, no mouth, no ears. Instead, two small, narrow slits from where it breathed. The acting foreman conferred with town elders, as was their custom, and he was consequently instructed to dispose of the infant as soon as possible. It's reported that the foreman swaddled the faceless child in a white blanket and then dumped the poor, pitiful thing into the mill's furnace to watch it burn. It was said that the child indeed perished; however, many months later, factory workers would later report hearing what sounded like the incessant shrieking of an invisible infant. Even more curiously, it's reported that when one of the larger machines was inspected after breaking down, a tattered, white baby's blanket—parts of the thing charred black and eaten away by fire—was dragged out from the sputtering machinery.

Although the discovery of the faceless infant is one of the darker blemishes soiling the town's already distasteful history, the community's most peculiar event occurred in the autumn of 1953, when it's reported that torrential rains pummeled Burnt Sparrow for seven days. On the eighth day, the submerged Main Street in town was littered with the corpses of large rats. Some residents claimed that the rats were swept into town from the flooded sewers; however, others insisted that the creatures were dumped there over the course of the seven days of rain, delivered there as some sort of cruel cosmic joke. Even more curious, the rats, like the strange infant discovered at the factory, were completely faceless.

No eyes, no ears, and no snouts. Their existence, like many living things in the town, is a curious testament to the familiar notion that almost every living thing will persevere no matter the agony, the deformity.

After the arrival and subsequent removal of the dead, faceless rats on Main Street, many reports indicate that Burnt Sparrow was left undisturbed until the spring of 2003, when a grisly murder occurred on the outskirts of the small village. Although the identity of the trespasser remains a mystery to this day, the unfortunate victim was later identified as a college student named Parker Hollis. It's reported that identifying the young man's corpse took longer than usual because the attacker had made every attempt to disfigure his target. When the body was first discovered by local law enforcement, it's said that the young man resembled a strange, otherworldly thing without a face. It's worth noting the timing of this tragedy as especially impactful, as several months later a family of three individuals descended upon the town of Burnt Sparrow and turned the Christmas Day parade into a bloodbath where it's reported over a hundred Burnt Sparrow civilians perished. Whether or not these separate incidents are related remains unknown to this day. Perhaps they are somehow tethered, in the way that all unfortunate events in the town of Burnt Sparrow seem to be a response to the town's previous misfortune. All horrible events throughout human history are like that—barbed responses to a prior hardship, terrifying answers to a previous devastation. Regardless, it's more than evident that there's a current of malice trickling gently beneath the surface of the land upon which Burnt Sparrow has been built. Does this misfortune truly mean anything to those who live outside the dismal community of Burnt Sparrow, New Hampshire? Unfortunately, it's quite obvious that it doesn't. Pain is not a universal feeling, as many would have you believe. Those who unfortunately find themselves in Burnt Sparrow have come to terms with this notion of isolated suffering. It's almost as if they're paying an impossible penance for the sin of those settlers who disturbed the balance of serenity and nature so many years ago. Nature reclaims everything in the end, and much to our collective dismay, humanity is nothing more than a fleeting idea—a waif of a miserable concept that deserves to be permanently extinguished.

GLADYS
ESHERWOOD

 It's early in the morning on a Wednesday in late January when Gladys Esherwood's maid, Veronica, knocks at her bedroom door.

Gladys knows that Veronica is always careful to remain unseen by the other members of the house staff when seeking out her companionship. But, surprisingly, Veronica seems to bash her fist against the door with an insistence, an urgency that cannot be denied. Gladys wonders to herself why Veronica would be so careless, so thoughtless in her delivery. *Christ in Heaven, does she want to be caught today?* Thankfully, Gladys's husband is in the workshop located in the cellar, so she knows he's not aware of their morning meetings. All the same, Gladys is bewildered by Veronica's urgent knocking so early in the day.

Gladys opens the door and is nearly trampled over when Veronica rushes inside the room. The poor young woman's face is heated red, her brow dotted and shining with beads of sweat.

"What's the matter?" Gladys asks, closing and locking the door.

Veronica swallows nervously. "He's asked me to tend to them once they arrive."

Gladys can hardly believe her. "He asked you—?"

"To see them as soon as they come here," she says, nearly spitting. "I'm expected to care for them!"

Gladys shakes her head. "Surely, he didn't mean—"

"What am I to do?" Veronica asks her. "What am I supposed to say? I don't want to be around those... *murderers*. Those monsters. I don't want them near me."

Gladys shushes her. "Keep your voice down. They'll hear you."

But Veronica can't be calmed. She starts to pace the floor. Back and forth. Back and forth.

"I don't want to even look at them," Veronica tells Gladys. "I'd rather scratch my eyes out. I couldn't bear it."

Knowing that Veronica can be comforted with physical affection rather than useless words, Gladys motions for Veronica to join her on the divan near her vanity. Veronica, rolling her eyes, sits beside Gladys with a groan of reluctance. But Gladys won't be put off by the young woman's childishness. Gladys runs her fingers through Veronica's hair, brushing some of the girl's strands from her face.

"You know I'd never let him force you to do anything that was against your wishes," Gladys tells her. "You were hired to be my companion. That's what you'll remain. Not some slave for a family of murderers."

Gladys notices how Veronica's breathing seems to slow as

she talks, her chest rising and falling—her breathing becoming more and more deliberate, each and every inhalation and exhalation calculated by measure.

Veronica shakes her head slightly. "But he already told me that he expects me to greet them as soon as they arrive this morning."

"My husband expects you to take care of me," Gladys tells her. "To see to my needs. That's what you'll do. That's what you've done up until now. Don't you think that suits you?"

Gladys notices how Veronica's cold guard seems to melt a little, more of her softness becoming apparent as Gladys leans closer to her.

"Yes. It suits me fine," Veronica says. "It's what I love doing most of all."

Sensing Veronica's breath heating her neck, Gladys pulls her close until their mouths are pressed against one another. Gladys pushes her tongue deep inside the pocket of Veronica's open mouth and circles there, attempting to unspool more of her nerve, her resistance. Her mouth feels warm, and Gladys would settle herself there if she could and bask in her heat until she begged to release her. But she never would. Veronica would never push her away. She'd probably sooner perish than allow that to happen.

Gladys figures it must be torture for Veronica to know that Gladys and her husband still have their intimate moments from time to time—sessions of uncontrolled fucking when she's humiliated, ravished, and defiled. It's her duty to perform the role of the obedient wife, the loving slave to her husband; however, lovemaking with Veronica has never been so rough, so degrading. Their moments together are tender and sweet, their hips locking together and the places between their thighs slowly becoming wet as they push back and forth against one another in perfect rhythm. For Gladys, it feels as though their bodies have perfectly aligned like planets in some kind of absurd celestial show, like they belong to one another and nobody else.

It feels like that for a moment—that indescribable sensation of symmetry—until Gladys pulls away from Veronica, dragging a thread of spittle from her quivering lips.

Gladys pushes her fingers into Veronica's open palm. "You know I'd never let him do anything to hurt you. I'd rather die."

Veronica smiles a little, her guard finally and completely lowered.

Gladys rises from the divan and moves over to the vanity, where she sits in front of the ornate, gold-flecked mirror.

"Brush my hair," Gladys orders Veronica.

Veronica doesn't hesitate for an instant. She approaches her mistress, swipes the diamond-embellished hairbrush from the bureau and then begins stroking Gladys's hair. Gladys smiles, watching her lover tend to her in the reflection of the looking glass. She believes if Veronica could comb her hair strand by strand, she would. Veronica would scrub and oil her feet too, just the same way Mary Magdalene had once tended to Christ. That's the true and complete depth of Veronica's unwavering devotion.

"When do you expect them?" Veronica asks her. "Soon?"

"Cyril says they should be here before ten," Gladys explains. "All of Burnt Sparrow will be present today."

"You're not frightened of them being in the house all the time? Always around?"

Gladys's eyes lower for a moment. Then her attention returns to Veronica. "I feel safe knowing that you're with me too… Promise you'll stay with me for the rest of the morning?"

Veronica pushes her hand into Gladys's. They squeeze each other's fingers until they feel a heartbeat between them—a sacred bond throbbing there, a wordless promise of affection and tenderness that can only be understood by another woman.

Gladys feels safe, protected.

Veronica continues to brush her hair and then, when she's finished, the two of them sit in silence, no words necessary— the dim sound of their heartbeats filling the entire room and eventually sounding as though it belongs to one monstrous heart, one vital organ that they share with one another and no one else.

———

Later the same morning, there's something upsetting about the way in which Gladys's husband calls to her from the downstairs parlor. His voice stretches, aching-sounding, almost. There's something curdled, stinking and rotted like carrion in the pit of his throat—something that immediately tells her that he's alarmed. She's unnerved by the thought of something upsetting Cyril. He's so stoic and so stately that she can hardly imagine anything ever coming close to troubling him. *My God, what on earth could it be?*

Gladys throws on her housecoat and hastens down the

corridor toward the stairwell. She passes the large, ornate oil portraits of the various deceased family members—the prestigious Esherwood bloodline—gazing down at her with birdlike senses and such scrupulous attention. All the painted figures seem to scowl at her, lips furrowing viciously and their eyes inspecting her with such condemnation and disgrace— silent voices whispering to her that she does not belong here, that she never belonged here.

Pushing the dreadful snarl of whisperings from her mind, Gladys tears down the staircase and sprints into the parlor where she finds her husband, Cyril, pacing back and forth in front of the fireplace. His mouth is twisted, crumpled in a scowl that softens whenever he takes a sip from his glass of brandy.

Gladys stands in the doorway for a moment, her ears perking at the sound of the record player playing "Rondo Brillant in B Minor." She chuckles to herself a little, knowing how Cyril only plays Franz Schubert when he's upset or sulking.

"Something's wrong?" she asks him, moving further inside the room and closer to the record player as the music serenades them.

"What's this nonsense about Veronica?" he asks.

"What about her?"

"She refuses to tend to our guests once they're here," Cyril says, setting the brandy down and crossing his arms.

"I would hardly call them guests."

Cyril seems to sense Gladys's dissatisfaction. Gladys is pleased with that. For now, at least.

"Oh. What would you call them?"

Gladys thinks for a moment. The word comes to her almost at once: "*Monsters.*"

"Whether or not they're monsters doesn't matter," Cyril tells her.

"All the people they murdered," Gladys says, her voice quivering. "You still can't bring yourself to call them *monsters?*"

Cyril stares at his wife for a beat too long. She recoils, a little surprised that she's still frightened of him. She knows he'd never hurt her. Or rather, she hopes that.

"Why is she refusing me?" Cyril asks. "What gives her the right to refuse something when I ask her?"

"Veronica didn't refuse you," Gladys reminds her husband. "I told you that I don't want her near those people. Whatever they are. Her role here was never intended to serve you and your needs. She works for me."

"I pay the little cunt," Cyril shouts. "She works for *me.*"

"She might work for you, but she follows my orders," Gladys says, shocked at her sudden brashness. "I don't want her near them."

Cyril uncrosses his arms for a moment and laughs politely—a laugh so harmless, so bland and uninspiring that it lowers Gladys's guard at once and she feels foolish, wondering why she feared the intenseness of his response in the first place. She's reminded immediately when Cyril lunges at her, grabbing her by the throat and squeezing tight against her windpipe.

"If you do anything to insult me, humiliate me today in front of our community, I will lock you down there in the cellar with those monsters," Cyril promises her, pressing his face against hers until he's practically spitting inside her mouth. "Do I make myself clear?"

Gladys struggles to answer, Cyril's steel-like grip on her throat tightening and tightening with every second. Stars pop, light blazing in the periphery of her vision as unconsciousness lingers nearby and threatens to claim her. But she fights it off and forces a weak nod that seems to appease her husband, because he releases her and then moves away. Gladys crumples against the sofa, coughing and struggling to catch her breath. Cyril's already at the parlor window, gazing out at the front of the house and, more precisely, the driveway where a few townspeople have already gathered and are waiting to be greeted.

"Some of them are here already," Cyril tells her.

Gladys swallows hard, wheezing and nearly breathless. "I'll go and change."

But Cyril tells her, "No. I want them to see the useless whore I married for what she truly is," he says, turning and moving toward the door.

"What about Veronica?" Gladys asks, calling after him. "What are you going to do with her?"

Cyril pivots for a moment, gazing at his wife with such disdain, such unreserved hatred.

"Veronica is expected to do what I ask her to do," Cyril tells her. "If I expect her to look after these people once they're placed in our care, she's supposed to do it. There are no other options."

Before Gladys can retaliate—say something, anything to wound her husband, or, at the very least, make him reconsider —Cyril flies out of the parlor and out of her eyesight.

Gladys, defeated and hurting, finds herself wrinkling onto the small couch beside the fireplace. She listens to the shrill chirp of the violins playing while the record spins, her attention eventually drifting to the small fire as it sputters and crackles. Feeling the warmth as it fills the room, Gladys thinks of when she was little and how her grandfather would wrap her in blankets and prop her beside the fireplace after she had finished playing outside in the freshly fallen snow. She hasn't been quite as happy, quite as content as when she was a child. Something in her has changed. She knows that. It keeps her up at night.

There's a part of her that wonders if Veronica knows this as well.

———

Gladys watches from the corner of the entryway as Cyril opens the door and greets the various townspeople already milling about outside. He receives them with the same lackluster enthusiasm that an owner might address an older dog who has delivered a branch or wooden stick. Despite his noticeable coldness, the villagers seem overjoyed to see him—to be welcomed by him, to be invited into his home.

Gladys loathes the fact that most people in town hold Cyril in such high regard. If only they knew him the way she knows him—the awful, monstrous things he's done to her in their quietest, most private moments together, the humiliations she's endured day after day simply for the sake of bearing the name "Esherwood." She often wonders why she married him, why she allowed her family to convince her to ever respond to Cyril's proposal with such tenderness and affection. He was once good to her. But something eventually awoke inside him—something that was once dormant came alive and flowered like a black root.

There are times when she reflects on the tender moments they shared with one another early on, when they were young and in love. That was so many years ago and, as Cyril often says, love withers two people away until they're threadbare and tattered. Love has such an agonizing way of destroying the familiar, the comfortable. Sometimes, Gladys wonders if she loved Cyril too earnestly, too enthusiastically from the very beginning. Perhaps she should have been less giving, restrained herself more. Still, there's not much to be said, because she knows for certain she would have eventually fallen in love with Veronica. She and Veronica were always meant to be with one another. All she can do is pray that Cyril never finds out. He'd destroy her if he had the chance.

Gladys watches as several townspeople traipse into their home, their heads swiveling as they admire the craftmanship, the opulence, the extravagance that Cyril and his family have fashioned here in Burnt Sparrow. It's not long before a small caravan appears in front of the house, several town elders departing from their vehicles and circling a small van that follows the procession of black cars.

One of the town elders—a gaunt-faced man wearing a large-brimmed black hat—approaches Cyril and offers him his hand. Gladys knows this man as Mr. Patefield, and has seen him in passing on the few times she's gone into town to shop.

"You have our precious cargo?" Cyril asks the town elder.

"We expected they might resist more," Mr. Patefield says. "It's shocking to see just how cooperative they are to things now."

Gladys glances up to the top of the nearby stairwell and notices Veronica observing from the second-floor landing. The young girl loiters there for a moment, watching, and then moves away when she realizes that Gladys has noticed her.

Several other town elders make their way into the foyer and come upon Cyril and Mr. Patefield while they chat.

"Lovely day for this grim business," one of the elders says to Cyril. "It doesn't seem right. Feels like it should be storming or pouring buckets instead."

"Careful, or you'll get your wish," another one of the elders says, laughing.

"Are they ready for us?" Mr. Patefield asks his constituents while removing his purple leather gloves. "We can't wait all day."

"They're waiting for your order," one of the elders informs him.

Gladys watches Mr. Patefield as he turns and motions to one of the guards dawdling near the van as it idles in the driveway. The guard accepts the order and motions for other watchmen to flank him as he prepares to slide open the van's rear door. As soon as the others with rifles prepared have come to his aid, the guard pushes the door open and reaches inside to grab the first prisoner.

Gladys strains to catch a glimpse of the captives, lifting herself up on her tiptoes as she cranes over the small crowd that's already gathered in the driveway. The guard pulls the first prisoner into the sunlight—a young teenage boy, no older than seventeen or eighteen, without a face. *How can that possibly be?* she wonders to herself. There's the small outlet—the tiny pinhole—arranged near where the boy's chin should be, but the damn thing has no eyes, no nose. Its existence seems impossible to Gladys. Surely it cannot be real.

She closes her eyes, willing the hideous thing far away until the driveway is clear, and all the people have left. But when Gladys pries open her eyes, she finds she possesses no such charmed powers.

Then the second and third captives arrive in the light as they descend from the idling van—each one more hideous, more abhorrent than the last. Gladys can scarcely believe that beings—creatures, more precisely—like this exist in the same world in which she dwells. It makes little sense to her. Then again, the monstrous things the family did at the town Christmas parade still make no sense to poor Gladys. She thinks of the families that were forever destroyed, the lives that were taken away. *How can such evil exist in the world?* she thinks to herself while the guards begin to prod the faceless family toward the front steps of the house.

As they draw nearer—the chains securing their hands and feet starting to clank loudly as they shuffle along—Gladys shrinks in terror. She thinks of ambushing her husband and throwing herself at his feet, begging him to reconsider everything—anything to keep them away, to keep them out of their home. But what would Cyril do? What could he possibly do even if she had the nerve, the audacity to sob at his feet like a beggar? He'd humiliate her in front of everyone. He'd make it so that she could never set foot in the town of Burnt Sparrow ever again. Is that what she truly wants? *Certainly not.*

Instead, she lets it happen. She pushes herself back until she's shrunk into the corner of the entryway. Inhaling sharply, Gladys can do nothing else but watch as the faceless family members amble across the threshold and move further into the house. The moment she had dreaded is now over. They are inside her home—soiling it, insulting it with their very presence.

"Can they understand me?" Cyril asks Mr. Patefield, who suddenly seems just as unnerved by the family's presence as Gladys. "If I say something to them—?"

Mr. Patefield swallows, nodding. His eyes never leave the faceless family. "We've found them to be responsive."

Cyril smiles. "Good."

Then, like a perverted master of ceremonies, Cyril receives the family with such joy, such excitement.

"Welcome," he says to them with a theatrical flourish. "I'm afraid I cannot lie to you and tell you that you'll be very happy here. But this is your home now."

The faceless family accept his warm welcome without comment. Instead, they linger in the hallway without movement like they have been lobotomized.

Cyril seems to deflate. Gladys figures he wishes they had resisted him more; Cyril seems to relish that.

Cyril motions for one of the servants to open the nearby doorway that leads downstairs to the cellar. The servant bows, obeying.

"Shall we see your new lodgings?" Cyril says.

One of the guards shoves the faceless teenage boy with the butt of his rifle, coaxing him to move. The boy stumbles forward mindlessly while the chains around his wrists and feet clatter like a rattlesnake's tail. His mother and father, secured on the same metal leash, move after their son until they begin to descend the cellar steps with the various rifle-wielding watchmen guiding the way.

Cyril looks at Gladys with a look that seems to say, *Come with us or else.* She immediately freezes. Fearing what he might do if she disobeys, Gladys reluctantly wrenches herself out of the entryway's corner and makes her way toward her husband. Together, they start to descend the cellar steps arm in arm. As they move lower and lower, the air around them cooling, Gladys feels as though there's a noose being tied around her neck—a lasso that's squeezing tighter and tighter until she finally chokes, a single name dribbling from between her lips while she dies: "*Veronica...*"

———

As the small group of people move down the cellar steps, Gladys tries to steal another peek at the shackled family while they descend lower and lower. To her, they resemble peculiar kinds of department store mannequins—faceless effigies that look almost and impossibly human, but just not quite.

Gladys recalls how she always detested the sight of mannequins whenever she visited the local mall with her mother when she was much younger. The mannequins had seemed to always leer at her with their imitation of friendliness, their inexact replications of joy and warmth. When she was little, there was one mannequin in particular that always frightened her: a model of a young pregnant mother situated in the maternity section of the store. For some reason, the figure's eyes seemed to haunt Gladys long after she and her mother had left the shop.

It was the coldness, the hollowness that had been carved into the model's very expression—dull and lethargic, completely unresponsive. Gladys always wondered how a mother-to-be— even a senseless replica—could resemble something so dismal, so bleak. Gladys realizes she sees that same kind of apathy, indifference, in each of the faceless family members as they descend the cellar steps.

The small group nears the bottom of the steps and Gladys watches as Cyril moves to the front of the procession, careful to avoid the faceless family as best he can. The cellar seems different since the last time she was down here. She's never invited, and, in fact, her husband has told her in no uncertain terms to keep away as much as possible. He argues that "loathsome, disgusting creatures" belong underground. Not her. "It would be an insult to your beauty," he's said in conversation at the dinner table. She supposes that's the most romantic affection Cyril is capable of offering her now.

Her attention then drifts to the three freshly made beds arranged in the far corner of the cellar, shackles fixed in the nearby stone wall. She imagines that's where the family will now sleep and thinks that the lodgings—as primitive as they may be—are still too good for them. *Why does he want them here? Why in God's name does he want these murderers in our home?*

A small wooden table is arranged near the three beds. The table is draped with fresh white linen and bears an assortment of various weapons—from kitchen knives to hatchets, from wooden spears to axes. She grimaces, shuddering at the very sight of them. It appears as though they've been lovingly arranged there by someone—probably Cyril—who's more than eager to make good use of them.

"Gentlemen," Cyril says to the watchmen. "Would you please introduce our guests to their new quarters?"

The guards prod the family members along until they reach the beds. The guards then release each family member from the chain-like tether that binds them and attach the shackles to the fixtures beside each of the small cots. When they're finished, the watchmen move away and watch as each of the family members stir in position, curious of their new, unfamiliar surroundings, like animals that have been relocated to a new paddock at the zoo.

For a few moments, everyone watches the prisoners as they become accustomed to their new residence. There's some kind of morbid curiosity shared among all the men that are present—a curiosity that seems to overcome any semblance of their disgust, an inquisitiveness that keeps them observing and forces them to inspect each murderer further and further.

"What about when they need to relieve themselves?" Mr. Patefield asks Cyril. "Surely, you've considered that."

Cyril replies by pointing to a small hole—a crude vent—in the nearby flooring.

"I'll have someone come down twice a day to take care of their needs," Cyril tells him.

"And you'll be present, of course?"

Cyril forces a little smirk. "I won't let them out of my sight."

Cyril seems to regard the faceless family with a perverted kind of affection, almost as if he were regarding the children they could never conceive. *Is that what these monsters are to him?* Gladys wonders. *Are these evil beings his new children?*

"Gentlemen, I propose we begin with the reason why we're here in the first place," Cyril announces.

Gladys observes while her husband circles the small table arranged with various weapons. He seems to admire each glistening blade, each perfectly thatched handle.

"It's not our intention to kill them, right?" Cyril says. "We want them to survive. To endure. To suffer for quite some time… We want them to feel everything, every pain, every agony they put us through."

Murmurs and whispers of agreement scatter throughout the small crowd of elders, some of them nodding.

Cyril picks up one of the butcher knives. "Mr. Patefield, would you care to do the honors?"

Mr. Patefield accepts Cyril's generous offer, bowing, and takes the knife from his hand. He approaches the faceless father who's been loitering beside the wall this whole time, standing there aimlessly like some dolt. Mr. Patefield inspects his first victim, his eyes seeming to pass over the faceless man with such scrutiny, such care—as though he were mapping in his mind the destruction, the utter desecration he's about to invite upon the poor unsuspecting captive.

"Remember: don't go too deep," Cyril says. "We don't want him to bleed out."

Mr. Patefield shoos him away. "I know. I know."

Gladys winces as Mr. Patefield approaches the faceless father until the two of them are uncomfortably close. Mr. Patefield stands there for a moment, the knife trembling in his hands. Then, suddenly, he slides the knife into the father's armpit and then drags it out from him. White shirt dying red from the spurt of blood, the man staggers back, seeming astonished. Before the faceless man can react any further, Mr. Patefield pushes the tip of the knife deep inside the thing's lower gut.

Cyril intervenes and elbows Mr. Patefield away.

"That's enough for now," he tells him.

But Mr. Patefield is clearly not satisfied. He scrapes past Cyril and stabs the faceless man once again. In the shoulder, this time. More blood sprouts beneath his shirt there. Just as Mr. Patefield is about to push the tip of his knife into the man once more, he sees something that troubles him—something that drains the healthy puce from his cheeks. He turns and glances at the other elders in the room, clearly wondering if they see it as well.

Gladys sees it: the three wounds that Mr. Patefield has recently opened in the faceless man have now completely closed, the blood drying and appearing to evaporate. It's as if he never stabbed him—threads of skin knitting themselves closed until the faceless man is complete once more.

"How can that—?" Mr. Patefield says, his voice trailing off, unsure.

Gladys watches as her husband snatches the butcher knife from Mr. Patefield's hands. He moves around the small cot and approaches the faceless woman, shackled and cowering in the cellar's corner. Without hesitation, he presses the knife into her exposed skin and drags the tip down the length of her arm until a stem of blood loosens there. He waits a few moments and then watches, dumbfounded, while the wound closes shut—the blood drying at once, the edges of her skin weaving together.

Mr. Patefield approaches Cyril, his breath growling while he moves. "This is an unwelcome development."

"What's to be done—?" one of the other elders shouts from the rear of the small crowd gathered in the basement. "We can't kill them."

"We don't quite know that for certain," Mr. Patefield says, studying each faceless family member with such hatred. "But we need time to discuss with the committee exactly what's to be done with them."

"What's to be done with them?" Cyril asks.

"Based on these new developments," Mr. Patefield says. "We need time to think."

Mr. Patefield turns and begins to move toward the stairwell. Cyril calls after him, but he won't reply. The guards and the other elders in the room shadow Mr. Patefield, following him up the stairs and out into the entryway. Soon the cellar has emptied except for Gladys and Cyril.

Gladys shudders, unnerved at the thought of being un-guarded in a room with murderers. Her eyes avoid the faceless family members stirring in the corner of the cellar. Instead, she stares at her husband, begging him to do something, say anything.

Finally, he does.

"They're going to take them away."

Gladys swallows, her throat itching. "Perhaps that's for the best."

Cyril grabs a hatchet from the wooden table and then tosses it against the wall. It clatters to the ground with a horrible thud.

He stands there for a moment—eyes lowered, shoulders dropped, utterly defeated. Gladys wonders why her husband is so fanatical, so devoted to this family of murderers. Surely he's engaged with unusual obsessions before. But it seems ridiculous even for him to devote so much of his time, so much of his energy to preserving a family of killers so that they can suffer day in and day out. *What's the point? Why does any of this matter so much to him?*

She watches as he observes each of the family members shackled to the wall, stirring in their confinement, unsettled in their captivity. She realizes why he was so adamant about relocating them to their home. It's not because he thought of them as the children they'll never bear; it's something else. Something far simpler to explain.

"You wanted to hurt these people," Gladys says. "Really and truly hurt them."

Cyril's face hardens, his lips curling. "I still can. Don't tell me I can't."

Gladys watches while her husband unzips his pants and then snatches one of the other knives from the wooden table. He approaches the faceless mother who's been wasting in the corner like a hospice patient muted by morphine, and then turns her around until her backside is facing him. He presses the blade of the knife against the poor woman's throat. The woman accepts his manhandling without comment, without pleas or pitiful supplications. How could she beg him? She allows him to expose her buttocks, stripping her of most of her clothing until she's completely naked. When he's visibly satisfied with his work, Cyril pushes himself into the woman until he's completely buried inside her and moaning. Gladys covers her mouth in disgust, observing while her husband slams himself against the poor creature again and again.

Back and forth. Back and forth.

Gladys wonders if she'll vomit. She almost does, bile surfacing in her throat for a moment and then dissolving right away.

She doesn't quite know how she manages to do it, but eventually Gladys pulls herself away from the obscene sight of her husband rutting the defenseless woman, and she starts to move toward the stairwell. Everything around her seems to blur, almost as though she were gradually awakening from some terrible dream. Gladys climbs the first step of the cellar stairwell, the sounds of her husband's animal-like grunts dimming to distant murmurs. She climbs the second step. Then the third. The fourth. The fifth. And so on.

Finally, she's out of the cellar. Away from the nightmare. For now.

She staggers toward the door leading to the parlor, wondering what she can do, what she could have done to stop him. Surely, she could have said something, could have tried to convince him not to go through with it. She wonders to herself how she'll ever touch him again, knowing what he's done—the horror he's invited into their home.

Without warning, her knees quiver and she's suddenly sent crashing to the floor. She lies there for a moment, unable to move.

Her imitation of strength comes apart completely and she begins to sob, wailing like a wounded animal and wondering if her very soul might split right down the middle.

RUPERT
CROMWELL

Rupert lies awake in bed, his eyes fixed on the ceiling fan as it hangs there without movement, and he listens to the sounds of his ancient childhood home—the creaking of wooden beams while they settle like an elderly person's bones at night, the distant chirp of the smoke detector from the cellar that his father has yet to repair.

Why has his father still not replaced the batteries in that stupid detector? His father was so much more on top of things when his mother was still alive. He had always expected things done a certain way, and was often exasperated at Rupert's disinterest and apathy toward what was considered "normal" for young boys to enjoy. Rupert concedes that from a very early age he realized that he and his father did not speak the same language.

That was fine when his mother was alive because she often served as a kind of interpreter. But now that she is gone forever, it is more than obvious that the two of them are incapable of properly communicating—perfect strangers destined to need one another in order to survive, and yet totally helpless of understanding one another's wants and requirements.

Just then, Rupert hears a soft mewling sound from the shoebox that he's tucked beneath his bed. He leans over the side of the mattress and pulls out the box, angling the lid open and revealing the small, black bird with the infant face stirring gently inside. Rupert had foraged in the backyard for all kinds of worms and beetles, but the creature seemed so disinterested and wouldn't eat anything that Rupert provided. The small creature straightens from where it has been lying and seems to regard him with such inquisitiveness, such obvious interest. He swallows, wondering what he can possibly do to keep this wretched thing alive. It seems like everything he brings to the bird is inadequate, useless. Do all caregivers feel this way when forced to look after their beloved? Are the weak and afflicted forced to endure torment day after day because their loved ones don't know how to properly tend to them?

For some inexplicable reason, Rupert feels compelled to touch the small bird—to rub the damn thing's bald head like some ritual to achieve a certain wish. Rupert points an index finger inside the box, about to touch the creature, when— *SNAP*. The little thing lunges for Rupert's finger, its teeth gnashing with such hideous intent. Rupert recoils. If he had gotten any closer, the wretched little thing might have broken the skin. *And then what?* Rupert would become infected, tainted, spoiled. Perhaps his wound would fester and sprout open with the birth of other strange, sewage-smelling, dwarf-like creatures that he'd be forced to care for.

Rupert curls inward, his limbs tightening beneath the bedsheets—almost as if he's anticipating something. Something he can't quite pinpoint. Something he can't quite describe. There's a rhythmic pulse coursing through the air. It's the same sort of anticipation he once felt at the local town fair, right before a car in the demolition derby crashed into one of the nearby bandstands and exploded upon impact. He recalls how he had smelled the unpleasant odor of gasoline and then first caught sight of the massive fireball plume stretching heavenward in the cloudless night sky. Then came the running and the shouting from where the derby was taking place—the ear-splitting shrieks from various guests to attend the wreckage, to save the driver. But it was far too late.

When law enforcement questioned most of the folks who had attended the fair, many people described how they began to suffer a sickening feeling in the pit of their stomach right before the explosion—almost as if they knew something was going to happen. It was the same awful feeling that Rupert had experienced. It's the same sickness he suffers from now, while he languishes in bed at four in the morning, staring at the ceiling. Something is about to happen. He can't quite tell what it is or why it might happen, but all the same, something terrible is fast approaching.

A few moments pass and he's proved correct, his ears perking at the sound of the floorboards outside his bedroom door creaking softly. He knows his father is standing on the other side of the door. *But what is he doing exactly? Listening to him sleep? Why should he even care?* His mother would often loiter outside his bedroom door when he was very little. She told him how she wanted to make sure he hadn't been ferried away by the woodland sprites that lived downstairs in the cupboard. As a curious five-year-old, Rupert had been enraptured with the idea of tiny creatures dwelling in their abode and capable of spiriting him far away from Burnt Sparrow. That is, until he realized that would mean he'd have to be far away from his mother. Then those ideas and desires began to subside.

Now, as a dispassionate seventeen-year-old, Rupert doesn't think there's any enchanted reasoning for his father standing outside his bedroom door. If anything, the reason is probably more related to his father's desire to kick Rupert from the nest—to discard the permanent reminder of his deceased wife's only living creation.

Rupert closes the lid to the shoebox and slides the thing underneath the bed. Before he can pull the sheets around him tighter and slip back beneath the covers, there's a gentle knock at his door. He leans over to the nightstand and switches on the lamp.

"Yeah?" he says.

The door swings open and reveals his father, fully dressed in his winter coat and galoshes, standing there with a look of expectancy—a look that seems to say, *Why are you still sleeping?*

"You know we're not expected to work today," Rupert tells him, rubbing his eyes. "We never go on Tuesdays."

His father stirs in the doorframe. The man clearly wants to cross the threshold but cannot for some inexplicable reason. He wants to say something—lips moving with muted words—but cannot. Rupert glares at him without any pity, begging him to say what he has to say and then be done with it.

His father seems to recognize his cruelty and pulls away for a moment, recoiling. Then he finally enters the room, starts moving toward the foot of Rupert's bed.

"I was debating whether or not I should come to you about this," his father tells him. "I didn't know if you'd be understanding…"

Rupert stifles a small laugh. That's rich. Rupert is the one who should be contemplating whether or not his father would be understanding about his sexual preferences.

"What is it?" Rupert asks.

"There's something I need to do in town," his father tells him. "Can you get dressed quickly and meet me downstairs—? I'll need your help with this…"

Rupert straightens a little. "Help with what?"

But his father doesn't answer. He's already moving out of the room and down the hall toward the stairwell.

Rupert sighs, uncomfortable. He slides out of bed and rubs his feet against the carpet, centering himself as best he can. Then he swipes a T-shirt draped on a nearby chair and a pair of pants that were tossed beside the dresser. He throws them on and darts out of his room, down the stairs to chase after his father. A little voice seems to whisper to him that he's heading toward something much like the explosion he witnessed at the town fair all those years ago.

———

Rupert and his father don't say anything to one another during the drive to town. *Why should we? What's there to say?*

Instead, Rupert listens to the car's motor humming painfully whenever his father eases his foot on the accelerator, the engine grumbling like some Biblical creature.

There are moments—as fleeting as they may be—when Rupert considers asking his father why the two of them are hurtling along the road to town in their old station wagon at four in the morning. There's a natural curiosity that accompanies something so odd, so otherwise outlandish and weird. But then Rupert admits to himself that asking such a question will force him to converse with his father, and that's a task he'd rather not have to endure at the moment.

While he sits in the passenger seat, Rupert wonders if every parent dies long before they actually pass away. Instead, parents self-destruct, annihilating themselves in the eyes of their children when they finally regress, when they evolve in reverse because of a disease or a sorrow that's claimed them. Rupert knows well enough already how a parent can become childlike and peculiar in their final days before dying. His poor mother suffered terribly, immolating in front of his very eyes, undoing years' worth of goodness and love in several moments of fleeting pain and agony. He wonders if it was worth it for her, if she found salvation in the strangeness, the absurdity she conjured in her final days before the illness eventually took her. Is there a point in every young person's life when they realize the horrible truth about their parents—how fucking weird they are, how strange they've become. Perhaps they were always queer; however, there's a distinct moment when that horrible realization makes itself known to every living person who's supposed to inherit their parents' space on earth. Rupert shifts in his seat, worried that such a day has finally arrived for him—the day when he will finally comprehend just how bizarre, how unusual his father actually is. He wants to care for his father and have a normal relationship; however, such things aren't possible now. Rupert has already peeled back the curtain. It's a threshold that cannot be turned away from ever again.

Finally, after what feels like a three-hour car ride in the dark, Rupert and his father arrive at the edge of the blocked-off main drag in town. There are police cars still idling with flashing lights at the end of the street, keeping all traffic out. Several officers are milling about the area, while a few Preservers traipse up and down the length of the partitioned roadway.

Rupert's father parks the car in a small lot near the entrance to Main Street. He switches off the engine and then glares at Rupert.

"I need you to do me a favor, Rupert," he says.

Rupert is silent, expecting the worst.

"I need you to speak with the officers stationed there," his father tells him, "long enough to distract them. To keep them occupied."

Rupert glances out the passenger window, gazing for a moment at the bright red and blue lights while they flicker in the distance.

"Keep them occupied from what?" he asks.

"Does it matter?" his father says. "This is why I brought you here. I thought you might be willing to help me."

Rupert thinks. He has no idea what his father is planning. But does he even care? For that matter, why should he? Still, there's a small part of him that wants to please his father. Even if he'd never actually admit it, there's a part of him that yearns for a conventional relationship with his father—something that seems so impossible and so unlikely with each passing day.

"What should I say to them?" Rupert asks.

"Think of anything," his father tells him. "Keep them occupied long enough for me to do what I need to do. Can I depend on you for that—?"

Once again, Rupert thinks. Surely he can trust his father. Even though he doesn't know him the way a son typically should, there's something to be said for the fact that the poor man raised him even if he didn't necessarily want to. Even if his father didn't want children and especially resented him after his mother died, Rupert could be safe in believing that his father still wants the best for him and cares for him in the way all fathers care for their young.

Rupert nods at his father, silently telling him that he's ready and willing.

Then both of them peel out of the car and begin to make their way toward the officers dawdling near the street's entrance. Rupert's father flashes his badge, and he's waved through. Rupert waits until his father passes through the barricade of police cruisers and then drops to the pavement, clutching his ankle. The officers, some rolling their eyes, rush to Rupert's aid and ask him what happened. Rupert explains how he must have tripped over an uneven part of the roadway and how he wonders if he's sprained his ankle. The officers tell him they can't be sure, but they try to lift him to his feet to see if he can walk. He hollers in agony, pretending to be sick. Out of the corner of his eye, Rupert watches in the distance while his father approaches the corpse of the nameless young woman that he's been paying close attention to for the past several weeks.

Rupert's stomach drops when he realizes the horrible truth of what his father is planning to do. His father clearly has every intention of prying her corpse from the roadway and transporting her away from what's supposed to be her final resting place. Rupert wonders if he can participate in something so wretched, so grotesque.

While the officers tend to his imitation of a sprained ankle, Rupert sees his father ladle the woman's corpse from the ground and sling her over his back. Rupert is surprised that his father can do something like this with Preservers loitering nearby. Then again, Rupert figures that his father already considered his options for removing the body. Late morning to early afternoon isn't possible because of all the foot traffic on the sidewalks with the various shops starting to open again despite the carnage in the roadway. Rupert's father was correct in his assessment of stealing the body in the early morning. The Preservers on duty at this time are usually the most dead-eyed, zombified dullards ever to occupy space in the town of Burnt Sparrow.

Rupert observes silently as his father props the corpse over his shoulders and then, with knees buckling, makes a dash down one of the nearby alleyways that cuts between two small buildings and leads to a quiet residential street. It's a matter of seconds before Rupert's father disappears from sight, vanishing down the narrow alley and away from the barricaded roadway.

When Rupert figures his father's work is complete, he

braces himself against one of the officers and struggles to lift himself off the ground. Finally, he does. He thinks to himself how he should have participated more in high school Drama Club. Perhaps he missed his calling. After he assures the officers that he's well enough to walk, he starts limping away from the barricade of police cruisers and makes his way toward the nearby abandoned parking lot. Just as he rounds the corner and arrives at the lot, he notices his father's car taillights flickering in the distance as his car pulls away and moves out onto the street, heading out of town toward home.

Rupert's guts twist and curl into themselves. It's obvious what's happened—his father has forgotten him.

He thinks what has to be done. He can stay here and wait for daylight. Perhaps wait for his father to realize his error and hope he'll return for him. Or he can start walking toward home.

Rupert steels his resolve and begins the three-mile trek toward his home on the outskirts of the village. As he walks, daylight begins to seep across the sky—the dim glow of dawn lighting his way.

———

Daylight breaks—the morning sky like paint melting on a warm canvas—as Rupert finally reaches the narrow driveway leading to his family's house. Eventually, he arrives at the front porch and half expects to find his father already changing the locks. Rupert feels foolish for not anticipating something like this earlier.

Rupert recalls how there was an ice-cream social fundraiser at the high school and how parents were invited to dine with their children during the event. Rupert waited for nearly half an hour, his bowl of chocolate ice cream melting, while he wondered if his father would show up. He didn't. When he went home later that day and asked his father why he hadn't shown up to the ice-cream social, his father had told him how he hadn't wanted to go. Simple as that. There were no tears, no heartfelt apology. Instead, his father told him rather matter-of-factly and then went on about his business.

Rupert slowly climbs the front porch steps, and when he reaches the door, he pulls down on the handle. The door sways open as he pushes and he's across the threshold in a matter of seconds. He doesn't have time to whistle. He looks about the entryway—downstairs is empty. The house is quiet—still, peaceful. He inches further inside, nervously looking around and feeling like an uninvited guest in his own home. Just then, he hears the gentle sound of music drifting through the corridor upstairs. He moves toward the stairwell and begins his ascent—slowly and hesitantly. It's not long before he's upstairs and realizes that the sound of the music is coming from the beyond the doorway at the end of the hall. The bathroom.

With hesitation, Rupert makes his way down the corridor until he arrives at the bathroom door. There's a sliver of yellow light spilling out into the hallway, the door almost completely shut. Rupert presses his nose through the small sliver and peers into the room. He senses his face whiten at the sight—his father kneeling beside the bathtub while he runs a damp washcloth over the nameless woman's naked body, her tattered clothing crumpled in a pile on the tiled floor. The music—some song played by a band from the 1940s—hisses through the radio speakers and fills the room while Rupert's father leans over the tub and tends to his beloved. He runs the cloth under the sink faucet, wetting it, and then returns to the tub to clean more of the blood from the dead woman's wax-like skin.

Rupert watches in horror as his father tenderly works the cloth up and down the length of her body—from her shoulders rusted brown with dried blood to her breasts and then eventually to her midriff and bellybutton. Then Rupert notices how his father's hands disappear below the poor woman's waist, scrubbing her there, and then his hands lingering with hideous intent. After a while, Rupert's father pulls his hands away from the woman. He lifts himself off his knees and towers over the bathtub for a moment, admiring the lifeless body. Then he does something that surprises Rupert. He loosens his belt. Lowering his pants until they're around his ankles, he kicks them off and then does the same with his shirt and underwear. Rupert thinks to look away but can't, for some strange reason. He's never seen his father naked before. Not even when he was a child.

He had thought he might turn away, might even shout out something in disgust, but he doesn't. Instead, Rupert remains kneeling at the bathroom doorway, peering inside and gazing at his naked father. His father climbs into the bathtub and positions himself in such a way that he's cradling the dead woman's body. Rupert thinks he might retch at the sight of his naked father spooning the poor young woman's corpse. Thankfully, he doesn't. He watches as his father lies there for a moment. Then he mounts her, groaning a little as he pushes himself to the hilt inside her. He rocks against her gently at first. Then, once he gets settled into the rhythm and the feeling of her lifelessness, he starts to thump against her with more force, more determination—a challenge to milk from her the last bit of fluid remaining in her dried out, desiccated cunt.

Rupert can do nothing else but merely watch. He thinks of the dead woman's family—her friends, her loved ones. Surely they never expected their beloved would end up in some pervert's bathroom, to be used as some kind of soulless object for leisure and enjoyment. Certainly, the young woman in question never expected that either. Rupert feels pity for her. That pity soon hardens to disgust for his father.

He knew his father was capable of horrific, monstrous things. But nothing like this.

Rupert thinks to pull himself away and lock himself away in his own room, but his attention is glued on his father. His father works his pelvis against the poor young woman again and again until he's satisfied—until he releases a soft moan of fulfilment, completely lost in the passion of a one-sided pleasure. Wondering if his father might pull away and show some visible remorse for the horror that he's accomplished here, Rupert waits. His father shows no such signs. Instead, he lies down beside the dead woman once more and pulls her close, until she's completely swallowed in his arms.

Rupert's father holds her with such tenderness, such carefulness—a crude imitation of the love and affection he once showed Rupert's mother. Rupert's hands tighten to fists, almost about to knock down the door and push inside to chastise and berate his father. But he can't do it. He can't bring himself to even go on another second gazing at his father while he lies there with his arms wrapped around a corpse that could never return the same love, the same fondness, the same softness and warmth.

Realizing there's nothing that can be done for now, Rupert pries himself away from the bathroom door and ambles down the hallway toward his bedroom. He shuffles into his room and then crawls into bed, kicking off his snow-damp sneakers and then slipping out of his pants so that he can be more comfortable. He stays in bed for hours, eyes glued to the ceiling fan once again and listening to the sound of splashing bath water from the room at the end of the hall. The God-awful sound of splashing punctuated by his father's almost inhuman grunting. It fills his mind. He thinks of the dead woman in the bathtub, wondering if she's intended to serve as his new mother—a hideous, grotesque replacement, an obscene imitation of maternal affection and tenderness. He thinks of his father, pondering how he could have abandoned him so easily, and questioning why he has chosen to act out such a perverted fantasy. Surely he'll be reprimanded for something like this if the elders in Burnt Sparrow ever find out. Rupert supposes it's not a matter of "if." It's a matter of "when." Perhaps there's some comfort to be found in that realization of the truth, he thinks to himself.

Pulling himself out of bed, he makes his way over to the desk arranged in the corner of the room. He swipes a notepad and pen. Then he starts to write. Anything and everything that arrives at the entryway of his thoughts. He writes: I fall in love with Finn Kitrick the day after my seventeenth birthday, and I tell him that I would gleefully undo my vertebrae for him if he ever asked. He thinks it's a beautiful sentence to begin a story with, and he quietly congratulates himself for thinking of something so poetic and yet so altogether absurd. *If only I could undo my vertebrae. If only there were a way out of this Godforsaken place!*

After an hour or so of writing, Rupert crawls out of his chair and drifts back toward his bed. Dragging himself under the bedsheets, he rolls on his side and closes his eyes. It takes him a while, but eventually he drifts off to sleep—a realm far away from the town of Burnt Sparrow, far from his father, from the nameless woman's corpse lying in the bathtub, from all the terrible monstrosities that poison his dreams and then turn them into Godless nightmares.

GLADYS
ESHERWOOD

Gladys watches as Veronica loosens the string securing her hair, letting it unravel until it falls past her shoulders. Veronica seems to delight in Gladys's attention—her unrestrained gaze, her eyes permanently locked on her and unwilling to let go. Gladys could spend all day gazing at her beloved.

They had already wasted so much of the afternoon making love in Gladys's bedroom, the bedsheets damp from sweat and the ceiling fan spinning tirelessly to cool the both of them down. Veronica sometimes glances at the doorway, as if expecting Cyril to barge in at any moment and catch them in the grotesque act of their lovemaking. But Gladys always comforts her, and tells her that the door is locked and he's far too preoccupied anyway.

Gladys watches silently while Veronica swipes a pair of shears from the vanity and pinches several strands of hair between her thumb and index finger. A single snip. She cuts a few strands of her hair and smiles, showing Gladys her handiwork.

"Seems like such an insult to you," Gladys says.

"It's what you wanted," Veronica reminds her, balling the hair in her fist and gently approaching her lover. "You still want it. Right?"

Gladys wonders if Veronica asks because the poor girl senses some kind of indecision from her, some sort of hesitation whenever Veronica draws near. If there's any reluctance residing within Gladys, it's because the cruelty of the world has planted it there—the hateful idea that two women should never couple with one another because it's supposedly unnatural and insulting to the sanctimony of traditional marriage and lovemaking. If Gladys appears hesitant to accept Veronica's offering—her desires, her passions, her sex—it's because she's endured enough hardship lying beneath her husband and pretending to be aroused whenever he penetrates her. But now he's sated with other objects to receive his affection—the family of murderers trapped in the house's dungeon-like cellar.

"I still want it," Gladys assures her, pushing aside any discomfort and dragging Veronica closer until they're pressed together. "I need it."

Gladys pulls Veronica into her embrace, their bare breasts touching and nipples firming as they rub together.

"It's going to hurt a little," Veronica says to Gladys, pulling away. "I'm afraid of hurting you, you know?"

Gladys smiles. "Sometimes you have to hurt someone to show how much you truly care."

She doesn't know if that is true or not. She says it convincingly enough that Veronica tilts her head and seems to accept the comment for what it is. But still, there's a part of

Veronica that looks distrustful—almost as if she knows that she shouldn't be doing this. Gladys takes Veronica's hand and kisses it.

"I promise this won't hurt me," she says.

Veronica inhales and then exhales deeply. She looks convinced. But perhaps not enough.

Gladys prepares herself as Veronica draws closer with the shears aimed at her left breast. There are only a few moments left before the irreversible is done. She could push Veronica away, could tell her that she's had misgivings about the whole thing and wants to reconsider. But she doesn't. She's not scared enough. She's excited. She's elated for the idea of Veronica cutting deep into her skin, the blood welling there, and some kind of ungodly tension being released in dark red rivulets.

Before Gladys realizes, Veronica's pressing the tip of the shears against her flesh and making a small incision there. Gladys flinches slightly, the metal blade cool at first and then heating her as it swipes across her bare skin. Soon a line of blood sprouts there, a thin current crawling down the slender curve of Gladys's breast. She looks down and feels queasy at the gruesome sight.

"Don't look yet," Veronica warns, bracing her. "I'm not finished…"

Then Veronica pokes her finger into the small blood-buttered pocket she's opened in Gladys's chest. Gladys shudders, shrinking at Veronica's touch, and feels guilty for pulling away. She knows she'd never abandon Veronica, would never willingly pull away from her as if she were a leper, as if she were some foul, diseased thing stewing in a gutter clogged with excrement. Gladys hopes that Veronica knows that. On some level, she believes that she does.

Veronica peels back the flap of skin and exposes some of the sinew beneath. Then, when she's satisfied, she stuffs the few strands of her hair inside the small pocket and closes the valve, elastic flesh pulling together as though they had never come apart. After she's buried the hair inside the small hole she has opened in Gladys's breast, Veronica grabs a needle and surgical thread she prepared on the nightstand beforehand.

"Almost done," she promises Gladys, working the needle through the skin and then drawing the lips of her wound close until they come together.

Finally, Veronica finishes binding the wound she has created and snaps the thread in half with her teeth. *Have I really asked my beloved to do such a thing?* Gladys wonders to herself. *Has she really and truly done that for me?*

Gladys can hardly believe it. She was slightly drunk on white wine when she first suggested the notion of Veronica donating something of hers that she can keep inside her for all time. She hadn't expected Veronica to ever agree to something so gruesome, so completely objectionable. Imagine her surprise when Veronica approved and showed a desire for it. At first, there was the issue of what item Veronica could donate. Some of the things Gladys had suggested seemed so inappropriate given the tenderness of their relationship—absurd things like teeth, fingernails, and pubic hair. Finally, they settled on a few strands of Veronica's head hair, because Gladys always runs her fingers through Veronica's hair any moment that she can. It had seemed like the perfect offering.

Gladys sits on the bed, naked, and feels a warmth vibrating inside her chest—the bristles of hair thawing inside her and spreading dark, luscious roots from her breasts to her feet.

"Where did you get the idea for something like this?" Veronica asks, setting the blood-soaked shears down on the nightstand. "It seems so... unusual."

Gladys covers her breast with her hand, sensing more vibrations quivering there.

"I saw it in a movie once," she tells her. "A woman takes the hair of her lover and sews it inside her chest."

Veronica seems a little concerned, her eyebrows furrowing. "How did the movie end?"

Gladys thinks for a moment, remembering. Then she senses her face hardening at the awful recollection. "The poor woman dies..."

Noticing that the light in the room has dimmed considerably since they first began making love hours ago, Gladys climbs off the bed and turns on the lamp until the room is glowing bright and alive.

"Not too much light," Veronica says. "He might come in here."

Gladys shakes her head. "He's been in the cellar all day. I doubt I'll see him tonight."

Veronica glances away and then back at Gladys, with a question she's been visibly aching to ask. "What does he do down there all day?"

Gladys thinks of what to say. Veronica must expect the master of the house to be a monstrous degenerate, a deplorable pervert; however, it's another thing to confirm those suspicions, to essentially out her husband to the world.

"He wanted me to watch him," Gladys tells her. "I refused… I don't know what he does. I don't care to know…"

"Do you think he's hurting them?" Veronica asks.

Gladys swallows, unsure. She feels her heart begin to beat a little faster, her cheeks reddening.

"What does it matter?" Gladys asks. "Don't you think they deserve to endure some kind of suffering? After what they've done—?"

"If he's hurting them, he's just as much of a monster as they are," Veronica reminds her.

Gladys softens a little. Perhaps Veronica is right. She doesn't quite know what to think. Does the faceless family in the cellar deserve pity? Or do they deserve to be tortured mercilessly day in and day out? Gladys recalls how she felt while she watched her husband mount the poor woman in the cellar—fucking her like some wild animal, subjecting her to cruelty after cruelty, humiliation after humiliation. She couldn't bear to watch any longer. But was it because the very sight of such a violent act troubled her? Or was it because she knew in her heart that it was wrong and that poor woman didn't deserve to be defiled by such a heartless, uncaring man? Either way, she won't be venturing into the cellar as long as the family is present and chained.

"This town is full of monsters," Gladys tells Veronica. "Sometimes, I dream of going far away."

"The two of us could, you know?" Veronica says, resting a hand on Gladys's thigh. "We could leave this place and go somewhere to be together."

Gladys smiles and then laughs at the absurd notion. "With

what money? Everything I have—everything I own—belongs to him. On paper, I have nothing."

"I have some money saved," Veronica tells her. "Enough to get by for a while. Enough for the two of us."

Gladys shakes her head. "He'd find me. And he'd kill you. You know that."

"You're just inventing excuses."

"You know what he'd do if I ever left him," Gladys says to her. "The greatest gift I could give you is to tell you to leave this place and go far away from here. But I'm too selfish for that."

Veronica looks away, tears welling in the corners of her eyes. "You just don't want to go with me."

Gladys swipes at Veronica's hands, but Veronica pulls away.

"You know that's not true, V," she says. "You know I want to be with you."

Veronica seems to harden, throwing her a hate-filled look. "But only on your terms. Here. In this house. The two of us: trapped."

"That's not fair," Gladys says.

But truthfully there's a part of her that wonders if Veronica's claims are accurate. She ponders if she's become comfortable in the relationship she's cultivated with Cyril, her love for Veronica budding in tandem and flowering side by side. She wants to take Veronica away from all of this—to be her savior, to be her fearless and daring protector. But, in her heart, Gladys knows she's none of those things. She's not the brave soul that Veronica clearly needs. She questions if it would be far kinder to wreck her, to ruin her in such a way that would make her never want to come back to End House ever again.

But she's far too self-centered for that. She could never exist in this home without Veronica. Veronica is the only thing that's kept her alive and sane for the last few years. Still, she knows that Veronica will leave one day, and she'll be left all alone with Cyril—the two of them seated across from one another at the dining room table and inventing new pleasantries to discuss with each other, before he inevitably becomes inebriated and decides to ravish her the same way he dishonored the poor woman in the cellar. Gladys doesn't know how much longer she can go on living like this.

Veronica doesn't stay to argue. She appears to be much too tired. Instead, she gathers her clothes and gets dressed, despite Gladys's repeated attempts to make her stay a while longer. Once she's dressed, Veronica unlatches the door and slips out into the hallway, where she picks up the tray of tea to return to the kitchen. Gladys watches her leave and then returns to her vanity, sitting naked in front of the large floor-length mirror. She admires the wound that Veronica has sewn in her breast— the lines zigzagging there, the rusted blood.

Even if Veronica does leave, she'll always have a piece of her. That's the real reason why she had argued so adamantly for Veronica to offer her something: because Gladys knows that she could leave any day now. She lives in fear of that, after all. She lives in fear of a lot of different things, but never quite expected to be fearful of her beloved Veronica.

In her quietest, most soul-defining moment, Gladys realizes that she yearns to be understood by another person more than anything. She feels that she's already wasted so much of her life not being understood by those who surround her, who claim to love her, who profess to understand her complexities, her most intricate delicacies. She's grateful to Cyril for rescuing her from a life of obscurity. Gladys knows what kind of life she was destined to lead given her upbringing—a God-fearing farmer's daughter raised by an alcoholic with a penchant for shouting and a meek, unassuming housewife who submitted to her husband as if he were her Lord and Savior. If her mother were stronger willed, she might have been a commendable role model. But she was so attached to the man she married that when he died, she perished not long after—as if he had called upon her from the grave. Gladys worries that she, too, will lose herself to the man she married, that she'll become a stain of her former self and won't recognize the woman staring at her from the mirror.

Gladys considers if she's ever really her true self around Veronica, or even Cyril, for that matter. Isolation truly and utterly forms a person. Isolation brings out the complexities, the unabashed truth of a human being, whether they are willing to reveal themselves or not. She spent so much of her childhood sequestered on the farm settled on the outskirts of Burnt Sparrow, she probably wouldn't know herself as well as she does if it weren't for those long periods of seclusion, those soul-emptying and tremendously uncomfortable moments of loneliness. Gladys remains thankful for those times when she was locked away in her bedroom—her once inquisitive nature forcing her teenage fingers to explore her own body, her burgeoning sexuality. She might never have discovered her queerness if it weren't for the loneliness she had endured on the farm as a teenager. Day after day. Year after year.

Despite her gratitude for those moments that defined her very spirit, Gladys concedes that she possesses an unquenchable thirst to be known, understood, and accepted by another human being. She feels foolish for once believing Cyril might submit to her whims, her fixation on both the male and female sexes. But she now realizes that the only thing Cyril truly cares about is power—his influence over others no matter their sex. He wants all to obey him, despite the obvious fact that he doesn't know himself. Gladys figures that's true of all people who want to exert dominance over other people—they're so focused on others that they don't really and truly know themselves. There was once a time when Gladys felt a semblance of pity for Cyril. However, all of that was erased the moment he defiled that faceless woman in the cellar.

———

It's later that same afternoon when Gladys hears a knock at her bedroom door. She sets down the book she's reading and meanders across the large room, unfastening the lock. There, standing in the doorway, is her husband. His forehead is dappled with sweat. His shirt is unbuttoned, exposing his dark chest hair and nearly perfect pectorals. Gladys notices how his sleeves are rolled up and parts of his white shirt are stained with blood.

"What happened?" she asks him, her voice thinning to a whisper at the gruesome sight of her husband.

Cyril pushes past her, walking into the room and looking around. "They're... miraculous."

Gladys rolls her eyes as soon as he utters the words. She knows exactly who he's talking about.

Cyril pants, wheezing as though he has been exercising for hours—toiling away without interruption. "I've been pushing them to their limits. They have none."

Gladys is afraid to ask. "What do you mean?"

"I took a hatchet and started cutting off their limbs," Cyril explains. "The tissue reconnects almost instantly, threading back together. You can't injure them…"

"Doesn't that frighten you?" Gladys asks. "They did something so horrible and now they can't be punished for what they've done."

Cyril sits in one of the chairs on the opposite side of the room, resting his feet on a small footstool. "It's clear to me that they can experience pain. But I'm not sure how much. That's why I'm testing them."

"When are they going to come to take them away?" Gladys asks.

"I've already spoken to some of the elders. They're going to remain here for the time being. Until they decide what's to be done, that is."

Gladys tries to prevent herself from saying anything, but the words come tumbling out all at once: "You want them as property, don't you?"

She recoils, surprised at herself for uttering something so brash, so careless.

Cyril smiles. "You know my tendency to want to collect things."

Yes, Gladys thinks to herself. *I know all about your collecting habits—your fondness for capturing people and keeping them as little trophies.*

"You don't have to play coy, Gladys," Cyril tells her. "I know you want to leave. I know you can't stand living here day in and day out... The boredom..."

Gladys is astonished. She's not normally one to hide her feelings, but she never anticipated her husband would ever acknowledge her unhappiness, let alone her desire to move far away from the town of Burnt Sparrow.

"Isn't that true?" Cyril asks her.

Gladys thinks for a moment. She could lie and pretend that she doesn't know what he's talking about—that she's happy here, that she's always been content here. But what's the point of pretending any longer? Especially now that he has his new little collection of misfits trapped in the cellar. He doesn't need her anymore for his amusement, his sexual deviance.

"Yes," she answers. "It's true. I want to leave."

Cyril smirks. "The house wouldn't be the same without you," he says. "I, for one, wouldn't be the same without you..."

"You once told me that you wanted me to be happy no matter what," Gladys says. "I hope that's still true."

Cyril rises from his chair and crosses toward Gladys. She shrinks away, but he's already backed her into a corner of the room. She's pinned there. Trapped.

"Then let me do what a husband should do when his wife is unhappy," he says to her. "Let me make it right. You know I'll always love you."

Yes, of course he says that. But does he truly mean it?

Gladys knows that Cyril doesn't want her to leave their

home. Who wants to be abandoned by their love? Cyril would never let that happen. Not to mention, there's something so comfortable, so familiar about him. Gladys loves and cares for Veronica, but she's been married to Cyril for over ten years. It's not always easy to walk away from a loved one—*more precisely, the obligation of a loved one*—even if that romantic spark, that all-consuming love has been snuffed out forever.

Before Gladys can respond, Cyril pushes his lips against hers. His tongue fishes inside her mouth, swirling there and teasing her softly. He grabs her breast and squeezes, forcing one of her hands onto his waist and then further down until she arrives at his crotch. Gladys had anticipated his advances, but she had expected she might resist more, might struggle to break free from his grasp and slip away so that he knew in no uncertain terms that she would never belong to him the same way ever again. But she doesn't do any of that, unfortunately. Instead, she merely allows the moment to happen. Their kissing becomes more intense, Cyril's hands frisking his wife and a few of his fingers sliding between her thighs.

Gladys pushes him away slightly, but that only seems to excite him more. They move, tangled in one another's arms, from the corner of the room toward the bed. Cyril eases Gladys down onto the sheet and then climbs on top of her, his mouth permanently tethered to hers.

Cyril rips Gladys's shirt open and his eyes seem to squint, questioning the small threaded wound on Gladys's breast. Realizing that he's staring, Gladys moves to cover herself. Her cheeks heat red, her heartbeat thumping away.

"What's this—?" he asks, his fingers about to touch the wound.

Gladys pulls away, shielding herself from him. "An accident from earlier. A clumsy moment with a pair of shears."

"You dressed it yourself?" Cyril asks, seeming a little doubtful. "With no help?"

Gladys swallows, trying to hide her nerves. She just nods.

Seemingly satisfied with her answer, Cyril resumes his labor —pressing his mouth against her neck and kissing her there, his mouth moving further down her body until his lips arrive at her left nipple. He sucks on it a little, teasing her, until it stiffens. Gladys cannot deny how good it feels. Even though she despises him, even though she loathes to dwell in the disrespect of his presence, she cannot pull herself away.

After a while, Cyril drags off Gladys's underwear and Gladys lifts her hips with an obvious invitation. It hurts a little when he first pushes himself inside her. She senses herself stretching, tearing under his force. He works himself in deeper with a single thrust, stabbing her, and Gladys closes her eyes. She feels unclean, knowing that the very thing inside her now had been inside the woman in the cellar. Gladys shudders, feeling as if Cyril has crawled and nestled somewhere—slowly polluting her body from the inside out.

It doesn't take long for Cyril to finish. It never does, after all. He isn't exactly a specimen of manhood, a paragon of masculinity when it comes to making love. A few quick thrusts and the matter has already been decided. He rolls over onto his side, his cock shortening and slimed with threads of pearly white spunk. Gladys, too, rolls over onto her side. But she faces away from him, nervous for him to bear witness to her humiliation, her shame. After a few moments, she climbs out of bed and excuses herself to the bathroom. She takes a warm washcloth and wipes the place between her legs—pushing more of Cyril out of her, hoping that no part of him remains. When she's finished, she sits in front of the mirror and stares at her reflection. She barely recognizes the hollow shell of a woman gazing back at her in the looking glass. The very sight frightens her, and she looks away, knowing that she'll begin to sob if she stares long enough.

WHAT EVER HAPPENED TO AMAYA RICHARDS? THE DISAPPEARANCE OF A BURNT SPARROW TODDLER

Originally published online at *Mister Jakes's Menagerie of Curiosities* (exact domain name currently unavailable) on May 11, 2022, at 3:33 a.m.

It's impossible to argue that one of the most sordid and unpleasant events in Burnt Sparrow's already tempestuous history has to do with the still-unexplained disappearance of a three-year-old named Amaya Richards. Born on July 8th, 1994, Amaya was the first and only daughter of Burnt Sparrow residents Ezra Richards and his wife, Beatrice (known affectionately throughout town as "Birdie"). Although Amaya was their pride and joy, many in town were unfamiliar with the girl's existence until she was reported missing by her parents in December 1997.

It's said that Birdie and Ezra contacted the police on Christmas morning with claims that their daughter had been abducted from their home. The police arrived at their residence and discovered visible signs of trespass on the property, with a bathroom window shattered and unlatched. Although the parents were inconsolable, the police assured them they would do everything within their power to locate Amaya.

Weeks passed and the search continued for the missing three-year-old. But something unexpected and grim occurred in the Richards household a week or so after they reported their daughter missing.

A sealed envelope arrived at their doorstep with no return address. When Birdie opened the envelope, she discovered a small, black feather tucked inside. Although she didn't think anything of the parcel at first, things became even more peculiar when another package arrived the following week with another black feather sealed inside a similar envelope.

More time passed and it was evident to both Ezra and Birdie that their precious Amaya would not be returning home. Matters became especially gruesome when a neighbor of the Richards called the police on February 13, 1998. When police arrived at the scene, they discovered Birdie leering over her husband's dead body, his mouth stuffed with black feathers. When she lunged at responding officers with a knife, they shot her.

To this day, Amaya's body has never been recovered. However, it's said that occasionally an envelope filled with black feathers appears on the doorstep of the home where the Richards family once lived.

Diary Entry Written By
RUPERT CROMWELL

February 2, 2004

There's a way to tell the future by spilling innocent blood. That's what I've been told, at least. I've never been present in the room when the monthly ritual takes place, when the axe is brought down upon some poor martyr's head, when a dark tide of blood curls across the empty floor. It supposedly occurs every three or four weeks, almost like a woman's menstrual cycle. Only a select few of the elders in Burnt Sparrow and the lowly, quivering wretch about to be sacrificed are permitted in the sacred space. I've been told by others what happens after the ritual—how the loose, random patterns of blood are examined by some of the elders, how predictions are definitively made. But it's something I will not understand until I'm finally in that small, windowless room, my shaved head fitted beneath the freshly sharpened blade about to come down. You see, when a throat is slashed, blood sprays hot like an unattended hose in the summer. At first, it's a heavy, difficult stream. An obscene flow with a godlike power almost, like some secret current that has been begging to be released but was constantly denied. It slows to a steady flow eventually, and then finally it weakens to a trickle, dark beads pattering the area. If you look closely at where the blood has been emptied, you'll notice certain patterns forming along the floor — curious little pathways, narrow ducts leading you toward a revelation, a secret that aches to be told. I don't recall when the elders first discovered that somehow you could reveal certain things, specific truths, from slaughtering innocent people. Like evolution, it's not merely one defining moment when everything was altered, but rather a gradual series of instances that finally led us to this. I can't tell you whether or not I believe what they tell me — that there's some specific way to regard the way blood is spilled when a sacrifice is made so that the future can be revealed. They seem to be under the impression that anything can be revealed with the right person observing the blood from a specific sacrifice, a person who's been molded, created simply for the sake of the offering.

RUPERT
CROMWELL

Rupert doesn't speak to his father much in the few weeks after the snatching of the dead woman. What can he possibly say to him after witnessing something so vile, so outright obscene? Rupert still feels sick to his stomach when he thinks of how he lingered at the bathroom doorway, watching his father undress and then make love to the woman's corpse. He wonders if his father loved his mother in the same way, if he was just as tender with her, just as delicate. Then he punishes himself for thinking of something so revolting, pinching his wrist until the skin turns dark purple and threatens to bleed.

Sometimes his father will try to speak to him at the dinner table, as if nothing's wrong, as if there isn't a dead woman's body lying upstairs in the bathtub—the same bathtub Rupert had enjoyed for years and now cannot use. Rupert worries that he smells and that the other kids at school will notice he's not washing himself regularly. He tries to dampen a washcloth and scrub his armpits with soap, but it's not the same as bathing properly. Rupert often worries that teachers might notice he's behaving oddly during class, his mind very much elsewhere. He's not sure what he would do if any officials came to him and asked why he was behaving so erratically and practicing such poor hygiene. He wonders if he would divulge his father's secret. To Rupert, it seems like some unspoken code that the two of them will never discuss the details of what his father has done. That said, there are times when Rupert yearns to tell someone, to scold his father for his monstrous perversions.

In an effort to soften some of the unpleasantness of the situation, Rupert decides to name the young woman so that he can refer to her in the privacy of his mind. He calls her "Agnetha." He names her after one of the members of the celebrated and iconic Swedish pop group ABBA—his favorite band. Rupert thinks it's fitting. Not to mention, he thinks Agnetha is such a pretty name, and the woman in the bathtub is so striking to look at even if most of her face is rusted brown with dried blood.

Rupert doesn't go into the bathroom where his father keeps her very often. It seems like another unspoken rule between them that Rupert will not interfere, will not knowingly put himself in the path of his father's shameful secret. Sometimes Rupert imagines asking his father why he did something so monstrous, so unforgiveable during their quiet drives to Main Street in town. Although the thought comes to him quite suddenly, the will to engage with his father never lasts and ends up abandoning him just as abruptly. He could question his father. He could interrogate him and beg him to reveal his true motivations for abducting and defiling that poor murdered woman. But what would be the point? The disgusting act has already occurred. They're well past the point of no return now.

There are many aspects of his father's relationship with Agnetha that Rupert doesn't understand. But the main thing Rupert seems to find himself bewildered by is his father's obsession with the dead woman. Very often, Rupert will peer through the bathroom door that's been left ajar, and he'll notice his father squatting on a stool beside the tub and gazing intently at Agnetha, almost as if he expects her to stir or say something. His father stares at the woman's rotting corpse with such focus, such patience. On more than one occasion, Rupert has noticed his father wiping away tears from his eyes while gazing at the dead woman. His father never regarded his mother with such tearful sympathy. He wonders why. He doesn't understand how his father can simply abandon the thought of his wife so hurriedly and turn to the embrace of another woman—even if she has already expired.

Rupert sits in the living room day after day, listening to the sounds of his father grunting and manhandling Agnetha's corpse in the upstairs bathroom. More often than not, he'll plug his ears with wads of cotton, or he'll turn up the music playing on the old record player.

One afternoon, the music is playing so loud that he doesn't hear the knock at the front door. It comes again. This time, louder—more forceful. Rupert switches the music off and crosses the room until he arrives at the front door. The doorway swings open to reveal a small pack of town officials—elders—dressed in their usual formal attire, all matching purple. One of the town elders crosses the threshold, pushing Rupert aside.

Rupert knows the man to be named Mr. Carmichael. He's older than most of the other gentlemen loitering at the doorway. The most distinguishing aspect of his withering features is that he bears a reddish-purple birthmark that obscures half of his face. His nose flares so exaggeratedly that Rupert can see the fat bristles of white hair blooming from his nostril. Like Mr. Patefield, Mr. Carmichael wears a wide-brimmed hat. The only major difference is his hat is adorned with a small yellow carnation.

"Is your father home?" Mr. Carmichael asks Rupert, surveying the room and sniffing the air.

Rupert can hardly answer. What's he to say? He can't possibly tell them that his father is upstairs defiling Agnetha's corpse for the second time today.

Rupert looks to the other elders crowding in the doorway. One by one, they begin to push past Rupert, filtering into the living room.

"I'm afraid it's urgent, Rupert," Mr. Patefield tells him. "We need to see your father at once."

"Has something happened?" Rupert asks the group of concerned-looking elders. "Something in town?"

Mr. Patefield glances at Mr. Carmichael, who already seems exasperated with the entire ordeal.

Mr. Patefield pulls Rupert aside. "There's been a theft. One of the bodies on the main drag in town. You wouldn't happen to know anything about that, dear boy?"

Rupert looks around the room, searching the faces of each elderly gentleman for a modicum of warmth, of understanding. There's none to be found.

He realizes he can protect his father, or he can sell his father's soul and cast him aside. He cares for his father. He loves him in his own unique way. But those feelings will never be reciprocated. His father will never adore him as his mother once did. His father will never care for him the same way. His father abandoned him already and forced him to walk all the way home. What's to say he wouldn't do something awful to harm Rupert?

Rupert swallows hard, his palms starting to sweat. He feels queasy and clammy all at once.

"My father's upstairs in the bathroom," Rupert tells Mr. Patefield. "The door at the end of the hall."

Mr. Patefield pats Rupert on the head like he is nothing more than a canine that has finally mastered the art of retrieving a ball. Then the elder motions for Mr. Carmichael to take the stairs, the remainder of the group of elderly gentlemen shadowing close. One of the elders from the group stays behind with Rupert like some sort of unnecessary chaperone. Rupert thinks to tell the gentleman to leave, but he doesn't have the nerve. Both Rupert and the lingering elder sit in silence, the quiet around them threatening to swallow them whole.

Suddenly, Rupert hears the bathroom door thud open, the door's handle presumably knocking the nearby wall. Shouting begins to follow, several of the elders hurling muffled profanities at Rupert's father. Rupert thinks to rise from his seat and head upstairs to see what's happening, but he knows that his chaperone probably wouldn't approve of him interfering in what's being done.

"*What have you done?*" one of the elders shouts, repeating it over and over again. "*How could you do this?*"

Rupert sinks deeper and deeper into the chair, wishing he could disappear, wishing he could pull the edges of everything around him further in and bury himself in the angry-looking wreckage.

———

Half an hour passes. Rupert knows this because he's been staring at the clock on the fireplace mantle. He listens to the creaking floorboards upstairs as the elderly gentlemen shift their weight from one end of the bathroom to the other, almost like a school of fish—operating with such unique precision, such unity. One goes one way. All the others follow.

Rupert tremors a little, worried that the elders will search his room and find the black bird with the human face in the shoebox he has hidden beneath his bed. He quietly prays that the damn thing doesn't cry while they're still in the house. He'll reward the wretched thing with anything it might desire once they go. He'll find the fattest beetles, the slimiest earthworms for the loathsome thing to feast on. But only if it stays quiet. Rupert can't bear the thought of attempting to explain to the inquisitive elders how the poor thing came to be, if they should find the vile creature nestled in Rupert's hiding place. *What on earth could he possibly say?*

More time passes and then Rupert hears a commotion at the top of the stairs. He turns and watches his father being led down the stairwell, dressed only in his underwear, and with a collar securing his neck and hands. The elders shove him down the stairs, inching step by step, until he arrives on the floor. One of the elders comes up behind Rupert's father and knocks him in the back of his knees. Rupert's father trembles, his legs giving way, and he crumples to the floor for a moment. Rupert leaps out of his seat, about to rush over to him, but his chaperone prevents him from moving any closer.

"Shouldn't we allow him to get dressed?" one of the elders asks Mr. Carmichael.

Mr. Carmichael sneers at Rupert's father. "And afford him a decency he doesn't deserve? I think not."

Some of the elders grab hold of Rupert's father and ferry him toward the front door, his feet dragging.

"Where are you taking him?" Rupert asks them.

The elders turn, their eyes collectively widening as if surprised Rupert would be bold enough to ask.

"The boy knew," one of the elders says. "Maybe he deserves to be punished as well?"

Rupert curls inward at the thought of punishment, his stomach churning at the idea of being subjected to cruelty after cruelty for a crime he never dreamed of committing.

"No," Mr. Carmichael says, waving off some of the elders who have already begun to gradually approach Rupert the way hunters might approach a wounded, dying fawn. "The boy's punishment will be bearing witness to his father's degradation. That's penalty enough."

Rupert breathes a sigh of relief, his whole body seeming to loosen at Mr. Carmichael's verdict. Still, that doesn't leave his father off the hook. Rupert watches as his father is dragged out of the house in his underwear. At first, Rupert wonders if his father will look at him—if his father will even acknowledge his mistake and look at him with a wordless apology, even a soundless plea for pity. But his father doesn't. His father won't look at him. No matter what. Rupert hopes he might witness a look of self-reflection from him, a realization of what he has done. But no such look comes from his father. Instead, he remains staring at the ground while he's dragged from the house and tossed into one of the black cars waiting in the driveway.

One of the remaining elders grabs hold of Rupert's arm and shuttles him from the living room to the front porch. Before Rupert realizes it, he's being pushed down the front steps and into another idling black car that's been parked in the driveway. The interior of the car is sleek and velvety smooth. Rupert feels guilty for indulging in the comfort of the leather seats. He sits gazing out the window at his childhood home. He wonders if the elders will allow his father to return home, if the two of them will be together once more as father and son. Rupert isn't certain, but he has an inkling that the elders plan to make it so that his father is held fully accountable for his wickedness.

Rupert's mind turns to Agnetha. He feels sorry for the dead woman—decaying bit by bit in a bathtub, abandoned there like a child's discarded plaything. But for the first time, a thought enters his mind that surprises him. Is what his father did different than the unusualness of the town elders leaving the slaughtered bodies to rot on Main Street? His father did things to the body—horrible, unspeakable things. But Rupert wonders if what his father did was just as hideous, just as disgusting as the town's way of grieving and mourning all the lives lost on Christmas Day. Rupert isn't sure. That uncertainty is what ultimately terrifies him.

All words seem so futile, so inconsequential to Rupert while he sits, hands folded politely in his lap, in the back seat of the black car. He feels cramped, sandwiched between two of the heavier elder gentlemen who had ushered him from his home to follow his father. As the car drifts along the road, Rupert keeps his eyes trained on the taillights of the other black car leading the way. The very same car his father had been thrown into when he was snatched away.

Rupert expects his father is bewildered and frightened. He wonders what that looks like for him. Rupert realizes that he's never seen his father afraid. He's never even truly seen his father display any semblance of emotion other than when he was in the company of Agnetha's corpse. Rupert worries what the elders will do to his father now that they know of his transgressions, his horrible perversity. He imagines that serving and protecting the remaining corpses littering Main Street— the ones that haven't been dragged away by wild animals, scavengers of carrion—will not be possible anymore. Once again, his father will be out of a job.

Rupert begins to worry that his father's unemployment might prevent him from leaving town once he turns eighteen. Perhaps his father will need him more. Perhaps he'll feel guilty for abandoning his penniless father. Rupert feels foolish for even thinking such a thing. His father has done very little to encourage him and display any modicum of tenderness or affection. It's not that Rupert requires that unconditional love from a parent. He has always felt unnatural around his father, even when his mother was alive. But he can't help but wonder if he'll ever be able to step away from the mess of a life he and his father have inherited from his mother's demise.

Rupert's attention drifts to one of the elder gentlemen sitting beside him in the crowded back seat. He notices how the old gentleman has a sullen-looking face and a wart sitting at the tip of his nose. The man sneers at him.

"How long have you known what your father was doing in there?" he asks Rupert, his voice grating and rough.

Mr. Patefield's eyes dart to the rearview mirror as he stirs in the driver's seat. He looks irritated.

"Don't ask the boy anything yet," he says to the gentleman. "Wait for Carmichael."

The gentleman eases back into his seat, sighing deeply.

The car continues to motor along the narrow stretch of tree-lined roadway, eventually passing through a large wrought-iron gate and gliding up an immaculately groomed driveway. Rupert peers out through the window and it's then that he sees where they're headed—End House. He's never been there, but he's certainly heard of the impressiveness of the Esherwood family home, one of the oldest and largest residences in the town of Burnt Sparrow. The house is so famous and celebrated in town that students at the local elementary school are taught about the Esherwood property. The house glares down at them as they circle the area, sweeping toward the house's front walkway.

Rupert feels so small, so insignificant. He recoils a little, some of the home's shuttered windows look like the teeth of an open-mouthed giant. Finally, the car parks and the two elderly gentlemen seated in the front climb out of the vehicle and then open the rear passenger doors. Rupert is about to climb off the seat when instead he's dragged out by hands far more eager to pull him along. He's tossed out of the car and lands in the driveway with a thud. He looks up and notices his father, still half-naked and shackled, being ladled from the other black car. Once his father is on his feet once more, the elder gentlemen responsible for him push him up the pathway toward the house's front door. Mr. Patefield grabs hold of Rupert's collar and pulls him along, keeping him at a considerable distance from his father's reach.

One of the elders pummels his fist against the door. They wait a few moments. The doorway parts open and a young woman appears in the sliver. Rupert thinks she's attractive enough, but there's something about her that immediately bewilders him. She looks so disturbed, as if she has seen every wealth that Hell has to offer. Moreover, she looks cautious and fearful of the old men lingering at the doorway. She seems to become especially unnerved when she notices Rupert's father dawdling there, dressed only in his underclothing, and shivering from the cold.

"Is Mr. Esherwood home?" Mr. Carmichael says, pushing his hand against the door so that the young maid is forced to obey and open the door further. "I'm afraid it's very urgent."

The maid retreats, allowing the door to swing open all the way. The men do not hesitate, storming the entryway and dragging Rupert's father until he's thrown on the marble floor.

"Where is he?" Mr. Carmichael asks the young maid, who looks too afraid to answer.

Without warning, Mr. Esherwood appears at the top of the

stairs like some deity prepared to receive his wretched offering. A somber-faced woman, probably ten years or so younger than he is, flanks him. Rupert assumes that must be his wife.

"Gentlemen," Mr. Esherwood says, drifting down the stairwell and commanding his wife to follow him. "To what do I owe the pleasure of your visit today?"

Rupert's father answers with a guttural moan, doubling over in agony from where he's been kicked in the ribs by one of the elderly gentlemen. Mr. Esherwood seems to take note of the prisoner all at once, studying him the same way a diner at an elegant eatery might observe a cockroach.

"This man has performed an egregious transgression against our town," Mr. Carmichael explains, spitting on Rupert's father. "Defiler of corpses."

"Since you and your household are tending to the town prisoners, we thought we'd convene here and discuss what's to be done with him," Mr. Patefield says.

Mr. Esherwood looks surprised, almost as if he hadn't expected the town elders to seek him out with such a grim and dangerous issue. Then his face softens, looking visibly pleased with the notion of the town elders requesting his counsel. He's excited, delighted almost.

"I see," Mr. Esherwood says. "What did he do exactly?"

"He stole one of the corpses from town and kept her in his home," one of the elders shouts from the rear of the small crowd. "The boy knew about it, too."

The room fills with whispers as the crowd of elders talks among themselves. Mr. Patefield issues a forceful motion, quieting them at once.

"This is the man's seventeen-year-old son," Mr. Patefield says, grabbing Rupert by the neck and pushing him to the front of the crowd. "It's obvious he knew about the ordeal before we did."

Rupert's eyes lower with humiliation. Then he glances at the woman standing beside Mr. Esherwood who looks at him with such pity, such sympathy, that it completely surprises Rupert at first.

"What do you think we should do with the both of them?" Mr. Carmichael asks.

Mr. Esherwood circles Rupert's father while he kneels on the floor and twitches. Then his eyes dart to Rupert with a look that seems to say, *You're guilty, aren't you?* Rupert looks away, too embarrassed to keep his eyes on Mr. Esherwood for fear that he's somehow been endowed with the gift of reading people's minds.

"The boy isn't guilty," Mr. Esherwood says to the crowd of elders. "He's not even a man yet, for God's sake."

The elders seem to respond in agreement, nodding with one another.

"But his father must be punished," Mr. Esherwood explains. "His kind of thoughtless and perverted disobedience deserves swift action."

"Like what?" Mr. Patefield asks.

Rupert notices how all the elders seem to inch closer to Mr. Esherwood, hanging on to his every word.

"I think he should be punished and should suffer quickly," Mr. Esherwood says. "Take him to the river and bind him with stones."

Rupert feels sick to his stomach, nearly bending over and vomiting. But he doesn't. Instead, he stares at the poor, quivering wretch of his father while he trembles on the marbled floor. Rupert glances at Mr. Esherwood's wife, and she seems distraught but hides it well. She gives him a quick look of pity and then turns away. For a moment, Rupert is grateful that someone else in this cruel, unforgiving town recognizes how greatly he suffers, how he bears such a worthless affliction for the world to view and then move along as if he were nothing, as if he was always less than nothing.

———

Rupert tightens his shirt collar, the icy wind whipping hard against him, as he's marched through a small thicket of trees on the outskirts of the Esherwood property. He's been walking single file with the elder gentlemen leading the way for the past half hour, and he feels tired. He wonders when they'll stop to rest or if where they're headed is nearby.

His father is near the front of the procession with elders guarding him as if he were some kind of deranged convict. Rupert supposes that in their eyes his father must be as worthless as scum. Sometimes certain members of the group of elders strike Rupert's father with such force that Mr. Carmichael or Mr. Patefield must intervene and tell them to refrain from killing him just yet.

As they march down a narrow path through the forest, Rupert glances back and notices Mr. Esherwood and his wife drawing close behind him. Mr. Esherwood seems so joyful, so excited to witness an execution. His wife, however, looks totally nonplussed. She appears nervous, her eyes dart about like captured prey.

Finally, after what feels like an eternity, the group reaches a steep embankment that leads down to a riverbank. Rupert had wondered if the river would be frozen this time of year, but since the weather has been so agreeable for the most part, the current flows and hums sweetly with a distinct call to all nearby living things—a call that seems to say, *Come to me. Drink from me.* Rupert muses how any body of water is a source of life—a beginning point for all living things, the very start of a sentence that ends elsewhere. He then thinks of how this same river will be the very thing that causes his father's demise—his drowning. The thought bewilders him, and he doesn't know what to do with himself while the elder gentlemen guide his father down the small incline toward the water lapping at the muddy shore.

His father stands near the river's edge, his bare feet careful to avoid the water until one of the elders pushes him and he topples down. He cries out, wounded, and he's helped to his feet immediately by two of the more merciful elders of the clan. Rupert grimaces while he observes his father standing there and shivering. The water has made his father's white underwear transparent and the poor man's shrunken manhood is clearly visible to all. Rupert feels such pity for his father. He knows that he's not responsible for what his father did, and that his father must be held accountable for his actions; however, his father's suffering is nearly unbearable for him to witness.

But not for Mr. Esherwood, it seems.

The steely-faced gentleman seems to delight in Rupert's

father's distress, his torment. He watches with such gleeful enthusiasm, occasionally commending the elders for their roughness and manhandling of the captive.

Finally, the moment arrives that Rupert had been dreading. He sees Mr. Patefield look to Mr. Esherwood for some kind of signal for approval. Mr. Esherwood motions for the elders to begin the execution at once.

Although the elders have already dispensed with any pleasantries when they first arrived, their yearning to make Rupert's father suffer becomes apparent when two of them—overseen and directed by Mr. Carmichael—grab hold of the poor man and force his face down into the water. Rupert's father struggles to resist them, but more elders flank him and steady his flailing arms. Then the two elders in charge of the execution take turns dunking Rupert's father's head in the stream. Rupert's father snaps back out of the water at their command, thrashing and gasping for air.

Rupert sees how panicky his father has become—so desperate to live, so afraid to die. The elders push Rupert's father down into the river one final time and they hold his head underwater for a beat too long. Then one of the elders picks up a large stone from the shore and smashes it against the back of his father's head. There's a sharp, cracking sound punctuated by the gentle noise of water lapping against the poor man's lifeless body. Then there's an uncomfortable stillness lingering over the group of onlookers, a quiet memorial for a grotesque man who did not deserve any pity. The elders eventually release his arms and let his head bob there in the water for a while, gazing at their handiwork and complimenting one another on their labors. Rupert feels sick to his stomach, his eyes locked on his father's corpse lying face down in the muck at the water's edge. The water has turned black and oily from all the blood emptying out of the gaping hole winking at him in the back of his father's skull.

Some of the elders pull out small notepads and fountain pens—to make notes on the execution, perhaps even to make predictions about next year's harvest from the way the blood ebbs into the passing current.

"What shall we do with the body?" Mr. Patefield asks.

"Strip him completely," Mr. Esherwood orders. "Let the fish eat him."

One of the elders tears off Rupert's father's underwear, exposing his ass. Rupert's heart sinks. He had never expected to see his father so exposed, so humiliated. It feels improper to see him fully naked now that he's dead.

Without warning, another elder steps forward and kicks the body further into the river, where it bobs gently for a moment and then is carried off by the current.

Rupert holds a private funeral in his mind for his father—all the things he wanted to tell him, all the things he wanted to do together. All those possibilities, those hopes, those dreams are now forever gone. To Rupert, it doesn't matter that he wasn't able to hold a proper ceremony for his expired father. He feels a semblance of jealousy for his father's corpse and how he's finally escaped the town of Burnt Sparrow. Although he's not sure where the river's unrelenting current will take his father's body, it must be far away from here—the most wonderful place you could ever dream of.

Some of the elders pass by Rupert with muted condolences, obviously fearful of upsetting anyone else and sharing sympathies with the child of some loathsome pervert. Rupert accepts their wordless pities without comment. He stands, frozen. Unsure what to do. Even uncertain how to move or if movement is even possible for him. Mr. Carmichael pulls him out of his daze, surprising him with a pat on the back and a muted look of pity.

"What's to be done with him?" Mr. Patefield asks Mr. Carmichael, referring to Rupert.

Mr. Carmichael then glances at Mr. Esherwood. "You believe the boy shouldn't be punished for his involvement in this?"

"We can't let him go back to an empty house," one of the elders says. "Someone needs to look after him."

"I will," Mr. Esherwood says.

All heads swivel and face Mr. Esherwood, unsure if they've heard him correctly.

"One of my servants will be sent to his lodgings to collect his things," Mr. Esherwood explains. "He'll come to live with us."

Rupert, mouth open, struggles to say anything or comprehend Mr. Esherwood's demands. Just as he's about to push out a few words, Mr. Esherwood turns and scales the embankment, heading toward the forest pathway. Rupert notices how Mr. Esherwood's wife lingers there for a moment, gazing at Rupert with an apologetic look. Mr. Esherwood calls to her from further up the path and she turns, hurrying after him.

One of the more compassionate town elders—a gentleman by the name of Alfred Gilchrist—is tasked with the role of accompanying Rupert back to his home to prepare the boy for his departure and relocation. Mr. Gilchrist puts an arm around Rupert and shepherds him through the woods toward the estate. As they move along the pathway, Rupert listens to the sounds of the forest—the water dripping from higher branches, the shriek of birds while they roost.

The world suddenly seems so different to him. Now that he's both motherless and fatherless, he doesn't feel the freedom he had once wrongfully imagined. Instead, he feels trapped—a small bird caught in a snare, wings beating tirelessly and about to succumb to exhaustion. Everything around him seems changed, almost as if he were wearing a special type of goggles that could see the heartache, the despair residing in each living thing—the very same despair that's spread its black, poisonous roots deep inside his very soul.

———

Not much can possibly comfort Rupert while he sits in the back seat of the black car, feeling as though he might sink deep into the leather cushioning and never reemerge. Perhaps he might like that. Perhaps there he would locate a modicum of comfort for what he's witnessed—the misfortune of his father's execution.

He never expected his father to die so violently. So pathetically. He realizes he never uttered a single word to his father following his awful conviction. He concedes his father never said anything to him either—probably too fearful, too humiliated to regard his only son and allow him to witness the unmanly wretch he had become in his final moments. Rupert had always felt as though he was waiting for his father to say something important, something vital to him. He realizes that his father was most likely waiting, unsure, for the same thing. Two people who care for one another will usually come apart because one isn't willing to bend. That's exactly how it had been with Rupert's father.

Rupert can mourn his father's unfortunate demise, or he can come to terms with the simple fact that things will never be the same for him ever again. It's more than evident in the way the two elders—Mr. Gilchrist and Mr. Patefield—climb into the front seat and regard Rupert in the rearview mirror as if he were damaged goods, as if he were a damaged clay pot once worth thousands and now worth only a measly pittance. Both Mr. Gilchrist and Mr. Patefield observe Rupert with a solemness, infrequent looks that seem to apologize for what they had to do. Still, in their awkward glances, there remains a firmness—a distinct harshness that whispers to Rupert they do not regret what they have done, that his father did indeed deserve to die.

Perhaps his father did deserve death after what he had done. But still there's a part of him that wishes it didn't have to be so, that his father had never became obsessed with Agnetha and remained the quiet, grieving widower instead. *Why did he have to try to cure himself?* That's exactly what Agnetha was—a temporary relief from the permanent affliction of grief. Rupert is certain that his father had tried to cure himself with Agnetha's corpse. He thought he might find absolution in her leaking wounds. He thought he might find grace in the cold touch of her waxen skin. Those things were not possible. There was no release to be found in her. Rupert curses his father for foolishly thinking there was.

As they motor away from End House and head toward Rupert's childhood home, Mr. Patefield instructs Rupert to pack enough of his belongings to last him a week or so. He explains how a servant from the Esherwood place will come later and retrieve more of his things. Rupert asks if he's expected to stay with the Esherwoods indefinitely, but Mr. Patefield won't respond. Even when Rupert asks for a second time, Mr. Patefield ignores him and keeps his eyes trained on the road ahead while he drives.

They arrive at Rupert's home, and he climbs out of the car, flanked by both elderly gentlemen as he moves up the front porch stairwell and into the house.

"Go upstairs and fetch your things," Mr. Patefield says. "We'll be waiting here."

Fearful of being chastised for not obeying, Rupert makes a quick dash up the stairs and heads for his bedroom. As he draws close to the open bathroom door at the end of the hallway, he wonders if Agnetha's body remains there or if anonymous officials from the town have already relocated her. He has no interest in seeing her, but he can't fight off his curiosity. He tiptoes toward the door, eases it open, and peers into the bathroom. The bath is empty, dark streaks of Agnetha's blood pattering the rim of the tub where it has dried.

Rupert leans over and inspects the drain, more of her blood has pooled there—an imprint of her body barely visible, but her ghost very much lingering in the ether of the small room.

Rupert's ears perk when he thinks he hears the faint chirp of a woman's laugh, but he figures it's probably just Mr. Gilchrist or Mr. Patefield downstairs, milling about. He doesn't have time to think about how people's presences dawdle in the spaces where they once were, even if they had already perished. It's possible Agnetha's spirit lingers in this house even though the town officials have obviously taken her body away. But Rupert can't think about that right now.

Instead, he moves out of the bathroom and heads into his bedroom. He starts pulling pants and shirts out of dresser drawers, stuffing them into a suitcase he finds under his bed. Then he moves over to his closet, flings open the doors, and starts dragging sweaters and sweatshirts from wire hangers. He pries open the nightstand drawer and swipes the tape recorder his mother left him. He crams the recorder into his suitcase.

Finally, he kneels beside the bed and reaches underneath the mattress until he slides out the small shoebox. He tips the lid open and finds the small, black bird still inside. It stirs slightly, eyes opening and closing to wink out some of the light.

"We're leaving," he tells the small creature with the human face. "We're going to live somewhere else for a while... I don't know how long..."

But the small bird doesn't react. It merely stares at him for a moment, then settles into the nest of twigs and branches Rupert has arranged in the far corner of the box.

Once he's finished closing the lid and easing the shoebox inside his duffle bag, something catches his eye on the dresser—the small, framed photograph of him and his mother kneeling beside that large, prehistoric-looking automobile. He stares at the photo for a moment, mining the sanctity of his thoughts for a recollection of when he was once happy. If he ever was once happy, it was when he was with his mother. It might very well be the same moment this particular photograph was taken. Before he can stuff the picture into his bag, there's a knock at the door. Mr. Gilchrist fills the door frame.

"Almost ready?" he asks. "Mr. Patefield is getting antsy, I'm afraid."

"Yes. Almost," Rupert tells him, shoving the photograph into his suitcase and zipping it shut.

Mr. Gilchrist passes over the threshold, his eyes scanning the empty walls of the room.

"No photos pinned to the walls?" he asks Rupert. "No posters? Nothing—? Seems like a waste of a bedroom."

Rupert shrugs.

He figures Mr. Gilchrist is right. Rupert has thought about fixing posters and photographs to the walls, but it would be too painful. Not to mention, he's never felt truly at home here. Especially since his mother perished. He figures if he had built a nest here after she passed on, it would be more difficult for him to leave. Rupert never imagined he'd be forcibly removed from his childhood home to live with a family he hardly knows.

Mr. Gilchrist kneels in front of Rupert, his hand disappearing inside his coat pocket. Rupert winces a little when Mr. Gilchrist pulls his hand out, expecting the worst. But he's surprised to find, instead, Mr. Gilchrist holding a small pendant—an emerald gemstone fixed in the center—dangling from a silver necklace.

"Hold out your hands," Mr. Gilchrist says to the boy.

Rupert does. Mr. Gilchrist passes the pendant into Rupert's open palms. Rupert gazes at the gift for a moment, admiring the way the jade green of the tiny gem catches the overhead light and glistens.

"Don't tell anyone I gave you this."

"What is it?" Rupert asks, his eyes still fixed on the pendant.

"It's a piece of protection," Mr. Gilchrist answers. "Something to guard you when you need it. I can tell you need it more than I do."

Mr. Gilchrist takes the necklace from Rupert and loops it around the young boy's neck. Rupert twists the pendant for a moment, then shoves it beneath his shirt so that it doesn't show.

"Come," Mr. Gilchrist says. "We'll be missed."

Rupert grabs his suitcase from the bed and hastens after Mr. Gilchrist down the corridor. When he moves, the pendant hiding beneath his shirt claps against his chest. The sound echoes in his ears: *Boom. Boom. Boom.* Rupert imagines it sounds like the noises of drums from far-away mountaintops —a God-like echo forever caught on a passing gust of wind.

GLADYS
ESHERWOOD

Gladys figures that any opportunity her husband had to be respectable has long since passed. She's terrified of asking him what his motivation was for taking the poor orphaned teenager under their wing. She concedes that any motivation he harbors deep inside himself must be similar in nature to his yearning for the faceless family to dwell in their residence. Cyril is a collector. He's always fancied certain things under his care, beneath his microscopic gaze.

It's not that Gladys opposes the orphaned child coming to live with them for the time being. Quite the contrary. She wonders if it might thaw some of the iciness lingering over End House. This troubled child could, in many ways, cure them. Still, Gladys finds it so bewilderingly peculiar how the elders have entrusted so much authority to Cyril, permitting him to command private citizens of the town. Even though it's alarming, Gladys has lived long enough in the town of Burnt Sparrow to know that traditions are unusual and certain authorities are kept as institutions in order to maintain regulation and balance. Many of the neighboring towns don't involve themselves much in the plight of the folks living in Burnt Sparrow. To Gladys, the town has always felt very much like a place that doesn't exist on any map outside of the one that the township had created themselves. She often wonders if she and the others dwelling in Burnt Sparrow are merely fantasists who have been caught dreaming the very same terrible dream. She's afraid of discovering the answer to such a dread-filled question.

Later that afternoon, Gladys pushes her nose against her bedroom window and watches as the black car returns and circles the small island of greenery situated in the front drive. The passenger door is opened and Rupert climbs out, his legs quivering a little when he stands. He looks about, his eyes obviously still captivated by the impressive size of the manor and how the house's dark shadow swallows him completely. Mr. Patefield wraps an arm around the sullen-looking teen and guides him up the front steps. Gladys can't fault the boy for looking so glum. Everything he's ever known has been taken away from him in a mere moment. Her husband destroyed his youth, his innocence, with a single command. Gladys feels some guilt for what her husband has done to Rupert. She knows in her heart that she doesn't bear any actual guilt for his father's gruesome execution; however, certainly, she could have interjected. She could have protested and questioned her husband's motives for ordering the poor man to be drowned. Would it have done any good? She can only speculate. She'll never know now.

Gladys makes her way toward the stairwell, peering down the stairs and observing one of the servants greeting Rupert and Mr. Patefield at the front door. She watches as Rupert passes his suitcase to the servant. Thinking not to interrupt Rupert's homecoming, Gladys lingers at the top of the stairs for a moment. But when she notices how Mr. Patefield awkwardly looks around, eyeing the servant for a hint of direction, she hastens down the stairs, calling out to the elder and to Rupert.

"I hope I didn't keep you both waiting long," she says to them.

"Not at all, Mrs. Esherwood," Mr. Patefield says. "We weren't sure if Mr. Esherwood might want to meet with the young man here."

Gladys tries to prevent herself from rolling her eyes. "He's downstairs in the cellar. I'm sure he'll be along later."

Her eyes fall upon Rupert. "In the meantime, I can show you to your room."

Rupert offers her a polite smile, but he doesn't look thrilled. Gladys can't expect the poor thing to force an imitation of joy when there's none to be had.

"The committee and I will be by sometime tomorrow," Mr. Patefield tells her. "We have more business to discuss with your husband."

"I'll be sure to let him know," Gladys says, sighing.

As soon as Mr. Patefield slips out through the front door, Gladys takes the suitcase from the nearby servant and eyes Rupert with an invitation for him to follow her. He does so willingly, and she prays quietly to herself that he'll go on to be agreeable during his stay here.

For the next hour or so, Gladys guides Rupert on a tour of the house. They wander the upstairs corridors from the Rococo-inspired East Wing to the French-provincial-styled North Wing. Rupert seems to accept everything Gladys says with a look of finality—a horror-filled look of quiet inevitability. He doesn't speak much. He certainly doesn't answer with more than a few words whenever Gladys asks him a question, so she tries to keep her inquiries to a minimum. After she's toured him through the various branches of the manor, Gladys guides him toward a large door situated at the end of the corridor in the West Wing. She pushes the doorway open and shepherds Rupert into the room, dumping his valise on the bed.

Gladys feels sad as Rupert looks about the room the same way a convicted prisoner might regard his final lodgings before an impending execution. Everything about Rupert seems to visibly twist inward—his arms shrinking, his neck shortening, secret parts of him probably reducing too. Once more, Gladys feels that familiar weight of guilt pile on her shoulders—an awful, gnawing feeling that overwhelms her all at once and then weighs her down with such force, like a giant hand forcing her head beneath a rising tide.

She curses her husband to herself. Most of this is his fault. Even though the poor boy's father was a deviant who did something he shouldn't have done, Cyril's verdict was extreme even for his cruel, unforgiving nature. But there's nothing she can do now for Rupert except try to make him as comfortable as possible while he remains as their house guest.

"Dinner will be at eight," she tells him. "We look forward to you joining us."

She lingers in the doorway, hoping Rupert might respond and tell her that he's looking forward to joining them as well. But he doesn't. Instead, he glances around the room, settling and gathering his bearings as much as possible. Gladys figures the best thing to do is leave him be for now, and she hopes that perhaps later he might be more talkative.

Slipping out of the room, she closes the door behind her and dawdles in the hallway outside. She's not quite sure what she's waiting for—perhaps a loud noise of exasperation from the other side of the door, perhaps a sign that the poor boy merely wants to be left alone. Gladys presses her ear against the door and listens. She hears a gentle, muffled sobbing on the other side. Gladys shivers, sensing the wound in her breast start to ache with a dull, relentless throbbing—an excruciating pulse that seems to mirror the cadence of Rupert's muffled cries.

She remains there for a moment, indulging in the pain, the agony of the poor boy's sobbing. Then, when she's finally had enough, Gladys pulls herself away and hastens down the corridor, away from Rupert's misery and hopeful that the sound of his crying—the horrible reminder of his pain, his torment—will not follow her.

———

Later that evening, Gladys sits at the dinner table and waits to be joined by Rupert and her husband. She stares at her glass of wine, swirling it in her hand with such impatience. It isn't long before Rupert appears in the doorway, dressed handsomely in new clothing. Gladys is taken aback. She hadn't expected the boy to know to dress for dinner, but she's delighted she didn't have to take the time to warn him.

"Please sit," she says, gesturing to the chair across from her at the table.

Rupert ambles further into the room, circling the head of the table, and sits in the chair. As he moves, his shadow flickers against the wall behind him. She thinks it's almost amusing how his shadow on the wall appears to be a very literal manifestation of Rupert's grief—his heartache, his despair—pursuing him wherever he goes. Gladys sees how his shadow shrinks in size when he sits. She almost thinks of mentioning it as something to break the ice, but she's interrupted by Cyril as soon as he crosses the threshold and enters the room.

"How kind of you both to wait for me," he says in a brash tenor, circling the table and sitting at the head. "I'm starved. What are we having?"

Gladys glances at Rupert, wondering if Cyril will say anything absurd to him immediately. She's surprised when he doesn't and merely goes about business as usual.

"I believe the chef is serving salmon tonight," Gladys tells him.

"Disgusting creature," Cyril says, sneering and eyeing Rupert as if hopeful the boy might agree with him.

Rupert says nothing. He keeps his eyes trained on the empty plate in front of him.

"It's supposed to be good for you, dear," Gladys reminds her husband.

"For what we pay him, the chef could try to come up with more appetizing options," Cyril says.

His gaze falls upon Rupert once more, eyes widening the way a predator might observe its prey.

"How do you find our home, young man?" Cyril asks him. "Everything to your liking?"

Rupert pauses, looking unsure how to answer.

"It's fine," he mutters, attention still fixed on his empty plate.

"Probably much more decadent than you're used to," Cyril says, taking a swig of wine. "Not like that hovel that pervert father of yours had you living in."

"Darling," Gladys says, hoping that her sudden interjection might challenge him and prevent him from saying anything else.

Cyril eyes her. He seems to soften a little bit, realizing his mistake.

"You're right," he says. "That wasn't very thoughtful of me."

An uncomfortable silence settles over the dinner table, the air around them thickening and churning with all the unsaid things obviously storming inside Cyril's mind.

"I imagine we'll have to order one of the servants to take him to school next week," Gladys says, taking another sip of wine. "The semester will be over soon, I gather?"

Rupert says nothing.

"The boy has been excused from school," Cyril tells her.

Gladys looks at him, bewildered. She notices how Rupert perks up as well, unsure of his claims and asking him a soundless question.

"The committee and I agreed upon it," Cyril says. "He won't have to return to school this year."

Gladys draws in a labored breath, unsure. She doesn't quite

know what to say. At first, she had enjoyed the thought of Rupert going to school to socialize and be with other children his own age. But now she realizes that he's very much a prisoner trapped inside the house. Just like her.

"I suppose we'll have to think of things that can occupy his time," she says. "He'll go mad without some sort of direction."

"You'll leave that to me," Cyril says. "I'll take care of it."

Once more, Rupert's eyes lower and his attention returns to the empty plate in front of him.

But Gladys is not as easily convinced. Although she's afraid to ask, she knows that she must.

"What kind of things did you have in mind?" she asks as quietly and as respectfully as possible.

"I'll be taking the boy down into the cellar this evening," he replies. "He'll assist me with things there. That should keep him more than occupied."

Gladys had been afraid of that. She swallows hard, knowing that it was only a matter of time before Cyril made his efforts entirely known to them both. Although she cannot possibly imagine the horrors that he wishes to subject Rupert to with those faceless prisoners, she knows that the poor boy does not deserve something so cruel.

"Do you think that's wise, dear?" she asks.

Gladys realizes that she's overstepped a little. She shrinks, leaning back in her seat and composing herself.

"I mean, do you think that's entirely safe?" she asks.

Cyril flashes a hideous grin at her. "Would you prefer to take his place?"

Gladys says nothing. Nothing could ever convince her to

return to the cellar and gaze upon those hellish misfits—those abominable, loathsome creatures that look neither human nor inhuman. However, there's a part of her that wonders if she's strong enough to sacrifice herself for Rupert's sake—to spare him the cruelty, the terror he might witness if Cyril succeeds in grooming him. That's exactly what he's planning to do, after all. Gladys knows it to be true. Cyril may not violate Rupert the same way he had violated the wretches in the cellar; however, he'll do things to the poor boy's mind that will be completely irreversible. If Cyril has his way with Rupert, the boy will become a living shell of his former self—a honeycombed exoskeleton to be filled with Cyril's most shameless and sacrilegious desires. Gladys would sooner die than allow that to happen. Cyril has already done enough to hurt Rupert.

"Perhaps he'll be entertained doing something else?" Gladys suggests.

"And what might that be?" Cyril asks, crossing his arms. "Following you around like a puppy dog all day?"

"I only worry for his safety," Gladys says.

Cyril scoffs at her. "He'll be safe. I'll be there every time he's there. Never unsupervised. I expect you to never question me about this again. Do you understand?"

Gladys doesn't answer at first. She wants to challenge him. She'd strip him bare and humiliate him right here and now if she could. She'll peel the skin from him—the very gristle from his bones—until he was without flesh and without manhood. But those dreams will never be. She'll never degrade him the way she secretly wants to, the way she imagines day after day. Instead of fighting him on the issue of Rupert's attendance in the cellar, she merely throws her husband a look and mutters: "Yes, darling."

Cyril leans back in his seat, uncrossing his arms and head swiveling about as he searches for a sign of dinner.

"Where's the food?" he asks. Then he glances at Rupert, looking almost hopeful that the boy might share his dismay. "We're wasting away, aren't we?"

Yes, indeed, Gladys thinks to herself, and flinches when she thinks of something so grim, so ghoulish. *We're all going to be wasting away until we leave behind nothing more than stains of our former selves—our wants, our needs, our most disgraceful transgressions.*

RUPERT
CROMWELL

There's something about Mr. Esherwood's face that perplexes Rupert. He winces whenever he's caught staring at the old man, almost as if Rupert's regarding something that's not meant to be seen by any unwelcome trespasser. That's exactly how Rupert feels: an undesirable visitor. He's not exactly sure why he should feel this way. Both Mr. and Mrs. Esherwood have gone above and beyond to try to make him feel comfortable, despite Mr. Esherwood's sneering whenever Rupert becomes too careless and is caught observing him for long periods of time.

Rupert doesn't quite know how to behave at dinner, especially since everything seems so formal between his hosts. The first course is served, and he's prompted by Mrs. Esherwood to wait to begin eating until Mr. Esherwood takes the first bite. Rupert has never felt so out of place before. He doesn't belong here, and he can't imagine why Mr. Esherwood has gone to such painstaking lengths to make it so that he's kept here following the demise of his father. He feels a twinge of hatred for Mr. Esherwood—hatred and loathing for the man who called for the unprompted execution of his poor father. Granted, his father had done some reprehensible things. But everything about the ordeal seemed so calculated by Mr. Esherwood. He wonders if Mr. Esherwood arranged his father's execution so that Rupert would be orphaned with nowhere to go. But why should he do such a thing? It makes no sense, especially given Mr. Esherwood's reputation in the community.

After dinner is finished and the three of them sit basking in the glow of the dim candlelight, Mr. Esherwood rises from his seat and orders Rupert to accompany him to the cellar at once. Rupert hasn't eaten much. The salmon they served him resembled the kind of fish that were probably feasting on his father's lifeless remains right now.

"You're certain you don't want to wait for dessert?" Mrs. Esherwood asks him, seeming to hope that a treat will pre-occupy her husband all at once.

But Mr. Esherwood waves her off and insists that Rupert follow him to the cellar. What else can Rupert do but obey? He looks to Mrs. Esherwood, feeling a bit foolish for expecting she might guide him in some way. She doesn't. She can't do anything but serve her husband's most capricious whim. She lowers her head, eyes avoiding him. When Mr. Esherwood notices that Rupert is not shadowing him, he turns and calls to him once more from the room's threshold. He sounds impatient, his voice straining and almost pained. Rupert doesn't hesitate this time, hurrying to his feet and following Mr. Esherwood out of the room and away from Mrs. Esherwood.

They cross the marble-floored entryway and come upon the doorway leading to the cellar. There are several latches securing the door—each one more expensive-looking and ornate than the last. Mr. Esherwood swipes a set of keys from a hook dangling beside the cellar door and then begins inserting the various keys into the locks, after explaining to Rupert how the brass-colored keys are for the cellar door while the black keys are for the prisoners' restraints. The locks release after he undoes them, some of them clattering to the ground with sickening thumps. Rupert asks Mr. Esherwood if he should retrieve them, but Mr. Esherwood tells him not to bother.

Finally, the last lock is opened, and Mr. Esherwood pries the cellar door open. A narrow staircase leading toward darkness sweeps in front of Rupert. For the first time in his life, he feels an overpowering fear. It's not the same fear he felt when he witnessed his father being executed by the town officials. No. It's something quite different. He hadn't felt fear when observing his father's death. He had felt an overwhelming sense of sadness, of pity. But not fear.

Rupert's stomach curls, his heart racing, as he regards the narrow cellar stairwell stretching down into a black pit of oblivion where candlelight doesn't seem to want to follow. He wonders what horrors Mr. Esherwood has in store for him. More to the point, he wonders what Mr. Esherwood will do to him if he doesn't obey his slightest command. Fearful of finding out too soon, Rupert starts to inch down the cellar steps while Mr. Esherwood pokes him along, pushing him further and further until they both reach the cellar floor. Mr. Esherwood switches on a flashlight and a bright halo of light blooms around them. Rupert glances around the space and notices how dirty and unkempt the cellar seems when compared with the rest of the house. Even the air feels as though it's unclean, and Rupert thinks of covering his mouth because he can taste the acrid odor.

Mr. Esherwood prods Rupert along like cattle, and before he knows it, Rupert is facing a corner of the cellar and observing a trio of dim silhouettes stirring where the walls come together. He squints, trying to make out what he's seeing. Mr. Esherwood aims the flashlight at the corner and it's then that Rupert sees them—the faceless family. They idle beside their cots, standing motionless like lobotomized inmates. As both he and Mr. Esherwood draw near, they start to wheeze, almost like they expect terror and misfortune from their captor. They make little mewling sounds—almost like kittens having their heads crushed—from the tiny pinholes fixed in the lower center of their waxen blank faces. Rupert shrinks a little when he notices how the light from Mr. Esherwood's flashlight reflects off the family's skin the same way it might for a deep-sea creature. Rupert swallows hard, too cautious to come any closer. Mr. Esherwood seems to notice the young boy's unease at once.

"Not scared, are you?" he asks Rupert. "There's nothing to be afraid of. They can't hurt you."

Rupert says nothing, his eyes fixed on the dark shapes loitering in the corner of the cellar.

"They're quite agreeable for murderers," Mr. Esherwood explains. "Very timid. Eager to obey, for the most part. We're still learning quite a bit about them and how they function."

Mr. Esherwood seems to immediately appreciate Rupert's

discomfort, eyeing him with all the disappointment of a father bearing witness to his uninspired offspring.

"Come closer," he says.

Rupert, stomach broiling with unease, takes a few steps forward and then stops. He can't move any further. He won't. Mr. Esherwood releases a heavy sigh, clearly exasperated.

Rupert's eyes widen with unequivocal horror when Mr. Esherwood pulls out a small pocketknife and brandishes it in front of him with such care and attention. He feels his stomach performing somersaults, his heart pumping furiously, while Mr. Esherwood approaches him with the pocketknife. The small blade glints in the glow of the flashlight.

"Would you like to see something?" Mr. Esherwood asks the wide-eyed boy.

But Rupert doesn't say anything. He tries to speak, but he's far too petrified to do anything.

Mr. Esherwood approaches the faceless mother. She seems to tremble at once, mewling softly and somehow sensing that her captor is drawing near. Mr. Esherwood grabs hold of her arm and holds it so that Rupert can witness what he's about to do. When he's certain that Rupert can see his labors, Mr. Esherwood pushes the edge of the pocketknife along the poor woman's skin until a line of blood unravels there. Rupert winces at the loathsome sight, more blood pooling and trickling from the woman's arm. But without warning, the bleeding seems to stop. The wound closes, the creeping line of dark red pulling itself back inside like a crimson string being threaded into fabric.

Rupert softens a little and feels filled with wonderment at the unexplainable sight. *How can this be?* Surely he had seen

Mr. Esherwood slice the poor woman's arm open, and yet the blood dried as soon as the wound laced itself shut. It makes no sense to Rupert, and he finds himself with an open mouth, struggling to comprehend such magic.

"They can't be hurt?" he asks Mr. Esherwood.

Mr. Esherwood offers a little smirk. "They probably suffer in many other ways."

He holds out the small pocketknife for Rupert to take.

"Here," he says. "Try it."

But Rupert isn't sure. He hesitates, eyeing the knife as Mr. Esherwood pushes the blade toward him. Sensing Mr. Esherwood's frustration when he doesn't immediately take hold of the offering, Rupert grabs the knife and then slowly makes his way toward the corner of the cellar, where the faceless family is waiting for him—waiting to be momentarily wounded, waiting to suffer.

Mr. Esherwood prods Rupert along until he's standing in front of the faceless teenager. Although he cannot be certain because of his nonexistent features, Rupert is confident that he and the boy are close in age. He stops himself, sensing an indescribable warmth pooling around the faceless teenage boy. Rupert is ashamed to admit that the momentary balminess feels nice, considering how cold Mr. Esherwood keeps the various compartments in the cellar. Of the three faceless family members at Rupert's disposal, there's something quite captivating about the teenage boy. *Is "captivating" the right word?* Rupert wonders to himself. He's a killer. Regardless, Rupert feels silly to admit that he pities the faceless teenager. He wonders why he feels this way. But he can't indulge in the internal questioning for too long, as Mr. Esherwood taps him on the shoulder every few seconds—reminding him that he's present, prompting him that there's excruciating work to be done on these faceless monsters.

"Take the knife," Mr. Esherwood orders him. "Slice his arm open. And look."

Rupert flinches, the knife trembling in his hands. He swallows nervously, unable to move at first. Realizing that Mr. Esherwood will make someone in this cellar suffer today, Rupert decides that it's not going to be him. He grabs hold of the teenager's bare arm and swipes the blade across his skin. At first, he misses slightly and only grazes the poor boy's transparent-looking flesh. Rupert recognizes his mistake at once, noticing Mr. Esherwood's obvious disappointment, and he tries to swing the knife at him harder this time. He does. The blood begins to flow, dripping there like a livid current.

A few moments pass, and as usual, the blood dries and the lips of the wound come together until the boy's arm is as it once was. Rupert is mesmerized only for a moment. His stomach churns, sick at himself for obeying Mr. Esherwood so mindlessly. What choice did he have? Mr. Esherwood is a man who will be obeyed no matter what. Even if Rupert does feel a semblance of pity for the faceless teen and feels guilty for slicing him open, those feelings don't matter to Mr. Esherwood.

The man wraps an arm around Rupert, visibly pleased with Rupert's handiwork. Rupert notices how Mr. Esherwood gazes at him for a beat too long, almost like Rupert has passed some sort of test that was planned from the moment he first set foot in End House.

Mr. Esherwood congratulates Rupert for a job well done and then tells him how they will return for more work later tonight or early tomorrow morning. As they start to leave the cellar, Rupert glances back at the faceless teen dawdling in the corner of the room. He wonders why he feels such pity for him. He wonders why he hesitated so much to hurt him. Doesn't he deserve to hurt after all the harm he's done? Rupert's afraid to admit that he's not certain. He's surprised to admit to himself that he doesn't hate the faceless family as much as he's been instructed to loathe them. This revelation puzzles him. But it certainly doesn't trouble him as much as when Mr. Esherwood gazes at him the same way an excitable mortician might regard a fresh cadaver on a chilled slab.

Rupert knows he's become nothing more than a corpse that Mr. Esherwood can poke and prod and inspect until his heart is content. Even though they leave the cellar and make their way to another part of the house, Rupert feels that he's been figuratively trapped in the basement with the faceless family. Overnight, he's somehow become another ornament in Mr. Esherwood's grotesque collection.

———

When he returns to his bedroom, Rupert makes a dash to his bed and swipes the small shoebox he had hidden beneath the mattress. However, when he lifts the lid to open the box, he isn't met with contended chirps of approval, little mewling noises the way an infant might greet its caregiver. Instead, he finds the small creature lying on its back, its little feet sticking up in the air and its mouth open as if in mid scream. Rupert shakes the box gently, hoping that somehow the movement might awaken the damn thing, might undo some of what's been done. But there's no such enchantment to be found here. Instead, Rupert finds himself gazing at the dead bird for what feels like hours, its infant-like human face shrunken and twisted in a look of agony as though it had expired in the middle of a question, in the middle of some kind of soul-defining plea to the unforgiving universe. Perhaps it had. Perhaps it had died when it needed Rupert most. But Rupert had been nowhere to be found. Rupert becomes sick to his stomach at the awful thought, the terrible reminder that he had been chosen to care for this wretched thing and had failed in his duty. Perhaps once he might have been a competent caretaker. But certainly not now. Rupert only knows how to destroy things.

He sneaks out of the room and into the nearby washroom, where he opens the medicine cabinet. Peering through capsules filled with pills, he eventually comes upon a small roll of white gauze. He returns to his room and then begins to wrap the dead bird in the bandages until the poor thing resembles some kind of being that might have once been buried inside a sacred tomb in Ancient Egypt. For a few moments, he holds the mummified corpse in the palm of his hand and feels the pressure of its weight there—the burden of its soul, the depth of its invisible breath. It is truly and unmistakably dead now. There is nothing on this earth that could ever bring this miserable thing back.

In his mind, Rupert holds a private funeral for the poor creature much like the little ceremony he held in his thoughts for his father. Faceless people weave around him—passing muted condolences, promising him that it's not his fault, that there's nothing he could have possibly done to save the vile thing. Perhaps Rupert knows this in his heart. Still, it's difficult to actually believe. He curses himself for not doing more, for not caring more for the little bird and providing all he could in such a short period of time. Maybe the thing wanted a different kind of nourishment from Rupert. Black beetles and earthworms were hardly loving companions for the damn thing. Perhaps the little bird required something far more tender—*love*.

TEN-LETTER WORD FOR PERNICIOUS: THE GRUESOME ACCOUNT OF ONE OF BURNT SPARROW'S MOST UNEXPLAINED MURDERS

Originally published online at *Mister Jakes's Menagerie of Curiosities* (exact domain name currently unavailable) on September 6, 2019, at 3:33 a.m.

While there has been a considerable amount of speculation and guesswork surrounding the unfortunate demise of both young men in the tragedy that took place in Unit 29B of 2004 Lafayette Avenue in Burnt Sparrow, New Hampshire, in 2008, the editor of this document wishes to assure readers that all details presented have been vetted by the authorities and all the information is available to the public at the time of this manuscript's publication. The documents presented in this manuscript have been offered to the public without significant redactions or modifications. Although there are other elements from this case that have been kept from the public, the editor would like to express their gratitude to the Burnt Sparrow Police Department for their compliance and generosity when compiling this information. Within these pages, one will find notes from video footage recovered at the scene of the tragedy. One will also find a detailed audio recording that was made by one of the parties involved on the night of the misfortune. These items are not intended to serve as a means of entertainment—to titillate the reader—but rather to provide the public with the pertinent information in the account of one of the most gruesome and baffling cases Burnt Sparrow, New Hampshire, has seen in its town history.

[NOTES FROM VIDEO FOOTAGE #093745]
The following notes were prepared and catalogued by Andre Lachlin of the Burnt Sparrow Police Department on November 2, 2008.

The following details are from a report written by a member of the Burnt Sparrow Police Department after viewing the photo footage recovered at 2004 Lafayette Avenue, Unit 29B. The details are intended to serve as a way to better understand the space of the apartment and the conditions of the tragedy.

THE UNIT RESIDES ON THE TOP FLOOR OF AN INDUSTRIAL WAREHOUSE THAT HAS SINCE BEEN CONVERTED INTO AN APARTMENT BUILDING.

THERE IS ONLY ONE MAIN ENTRYWAY THAT ACCESSES THE SPACE—A GIANT, STEEL-REINFORCED SLIDING DOOR THAT OPENS OUT TO A DIMLY LIT CORRIDOR.

THE ONLY OTHER MEANS OF ENTRY IS THROUGH ONE OF THE LARGE DIRT-CAKED WINDOWS THAT LEADS TO A LESS-THAN-STABLE-LOOKING FIRE ESCAPE LADDER SCALING THE SIDE OF THE BUILDING.

THE BRICK WALLS ARE CEMENTED WITH DRIED FLUIDS AND OTHER PERMANENT MARKINGS PRESUMABLY FROM PREVIOUS TENANTS,

SUCH AS UNDECIPHERABLE LETTERS AND UNREADABLE SYMBOLS WRITTEN WITH SPRAY PAINT, BODILY FLUIDS, AND DRIED FOOD.

A TOILET SITS EXPOSED IN ONE CORNER OF THE ROOM WITHOUT EVEN THE DECENCY OF A PARTITION OR CURTAIN FOR THE USER'S PRIVACY. BOTH THE BOWL AND HEAD OF THE FIXED RECEPTACLE ARE STAINED WITH URINE AND EXCREMENT.

A MATTRESS SITS IN THE OPPOSITE CORNER OF THE ROOM. THE PILLOWS ARE TORN AND TATTERED, FEATHERS SCATTERED ABOUT.

[TIMESTAMP: 09:05:45 PM] SUBJECT A **[DARREN LEACH]** LIES MOTIONLESS ON AN UNDRESSED, BLOODSTAINED MATTRESS. DRESSED ONLY IN A WHITE SHIRT AND UNDERWEAR. BLOOD AS THICK AS HONEY TRICKLES FROM BENEATH HIS HAIR. HIS FOREARM IS WOUNDED, LEAKING BLOOD AS WELL.

EYES CLOSED, DARREN STIRS GENTLY. HANDS AND FEET BOUND WITH WIRE, HE RESISTS. WHIMPERING, HE SLIPS IN AND OUT OF CONSCIOUSNESS. HIS HEAD BOBS, MORE BLOOD TRICKLING FROM THE STRANDS OF HAIR ALREADY GLUED TO HIS FOREHEAD WITH SWEAT.

THE SONG "YOU'RE NEVER FULLY DRESSED WITHOUT A SMILE" FAINTLY DRIFTS IN FROM A DISTANT ROOM.

[TIMESTAMP: 09:10:24 PM] ANOTHER FIGURE—SUBJECT B **[BRADLEY MILTNER]**—ENTERS THE SPACE.

BRADLEY HOLDS A HAMMER, THE TIP DRIPPING WITH BLOOD AND KNOTTED WITH CLUMPS OF HAIR. A TRADITIONAL PVC BONDAGE HARNESS BELTS HIS BARE CHEST AND SHOULDERS. HE ALSO

WEARS A BLACK LATEX JOCKSTRAP. HIS FACE—A SHIMMERING MASK OF GORE.

EYES SCANNING THE ROOM, DARREN'S BODY MOVES SLIGHTLY AS BRADLEY ENTERS.

BRADLEY APPEARS INDIFFERENT, NOT EVEN SEEMING TO NOTICE THAT HIS PREY HAS WOKEN UP AND THAT HIS BREATHING HAS GROWN SHALLOWER WITH EVERY GASP.

BRADLEY DRIFTS ACROSS THE ROOM TOWARD THE CAMERA AND SHUTS IT OFF.

THE VIDEO GOES BLACK.

THE AUDIO CONTINUES TO RECORD.

[END OF VIDEO FOOTAGE #093745]

[AUDIO TRANSCRIPT #062186]
The following audio transcript was prepared and catalogued by Andre Lachlin of the Burnt Sparrow Police Department on November 3, 2008.

[;;;INDECIPHERABLE;;;]

DARREN: …Bradley—?

BRADLEY: …You've lost a lot of blood…

SOUND: The hammer slips from BRADLEY's hand.

DARREN: Bradley, wh-what are you doing?

BRADLEY: Don't speak…

DARREN: What happened?

BRADLEY: Didn't you fucking hear me?

SOUND: DARREN stirs again, groaning.

[;;;INDECIPHERABLE;;;]

DARREN: …My head hurts.

BRADLEY: Hold still or I'll use the hammer again.

DARREN: Wh-what did you do to me?

BRADLEY: To you—? What about to me, you cocksucker?

DARREN: What?

BRADLEY: You wet yourself. Did you know that…? Pissed yourself like a little kid.

DARREN: Please. Nothing's happened yet. You can stop.

BRADLEY: Why do you insist on embarrassing yourself?

SOUND: DARREN screams for help, but his cries are soon muffled.

BRADLEY: If you make one more noise, they're going to be hand-picking the greasy bits of your brain from the end of this hammer. Do I make myself fucking clear—?

SOUND: DARREN releases a muffled whimper.

BRADLEY: I have to think…

DARREN: About what—?

BRADLEY: What's to be done.

DARREN: Done?

BRADLEY: Something has to.

DARREN: It hurts.

BRADLEY: Those teeth of yours.

DARREN: My teeth?

BRADLEY: Something must be done about them.

DARREN: Please. You don't have to do this.

BRADLEY: What's a ten-letter word for "necessary"?

DARREN: What?

BRADLEY: A ten-letter word for "necessary". A synonym.

DARREN: What are you saying?

BRADLEY: Didn't you say you liked playing games? What's a ten-letter word for "necessary"?

A LONG PAUSE.

DARREN: …I—I don't know. Please.

SOUND: *A glass shattering against the wall.*

BRADLEY: What's the fucking word?

DARREN: Ten-letter word for "necessary"? …"Absolute."

A LONG PAUSE.

BRADLEY: Wrong. Eight letters. Different meanings, too. You know what a synonym is, don't you? A word having the same or similar meaning as another… I thought I was being obvious. The arrangement you and I had made was obvious too, wasn't it?

DARREN: The money's on the dresser… Take it. Please.

BRADLEY: You think I give a shit about the money—? I knew the kind of risk I was taking when I first sought you out months ago. Wouldn't have even bothered if I didn't keep hearing how most guys are better than women at giving head.

DARREN: Please.

BRADLEY: Your kind disgusts me… Faggots.

SOUND: *DARREN sobs gently.*

BRADLEY: What's the word?

DARREN: Ten-letter word for "necessary". What about "inescapable"?

BRADLEY: Eleven letters. It's not your fault. You're not thinking clearly… I suppose the consequence is inescapable…

SOUND: *DARREN squirms, resisting.*

DARREN: No. It doesn't have to be.

BRADLEY: Is that what you think?

SOUND: *DARREN gags on quiet sobs.*

DARREN: Please don't do this.

SOUND: *DARREN groans, fidgeting.*

BRADLEY: There's no way to disguise the unpleasantness of the task. I'm afraid the ordeal is a ten-letter word for "necessary."

SOUND: *DARREN howls in agony, rolling over on his side.*

SOUND: *The hammer slips from BRADLEY's hands.*

SOUND: *Vomiting.*

BRADLEY: I—can't—finish… I can't do it… Nine-letter word for "silence." Quiet. No. That's only five. Secrecy. That's seven.

DARREN: Why are you doing this?

BRADLEY: Playing a word game with myself… It calms me down…

DARREN: I won't say anything.

BRADLEY: Why should I believe you? Is that why you kept insisting on coming back here?

DARREN: You said it's what you wanted.

BRADLEY: Is this what you practice with all your other clients? What is it for you? Boring routine—?

DARREN: The money's on the dresser. Take it back. Please.

BRADLEY: What did you want from me—? For me to beg for my life? Did you think I'd wet myself? Is that what you wanted to see—?

DARREN: What?

BRADLEY: How did I taste, you sick fuck?

A LONG PAUSE.

DARREN: Is that what I did—?

BRADLEY: As if you didn't know.

DARREN: What was it?

BRADLEY: *What was it?* I go to the bathroom for five minutes and I come back to find you—

DARREN: What—?

BRADLEY: Eating yourself. The way your eyes widened when you saw me. And those awful little noises you made when you leapt at me… Your teeth. I only did it so that you couldn't do it again. I should've finished taking each one.

SOUND: *DARREN coughs violently.*

DARREN: Don't you see that I'm sick?

BRADLEY: No fucking shit.

DARREN: I thought you could—help me.

BRADLEY: You tried to eat me.

DARREN: No.

BRADLEY: Why don't you have a heartbeat?

DARREN: Because—I need a conduit.

BRADLEY: I didn't think you knew the word.

DARREN: He had given it to me. He had—left me… Haunted me…

BRADLEY: Who?

DARREN: I wouldn't have left you like that. I promise I would've told you.

BRADLEY: Told me what—?

DARREN: What do you think happens right before you die—? More of you is on the outside than there is left on the inside. This—does the opposite. It gnaws at you until all your outsides are on the inside. It's a curse.

BRADLEY: You're messing with me.

DARREN: It's like getting your foot stuck in a steel trap. The more you pull, the tighter it gets.

BRADLEY: What the fuck are you saying?

DARREN: Shh. Not too loud.

BRADLEY: What are you doing?

A LONG PAUSE.

DARREN: It's—in the room again… It's with us now…

BRADLEY: What?

DARREN: Don't you see it—?

BRADLEY: See what?

SOUND: *The trill chirp of a small set of rusted wheels slowly approaching.*

DARREN: It's looking at me right now. It looks—just like my mother. Sounds like her, too. But the skin on her face is silvery and shiny like a mirror. Both of her arms and legs are gone. They look as though they've been… devoured. She wheels toward me on a child's wagon made of wood. Staring and repeating just one word to me. *"Eat." "Eat." "Eat."*

BRADLEY: You're full of shit.

DARREN: Don't you see her?

BRADLEY: You're fucking with me.

DARREN: Look.

BRADLEY: You think I believe you enough to take my eyes off you?

DARREN: He said it's different for everybody. What it looks like. *"You're always haunted by the thing that you love the most,"* he told me.

200

BRADLEY: Sounds like he told you a lot of things.

DARREN: He would know. He gave it to me.

BRADLEY: Who—?

DARREN: The young man that paid me for twenty minutes. Last night. He was missing one of his eyes. All his fingers on his left hand, too. Said he had eaten them one night while jacking off.

BRADLEY: What was he paying you for then?

DARREN: Only a bite. But he said it would leave me, too. Once I found another host to pass on the spirit… the suffering…

BRADLEY: What is it—? A kind of AIDS?

SOUND: *DARREN coughs again.*

DARREN: I thought about not telling you. Just leaving you there. I thought about it and how eventually, if you kept eating, you'd be nothing but a—

A LONG PAUSE.

BRADLEY: A what—? A shining red stump of muscle and bone?

DARREN: I would've given anything to see you like that. To hurt you.

BRADLEY: You could've done that to me?

DARREN: Why not? It's easy for you to do it to me. You don't love her.

BRADLEY: Until tonight, you were the one thing that hadn't tried—to hurt me.

DARREN: A person's not a vending machine. I can't pretend to be yours anymore.

BRADLEY: What was it—? You thought I'd stay here with you if you made me sick?

DARREN: You know I could never leave you like that. We'd be siblings of the same affliction. And we would have to find another to pass on the spirit. Together.

BRADLEY: And what happens if we don't?

A LONG PAUSE.

BRADLEY: You actually think I'd leave my family for you?

DARREN: How could you not?

BRADLEY: How could I not?

DARREN: …You don't love them.

BRADLEY: They need me. My little boy especially. His name's Gabriel… He's only four. He upsets my wife, and she gets angry with him… She screams and pinches the nape of his neck, leaving little bruises… Last week I found him crying, stuck inside the washing machine. She said he had crawled in there by accident. But now Gabriel screams whenever she goes to touch him… And we're having another baby. She's due in seven weeks… She shouldn't be a mother. She's not who she pretends to be. Just like you. Just like me, too…

DARREN: Why do you keep coming back here to me if you didn't want this?

BRADLEY: …I was going to end it tonight.

DARREN: After you said you loved me—?

A LONG PAUSE.

BRADLEY: Darren, I'll see to it that you get help—and get better—from whatever it is that you have. But that's all.

DARREN: I'm not going to get better… It's a fag-eat-fag world. I've already been bitten.

BRADLEY: The offer is on the table…

[;;;INDECIPHERABLE;;;]

BRADLEY: …That's it.

DARREN: You don't think you owe me anything else?

BRADLEY: Did you expect I'd say anything different?

DARREN: This… *sickness* didn't give me a heart with sharp teeth. I already had that… It'll rip everything out of you… It's—

inevitable. That was the ten-letter word for "necessary," wasn't it?

BRADLEY: Yes. It was.

SOUND: *DARREN coughs, laughing.*

BRADLEY: Darren...

A LONG PAUSE.

SOUND: *DARREN screams, biting BRADLEY.*

SOUND: *A hammer smashing against DARREN's head.*

SOUND: *A vulgar thud as DARREN's body crashes to the floor.*

A LONG PAUSE.

BRADLEY: Fuck... No...

ANOTHER LONG PAUSE.

SOUND: The faint chirp of a set of rusted wheels slowly approaching.

BRADLEY: Gabriel—?

[;;;INDECIPHERABLE;;;]

[END OF AUDIO TRANSCRIPT #062186]

RUPERT
CROMWELL

In his dreams, Rupert is a young boy—no older than seven or eight. He dreams of a quiet Sunday-afternoon drive through the countryside surrounding the village of Burnt Sparrow, Mr. Esherwood steering the car and Mrs. Esherwood sitting in the front passenger seat. The perfect family.

He dreams how Gladys tells him that young boys his age are always so unpleasant, so unforgiving and needlessly cruel. She tells him how the boys in her neighborhood when she was a child would torture frogs or newts and would smash mailboxes with baseball bats. She tells Rupert how the boys would tease her with unpleasant nicknames and then would intentionally leave her behind on her own while they drove to the market in town. Mr. Esherwood tells him about the same awful stories from when he was little, and typically praises Rupert for possessing such level-headedness at such a tender age.

He recognizes how he was once a menace—a terror as well—but seems grateful that young Rupert has never been touched by such cruelty. Mr. and Mrs. Esherwood appear so astonished by Rupert—flabbergasted by his composure, his even temperament. They tell Rupert how fortunate they are to be the adoptive parents of such a calm and collected young boy like him. Seeing as both Mr. and Mrs. Esherwood only seem to offer disparaging remarks about the other boys from town his age, it perplexes him when they slam on the brakes and veer onto the shoulder of the dirt road to pick up the small boy without a face who they had just passed.

Rupert can't see much of the faceless boy at first in the rearview mirror. His hair is long and covers most of his non-existent expression, especially when he looks down. He's dressed from head to toe in white—from his neatly pressed corduroy pants to his buttoned jacket with an emerald lapel embellishing the collar. Rupert wonders if his adopted parents will make a comment about the peculiarity of how the young boy is dressed—how he's outfitted in such expensive-looking clothes while stirring there in the summer heat. They don't comment on this for whatever reason.

The faceless boy doesn't notice the car has stopped in front of him at first. His attention is instead fixed on a small green apple he's carefully holding in both hands. He twists the apple's stem over and over again, but never seems to be able to pull it apart. Whether he can't bear to or he's merely unable to, Rupert cannot be certain. Regardless, he seems so fixated on the apple that Rupert wonders if he'll ever glance up at them and realize that they've stopped for him.

For a moment, Rupert questions if he recognizes him. He's probably no older than seven or eight. It's possible he goes to school in the same town where they live, but Rupert cannot be sure.

Mrs. Esherwood leans across the seat, the large brim of her hat blocking out some of the sun when she moves in front of Rupert and asks her husband to get out of the car and flag the boy down. He obeys without comment, shifting the car so that he can park on the shoulder of the road. He lurches out of the driver's seat, circles the vehicle, and then ambles toward the young boy, who immediately seems to shrink from him, obviously frightened by the mere sight of Mr. Esherwood looming toward him.

Rupert struggles to his knees and peers out through the backseat window, watching Mr. Esherwood approach the young boy stranded on the side of the road. Mr. Esherwood's lips move with muted words which Rupert cannot hear, because the car's air conditioning continues to hum and blast them with cool air. Rupert glances at Mrs. Esherwood in the front seat, who also seems transfixed at the very sight of her husband lazing there on the roadway, chatting with the little boy. Just then, Mr. Esherwood wraps an arm around the child's shoulder and starts to guide him toward the waiting car. Rupert's stomach curls a little, a twinge of jealousy heating there when he notices how lovingly Mr. Esherwood shepherds the boy.

Mr. Esherwood pries open the backseat passenger door and Rupert watches while the child climbs onto the seat and sits beside him.

"This young boy is going to join us on our ride today," Mr. Esherwood tells them.

Rupert forces a polite "Hello" and a half-hearted wave at

the young boy while he settles himself on the leather seat. Mr. Esherwood pulls the seatbelt across the boy's chest and then clicks it into the lock, securing him tight.

"Comfortable?" Mr. Esherwood asks the boy, tugging on the belt and testing it.

The boy, stirring slightly, nods in return.

Then Mr. Esherwood slams the door shut and climbs into the driver's seat, greeting Mrs. Esherwood with a peck on the cheek. Rupert is quiet for a moment—wondering if he should say something to the boy, wondering what the etiquette might be. Rupert doesn't interact much with kids younger than him. Rupert doesn't even feel at ease around other kids his own age. That's why he's always immediately gravitated toward adults. Mr. and Mrs. Esherwood seem to know this about him and, thankfully, Mrs. Esherwood takes charge of the conversation as she swivels around in her chair and greets the young boy with a hideous, all-too-polite grin.

"What were you doing so far out here, dear?" she asks him.

The faceless boy's head lowers, his fingers twisting the stem of the apple once more. He doesn't answer her.

Mrs. Esherwood seems to recognize the boy's distress. Her lip pulls downward, and she eyes him with a look of such sympathy.

"Did your parents leave you here?" she asks.

The boy hesitates to answer at first, turning away from her. Finally, he responds, shaking his head *no*.

Rupert watches Mr. Esherwood adjust the rearview mirror so that he can now spy on both him and the faceless boy while they sit in the back seat.

"We're heading back into town now," Mr. Esherwood tells the boy. "We can drop you off there, if you'd like?"

The boy nods slightly.

Seeming satisfied with the young boy's compliance, Mr. Esherwood shifts the car into gear and eases on the accelerator. The car wobbles forward and they drift from the shoulder onto the main roadway, and then further down the tree-flanked lane.

Rupert and the boy sit in silence. Rupert wonders if Mrs. Esherwood will take charge again and carry the conversation. But instead, she keeps her eyes trained on the open road ahead while Mr. Esherwood steers them along.

Rupert wonders if he should say something, but he can't think of anything notable or worthy. It pains him to realize just how out of place he feels when confronted with the task of mingling with another child. He knows that he's never been comfortable around his peers; however, it feels so unequivocally agonizing to realize just how unsure and suspicious he becomes when he's around another boy. Rupert wonders why he's so inherently cautious, why he remains so guarded with the faceless boy.

It's not that he appears untrustworthy or seems capable of unraveling whatever resolve Rupert has imagined for himself. It's quite foolish to think of how Rupert assigns so much power, so much worth to others. He suddenly views the faceless boy as if he were capable of his destruction, as if he were somehow qualified to shatter the peacefulness he's come to know with the imitations of Mother and Father. Rupert knows this cannot be true. He seems so average. Even if he's dressed in white and he doesn't communicate much with them, Rupert must realize that there's nothing fundamentally dangerous about him. He's so quiet because he's also unsure of what's to become of him.

Thankfully, Mr. Esherwood answers that question almost immediately when he asks if they would like to stop for ice cream. Mrs. Esherwood claps her hands in childlike excitement and then swivels around in her chair, asking the faceless boy if he'd like some.

The boy, still appearing guarded and distrustful of them, nods in agreement. He quivers slightly whenever he shakes his head, almost like he is desperate to say something but far too exhausted to summon the words to speak. Rupert figures that his fatigue must be from the summer heat. Who knows how long he was strolling on the road with the sun beating down on him? It's a miracle they came along to rescue him from certain harm.

After a short while, they arrive at the roadside ice-cream stand—a small cottage with bright red trim, and a faded sign with lettering which has already begun to peel away that reads: *The finest treats you'll ever eat!* On the sign, there's a large portrait of a young boy, smiling a grotesque, toothless grin, as he snacks on a cone topped with melting strawberry ice cream. Because parts of the sign have been eaten away by the carelessness of time and the cruelty of New England weather, the boy's portrait is a frightening vision—bits of his painted face flaking off, his eyes now shattered and rusted-looking.

Mr. Esherwood aims the vehicle at the cottage and pulls into an empty parking spot. Twisting around in his seat, he asks what flavors Rupert and the boy would like.

Rupert tells him his usual: "Chocolate."

Mr. Esherwood's eyes flash to the faceless boy for an answer. But the young boy hesitates once more. Whether he's still deciding or painfully shy, Rupert cannot be totally certain.

Finally, he responds:

"Vanilla please," he somehow says, despite not having a mouth.

"Would you like me to throw that apple out?" Mr. Esherwood asks him. "I'm sure you'll be happier with the ice cream."

But the boy shakes his head, pulling the apple tight against his chest like it is the very thing keeping him together, preventing him from completely falling apart.

Mr. Esherwood climbs out of the car and makes his way toward the small line of guests milling about and waiting for their order to be received at the takeout window.

They wait, observing Mr. Esherwood as he eventually reaches the counter and speaks to the young redhead in the blue pinstriped uniform. Once more, Rupert thinks of saying something to the faceless boy. But what on earth could he possibly say? If anything, Rupert feels as though the boy owes *him* explanations. Mrs. Esherwood does as well. It had seemed so out of character for her to request to stop to tend to the young boy. Why on earth should she care? She's always droning on and on about how youths today are so violent and capable of the most shocking and heinous transgressions. It makes little to no sense why she and Mr. Esherwood would make such an effort to be so polite, so gracious when confronted with some bewildered child. Her willingness to assist the poor boy makes Rupert wonder about the integrity of everything she's ever told him. Perhaps others aren't as cruel and vindictive as she claims.

But then why would she make such an effort to convince him otherwise? Surely, there's not much reason to be had when he considers Mrs. Esherwood's true motivations.

Finally, after fifteen minutes or so, Mr. Esherwood returns to the car. He carries two large ice-cream cones—one chocolate, one vanilla—and he passes them to Rupert and the young boy through the open crack in the backseat window. He waits for them to try a taste before climbing into the front seat once more.

"Everybody happy?" he asks.

But the boy and Rupert are far too distracted with their melting ice cream. Rupert wonders how the boy will eat the ice cream without a face, but he's too hungry to consider that right now.

Mr. Esherwood shifts the car into reverse and pulls out of the parking lot, drifting back onto the roadway and motoring down the empty lane toward town. When they have finished their desserts, Mrs. Esherwood takes their uneaten cones and stuffs them into the large plastic bag she keeps in the front seat for trash.

Rupert doesn't quite know why but he suddenly feels his eyelids becoming heavy, the whole world around him starting to blur as though he were already dreaming. He notices Mr. Esherwood's eyes shoot to him in the rearview mirror.

"You can go to sleep for a bit, bud," he tells him. "Still half an hour until we get back to town."

Before Rupert can utter another word, he hears the distant shriek of a small bird calling to her mate. His eyelids flutter open, and he finds himself sprawled out on the empty back seat. His attention drifts to the car window above his head and he notices the night sky framed there—a dark curtain dappled with the rusted silver of faint, faraway starlight. His heart begins to thump over and over again inside his chest when he glances at the front seat and sees the chairs are empty and that the car has been parked beside the base of an old oak tree, the headlights aiming ahead at a grassy knoll and tearing two bright halos into the surrounding dark.

Rupert scrambles to his feet and pries open the rear door, toppling out onto the grass. Mosquitos hum all around him and he swats them away. He doesn't recognize where his parents have brought him.

Surely they couldn't have left him here all by himself. The car has been parked and the keys are still in the ignition while the unattended vehicle sits there quietly. Just then, he hears the soft whimpers of a young boy followed by a series of strained, controlled grunts. Next, he hears a sickening thud like a bag of potatoes being dropped on the ground. He drifts around the base of the old oak tree and comes upon a horrible sight that perplexes him and alarms him all at once.

There, sprawled out in the dirt, is the faceless boy, with Mr. Esherwood kneeling on his chest with his hands wrapped around the poor boy's throat. Mrs. Esherwood is holding the plastic bag she kept in the front seat of the car over the boy's head, the bag crinkling while he wheezes and gasps for air. Rupert watches Mr. Esherwood as he presses down harder against the boy's windpipe, crushing his little throat until the poor thing is finally limp and without movement.

When they're both certain he's dead, Mrs. Esherwood

undoes the plastic bag and rips it from the boy's head, uncovering him.

Rupert watches in silence as Mr. Esherwood rises from where he had been kneeling. He kicks the boy's shoe to properly gauge whether or not the boy is actually dead. The boy makes no movement. Satisfied with his labors, Mr. Esherwood moves away from the little boy's corpse and then notices Rupert standing there, observing the whole scene. He doesn't seem worried or bewildered by the fact Rupert has seen him and what he's done. Instead, he seems glad. He appears giddy, delighted to show off his handiwork to his only son. He passes Rupert, gently patting him on the head and then ambling to the car to catch his breath.

Rupert searches the thing pretending to be his mother for an explanation—an admission, a sign, anything. But she says nothing to him. She, too, appears almost delighted that he has witnessed their private ritual. She rests a hand on Rupert's shoulder and gazes at him with such love, such unreserved devotion.

"Come along," she murmurs to him. "It's getting late."

Rupert tries to elbow himself out of her reach, but he discovers that he cannot move. It's like he's been bronzed there, as though she's the only one who's permitted to command him to stir from where he's standing. She does so, pushing him along toward the idling vehicle and Mr. Esherwood waiting for them. Rupert feels numb. He thinks to say something, to question the Esherwoods for what they have done—the permanent nightmare they have brought upon that poor, defenseless boy. But Rupert can't bear to ask them that right now.

Mr. Esherwood opens the backseat door and lets Rupert climb into the chair. He drags the seatbelt across his lap and chest until he hears a soft click. Mr. and Mrs. Esherwood lunge into the front seats, Mr. Esherwood shifting the car into gear and then guiding them further away from the place where the young boy had been killed.

Rupert glances down on the floor and notices the dead boy's discarded apple rolling beneath Mr. Esherwood's seat. He swipes at it, pulling it close to his chest and inspecting it with such fondness, such care—the very last remnant of that poor murdered boy in this world. Rupert pinches the tip of the stem and pulls tightly until it snaps apart in his hands.

As the vehicle drifts out onto the open lane, Rupert lowers the window beside him, and he's blasted in the face by a cool gust of wind. The nighttime chill beats tirelessly against him, and he gazes ahead at the dim silhouettes of the Esherwoods sitting there in the front seats of the car. They don't say anything to each other. They won't even look at one another, for that matter. Instead, they stare blankly ahead at the empty road like a chance meeting between two soulless strangers, the car headlights wiping away more and more darkness as they drift along—their little vehicle splitting the curtain of night open with the unbearable weight of a horrible secret that only daylight can possibly smear away.

The dream comes to an end.

Rupert wakes, sweating and pining for the comfort of his real mother. He wipes his face clean with a cool, damp cloth and then tries to sleep again, even though he knows his mind will forever be diseased with the fresh rot of nightmares.

———

Later that same night, Rupert still finds himself unable to sleep.

He kicks off the bedsheets and straightens from where he had been lying, pulling his knees tight against his chest. Rupert listens to the thumping of his heart. The familiar *boom, boom, boom*—that loathsome internal clock ticking away inside him, counting down the moments until he's inevitably no more. Rupert has always felt as though he's running out of time. The mere fact he's lived all his life in Burnt Sparrow—a town where nothing ever happens and where everyone seems subject to the same accelerated entropy and decay—might have contributed to that all-consuming anxiety. Regardless, he figures it must be true.

Even though he's only seventeen, he worries he's passed an important expiration date—the date when he was supposed to leave Burnt Sparrow, a time when he could have once escaped. Has that moment now forever passed him? Do the Esherwoods intend to keep him as a permanent prisoner of End House? Surely, when he turns eighteen, he can do as he pleases. But that's not for another several months. He might die from the boredom before then.

Rupert climbs out of bed and then begins to pace the floor like those poor, frightened animals he used to observe at the zoo when his class took a field trip to the nearest city. Even though he feels like some captive wild animal, he thanks God he's not shackled to the wall and incapable of moving freely about the house. He thanks Mr. Esherwood for his benevolence, for not keeping him bolted and chained in the cellar like that faceless family of killers.

He's surprised at himself, when he thinks of the faceless teenager, that he holds no hatred in his heart for him. Instead, his body seems to soften—almost like he feels a semblance of unearned pity for the teenager. Why should I feel this way? What's wrong with me? The teenager is just as guilty, just as culpable as his parents. Still, there's something about him that thaws Rupert entirely. He can't possess any hatred or resentment for that boy. It's entirely possible that the parents coerced their son into pursuing their gruesome plans to slaughter those poor, unsuspecting townspeople on Christmas Day.

Comprehending that he cannot harbor any ill feelings for the faceless teen, and finding himself disgruntled at this awful realization, Rupert wonders if his feelings might shift considerably if he spent more time in the cellar. He figures he might learn to hate the faceless teenager in time. He hopes for this.

Easing across the bed and reaching underneath the mattress, he pulls out the shoebox and tips out the contents. The mummified corpse of the little bird spills out onto the bedsheets like a small, white egg bound in fresh cloth. At first, he's afraid to touch the little creature—worried that the insult of his hands might spoil the memory of the deceased thing, might undo the tenuous resolve of the damn creature to remain in this world despite its agony, despite its affliction. Just as Rupert is about to reach out and touch the bandage-wrapped shape, it seems to deflate suddenly as if a hole has been punctured in its side. Rupert, eyes searching the shape for an explanation, unspools some of the wrappings and finds the bird has completely disintegrated. In its place are nothing but broken bits of black ash, like the remnants of precious innocents who had been lost in a house fire. He mourns the creature for the second time. Somehow, it's even more unbearable, more excruciating now. He scatters the bits of ash into the shoebox and then closes the lid, sealing it off.

Rupert is motionless for a while. He feels dirty for having touched the remnants of the little bird with the human face. He feels unfettered, unbalanced at having caused so much destruction in such a short amount of time.

Pushing his feet into a pair of slippers, Rupert moves out of his room and creeps down the corridor until he arrives at the stairwell leading down to the expansive foyer. Gripping the railing, he makes his descent and eventually reaches the final step. He notices how the lights in the nearby parlor room have gone out, the entire house dark except for a few lights positioned in various windows throughout the entryway.

Rupert hastens over to the cellar door and snatches the set of keys from the hook pinned to the wall. It takes him a while to figure out which keys should be inserted into which specific lock; however, after trial and error, he unfastens each lock securing the door shut. He grabs the flashlight that Mr. Esherwood left on the nearby credenza when they emerged from the basement earlier this evening.

Aiming the light in front of him, Rupert opens the door and makes his way down the cellar steps until he arrives at the basement level. Rupert had thought it was impossible for the cellar to be even more unsettling and strange than it was in Mr. Esherwood's presence. He's unnerved to find out how greatly he's underestimated matters. The cellar is eerily quiet, cool air blasting him in the face all at once. He scowls and makes his way further into the dark and toward the corner of the room, where he finds the three shapes occupying each of the small cots arranged there for their minimal comfort. Rupert notices how each of the family members' arms hang over the side of the bed, their wrists shackled and chained to the nearby concrete wall.

Rupert thinks it curious to find the faceless family sleeping. For some reason, he could never envision them at rest. He figures beings that are evil incarnate must not need to rest the way humans do. He's unnerved to find his theories were false, watching each one as they doze softly—their chests rising and falling beneath the white bedsheets.

Rupert, cautious at first, starts to draw closer to the beds arranged in the corner of the room. Just as he's about to reach the foot of the first bed, the teenager shoots up from sleep. His head swivels around with such frantic desperation, the same way a blind man might awake if startled late at night. Rupert recognizes the boy's discomfort at once and tries to calm him. He sits on the edge of the bed and rests a hand on the teenager's arm. The faceless teen, surprised at the touch, cowers a little—obviously fearful. He makes soft whimpering sounds, the noises whistling from the tiny pinhole where his mouth should be. Rupert grabs his arm a little more forcefully, begging him to quiet. After a few moments, the worried teenager relaxes, his shoulders visibly dropping and his breathing becoming less erratic. Somehow, he seems to know that only Rupert is present, and that Mr. Esherwood is not here.

For a few moments, Rupert and the faceless teen sit in silence. Rupert gazes at him, eyes unable to pull away from the unsettling sight of the teenager without a face—his wrist shackled to the wall and the chains rattling whenever he stirs to become more comfortable. From the looks of it, however, comfort is an elusive creature for the poor boy. That's obviously Mr. Esherwood's intent—to see to it that the family of murderers never have a moment's peace as long as they're prisoners in his home. Still, there's a part of Rupert that wishes he could do something for the faceless teen. Even though he had once wondered if being in the boy's presence might encourage hatred for him, he knows this will never happen. There's something about the boy—something that vexes him, surprises him, astonishes him. He can't quite describe it, but Rupert knows it to be true.

That's not to say that Rupert completely overlooks the fact that the boy is an ice-blooded murderer. He knows this to be a fact whenever he gazes at the boy, whenever he catches the dreadful teen in a private moment of reflection. Rupert wonders why the boy did such a thing. If it was his parents' wishes, why did he so blindly follow suit? Why didn't he stop them? He won't know the answer until he asks the boy. So, he does. He rubs his hand along the teenager's arm. The boy's bare skin feels rough like sandpaper.

"Why did you do it?" Rupert asks him, his voice quivering a little. "Why didn't you stop it from happening?"

The teenager makes quiet, muffled whimpering noises once more, wanting to say something. But what exactly? To confess? To seek forgiveness? Rupert waits, almost anticipating the boy being granted the miracle of speech. But no such wonder occurs. Instead, the boy and Rupert are left sitting on the small cot in the dark corner of the cellar like ghosts who have grown weary of haunting the same house after centuries.

Rupert glances down and notices that the boy is dressed only in his white underwear. Even more curious, Rupert can see the outline of the boy's limp cock through the tightness of the material. He holds his gaze there, observing as the teenager grabs himself a little. Rupert then becomes firm, the front of his pajamas tightening. Cheeks heating red, Rupert flies off the bed and hastens out of the basement and up the stairwell until he's out of the cellar. He feels guilt for leaving the boy without any light, but he couldn't have stayed there even if he wanted to. He's afraid of what he might have done. Rupert can imagine himself performing lewd, lascivious sexual acts on the boy's helpless body—sucking him off before eventually mounting him and then pushing himself inside the warmth of his guts until he spills his seed deep inside him. But Rupert can't bear to think of any of those things right now. He tucks his firming manhood to the side so that it's not as visible when he moves, and then begins to walk away. As he does, he slams his knee into the edge of a small table and knocks a few items off. Scrambling to catch them, Rupert swipes at an ornately bound leather journal.

He brushes the dirt from the book's cover and reads the words printed there: CYRIL ESHERWOOD. He can hardly believe it. How can this be?

Unlatching the decorative golden clasp, Rupert tips the book open and holds it beneath the nearby lamp to read. He discovers that it's a journal containing merely five handwritten entries—each entry written in exquisite penmanship.

Rupert reads:

I am ten years old—a freckle-faced tenderfoot who often bites his nails until they're raw and blistered red—when my older brother first touches me below the waist. His hands are larger than mine and his fingers feel cold pressing hard against my skin, almost like long, thin tubes of pork sausage that have been left too long in the freezer. Even though his face shows visible signs of panic—his forehead popping with little beads of sweat, his bottom lip quivering—he keeps assuring me that this is fine, this is okay.

"It's normal for brothers to do these kinds of things with each other," he whispers to me, cupping my testicles the same way your hands form a small bowl to drink water from a mountain spring.

Is that what I am? I wonder to myself. A sacred mountain spring? Something to keep him from becoming parched?

"It'll bring us closer together," my brother assures me.

When he thinks he's pacified me, he starts to rub his hand up and down the length of my limp penis until it begins to firm and grow heavy with the weight of blood in his fist. I pretend to be shocked at the sensation and how good it feels, but the truth is that one of my classmates, a boy named Matthew Fletcher, has already showed me how to do this a few months ago. I didn't want my brother to know I was regularly pleasuring myself, so I continue to pretend this is the very first time I've felt something so enjoyable. My brother seems pleased at the sight, and then when I'm fully erect, he gets on both knees and gazes up at me with a look of frightened devotion I've never seen before.

"You promise not to tell?" he asks me.

I don't quite know how to answer him. I think to shake my head, but before I can respond, he opens his mouth wide and swallows me to the hilt. He wraps his lips around me tight, tongue circling the head of my penis, and it isn't long before I finish. He swallows me and then pulls away, wiping his mouth clean. I'm left standing there in the corner of my bedroom, my penis dribbling wet and slowly shriveling until it's buried inside a nest of pubic hair.

My brother sprints out of the bedroom for a moment, and I hear his weight shifting from one end of the corridor to the other. I wonder if I've offended him somehow as I hoist my underwear up and zip the front of my jeans. It isn't long before he returns with a twenty-dollar bill. He passes the crumpled money to me, squeezing the bill into the palm of my hand until my fingers curl around it and hold tight.

"What's this?" I ask him.

"For letting me," he says. "You promise you won't say anything?"

I glance at the money balled up in my fist—a horrible reminder of what we did.

"I won't tell," I say to him.

He seems comfortable with my promise; however, there's a part of me that truly wonders if he believes what I tell him.

I am eleven years old—face pitted with acne, arms shriveled and withered looking because I've always been such a frail child—when my older brother first kisses me on the lips. His mouth feels warm against mine. He slips his oily tongue between my lips and fishes around inside my mouth for a few moments. I try to shrink and pull away, but he pulls me closer against him with his large hands. His breath doesn't smell bad, thankfully, and sometimes he releases little gasps of pleasure while he keeps pushing his mouth against mine.

Eventually, we come apart and he regards me with such tenderness and care. Still, there seems to be a quiet part of him that remains cautious, perhaps even a little fearful of what he's done—the shame we've summoned together.

"I've been practicing with some girls at college," he tells me, buttoning his shirt until his hairy chest is covered from me. "They say I'm pretty decent."

Then he looks at me with so much distrust, as if he knows that he's already crossed some invisible threshold and can't take any of it back.

"Was I?" he asks, nervous. "Was I decent enough?"

I nod, feeling a little sorry for him, feeling a little

pitiful for him that he remains so unsure of himself even at the age of eighteen.

"I tell them that I love them, that I care for them," he says, his eyes lowering until he won't look at me. "I don't mean any of it. I've never meant it."

A long, uncomfortable silence lingers over the room and fills the space between me and my brother. I don't quite know what to say, what to ask him. Everything I can think of seems so artificial or insincere. I had expected he would meet young girls at college, and he would have his way with them because he's usually so charming. But I hadn't realized how much it would devastate me to know that he's been with others the same way he's been with me. I'm not quite prepared to admit to myself that I want him entirely and want him only for me.

"Why do you tell them that?" I ask him. "If you don't mean what you say?"

He looks at me, a little shocked by the brashness of my question. He probably thinks an eleven-year-old boy isn't supposed to be so perceptive, so shrewd.

"Because they'd leave me if I didn't tell them that," he says, his voice quivering a little. "How am I supposed to keep anyone around if I don't give them things? Or at least tell them what I know they want to hear?"

I probably shouldn't be so surprised by his confession, since my brother had remained so guarded with me until the first time we touched each other last summer. Now, after a year at college, he comes back to me and doesn't want anything physical like last time. Instead, he wants

225

to cuddle in his bed and spoon each other in only our underwear while he kisses the nape of my neck. When we're finished lazing in bed for the afternoon, he goes over to the bureau in the corner of the room. He opens his wallet and pulls out another twenty-dollar bill, passing it to me.

"You promise you won't tell Mom and Dad?" he asks, his voice trembling.

I think of swatting the money away. I would spend time with him even if he didn't pay me, even if we didn't touch each other and fool around underneath the bedsheets. But, out of politeness, I swipe the money from him and pocket it.

"I won't say anything," I promise my brother.

I ask him if he wants to go to the ice-cream shop in town or if he wants to see a movie at the old cinema a few towns over. But he tells me he has plans with his hometown friends later tonight and can't. I pretend to understand even though it hurts me. After I get dressed, I take the money he gave me and make my way to the ice-cream shop. I think of my older brother, still tasting him in my mouth, and wonder if he might be thinking of me.

I am twelve years old — dark hair falling past my shoulders, much to my father's disappointment — when my older brother first makes love to me. He's gentle with me at first, peeling off my clothing bit by bit the same way you might strip the white, tattered bark from a sun-bleached birch tree.

Once I'm naked, he asks me to take his clothes off and I obey without comment. He's much more muscular than I remember when I saw him last summer, veins bulging in his arms and nipples firming at the slightest hint of my touch. I glance at myself in the floor-length mirror across the room and I notice how withered and unseemly I appear in his presence. My penis is shriveled and limp, hidden behind a nest of pubic hair. My arms are thin, toothpick-like almost. My belly is bloated and obscene-looking from too many cheeseburgers and diet sodas. I can't help but wonder why my brother wants me the way he does.

He tells me to turn around and face the wall, so I obey. I feel him press himself against my butt cheek, his cock stiffening until it's completely erect. His warm breath heats my neck and I feel myself soften a little, prepared for the pain he's often warned me about. When he's certain I'm completely relaxed, he pushes himself inside me and rests there for a moment. I shrink, my eyes beginning to water when he slides a little deeper this time. Finally, I sense he's buried there.

He pumps against me once or twice, his hands holding onto my waist, and then he finishes inside me with a deep, guttural groan. I feel my brother pry himself out from me and he releases short, shallow gasps while he admires the spunk he's sprayed across my backside. He grabs a rag from the nearby dresser and cleans me off.

"I'm sorry," he whispers to me, tossing the dirty rag onto the floor.

I watch him sit on the edge of the bed, his eyes lowering.

"I know it didn't feel good for you," he says, eyes avoiding me. "But we can keep trying, maybe? We can try different things. Different positions…"

But we don't.

The following day, I go into the kitchen and my mother tells me that my brother returned to campus early last night and won't be back again until next summer. I don't say anything. I don't tell her about what my brother and I have done. How could I? I certainly don't tell her how I've been bleeding from my backside all morning and have stuffed tissues in my underwear to soak up the mess.

I am thirteen years old—eyes dimmed and glass-like with a look that my mother and father detest with every fiber of their being—when I'm told that my brother won't be returning home this summer. Instead, he's participating in a foreign exchange program and will be spending the summer months in a small town in northern France. I ask if we'll see him for Thanksgiving or Christmas, but my parents aren't sure. They push me away and tell me not to ask so many questions.

I spend most of the summer with my friend, Matthew. We ride our bikes to the old rock quarry and try to catch frogs with nets in the nearby lake. Sometimes we head into the woods to get undressed and touch each other. I show Matthew some of the things I've learned from my brother, and he likes it when I swallow his penis with my mouth.

Matthew tastes different, though. It's a pungent, bitter

taste that makes me gag almost. He smells like he doesn't wash himself regularly and I try to remain as dedicated as possible while working my mouth and hands on his shaft, even though the awful stench nearly makes me vomit.

When Matthew asks me how I've learned so many different tricks, I lie and tell him that I've watched a few pornographic films. He seems to believe me, raking his head back against the tall grass while I devour the area between where his thighs meet. I listen to him make little whimpers, almost like a kitten caught in a steel trap.

For the first time in my life, I feel dreadful and terribly unhappy.

I am fourteen years old—somber-faced and permanently exhausted from sleepless nights and eating junk food by myself—when I'm told that my brother has died. My mother and father, choking on quiet sobs, call me into the parlor one morning and tell me that they have terrible news—my brother has been found dead in his college dormitory after an apparent overdose.

We hug and cry together, my mother and father squeezing me tight in an embrace that feels permanent. We spend time talking about my brother and then we spend just as much time avoiding conversations about him. I don't quite know how to behave around my parents until the funeral is held at our local church.

I find myself lost in a sea of unfamiliar faces, weaving through the tide of mournful guests dressed in black and

229

offering me sincere condolences when I pass them. After
a while, I peel myself away from the crowd and make my
way toward my parents' car parked in the church parking
lot. I pry open the door and slide onto the back seat, the
leather cushion squeaking when I stir there.

I laze there for what feels like hours, listening to the
hum of little birds roosting in the nearby trees. I think of
touching myself, so I lower my pants and pull myself out
until I'm firm. Sliding my hand up and down, up and
down, I can't help but think of my brother. I think of how
it feels to know that he's forever gone—how he left me in
the middle of a sentence. Part of me wonders if he took his
life because of what we had done together—the passion our
bodies had wrongfully invented. However, there's another
part of me that wonders if he left so abruptly because he
knew in his heart that we could never be together the way
he had always intended—the way he had once dreamed
about.

I finish pleasuring myself, spurting all over the back
seat. I grab a towel from the trunk and clean the mess
I've made. When I'm done, I lay my head down and curl
myself into a ball. I pull the crumpled twenty-dollar
bills that my brother had once given me from my pocket.
Knowing that I'll never spend them, I push them between
the seat cushions until they're completely buried.

I wish I could bury my brother—the tender memory
of his scent, his gentle touch, his lovemaking—in the
deepest grave I can dig inside my mind. But instead, I ladle
him into the shallower pastures of my thoughts. Sometimes

I find myself hesitating before I enter rooms, wondering if I'll find his ghost there—pants around his ankles, a pitiful look in his eyes, an invitation to come closer toward him, a voice that tells me not to be afraid—exactly like the day it first happened when I was ten years old, the day when he sewed his shadow to mine with dark thread and taught me a secret language that only we, brothers, would ever know.

When Rupert finishes reading, he closes the notebook and pushes it aside. His breathing is shallow, almost forced. It feels weird to learn something so intimate about his captor.

Regardless, it explains some of his cruelty. Perhaps not all of it, but enough to justify why he's such a monster to almost everyone.

He feels a sense of satisfaction at learning of Mr. Esherwood's infatuation with his brother. It seems so easy to accept that he once felt love for someone, so unreservedly—a person he could never truly possess, a lover he could never wield his power over completely. It explains almost everything about him to Rupert—the power over others he seems so determined to enforce, the way he questions others with a kind of learned suspicion.

When Rupert eventually returns to his bedroom, he locks the door. He crawls into bed and lies there, staring at the ceiling. He thinks of touching himself—surrendering to the pleasure, to the thoughts of coupling with the faceless teenager in the cellar. But he doesn't. Instead, he tries to think of things that upset him so that he's no longer aroused. The list is long. He could think of his mother's funeral. He could even think about the time he cut his hand on a decorative clay pot in the backyard. But eventually a thought enters his mind that he cannot push away, and he immediately regrets inviting such a sickening image to his brain—the grotesque sight of his poor, dead father lying face-down in the mud on the side of the river that carries all his secrets far away.

Eventually, Rupert drifts off to sleep, the horrible image of his father's face distorted in terror feeding off his mind like a blood-sucking leech and poisoning his every pleasant dream.

———

It's very late in the afternoon—almost dusk—when Rupert hears a commotion downstairs.

He has spent most of the day in bed after telling the maid, Veronica, that he was too ill to partake in any activities Mr. Esherwood had planned for them. He has paced the room thousands of times, wondering about his infatuation with the teenage boy in the cellar. He has tried to guess the reason for his fixation, tried to explain it as best he could. But no matter how he has attempted to justify his obsession, there seems to be a glaring obvious fact standing in the way: he was smitten with the boy. *Why shouldn't he be?* The boy had been so tender with him, so unguarded, and so unlike any other young man he has known in the town of Burnt Sparrow.

Hearing the uproar continue downstairs, Rupert slips into his housecoat and then meanders out of his bedroom toward the stairwell. When he reaches the landing, he peers over the banister and notices a group of elderly gentlemen dressed in purple gathered in the foyer. They're greeted by Mr. Esherwood and his wife, exchanging pleasantries. One member of their group stands out to Rupert. The dark-haired man is disheveled looking—his hair wiry and unkempt, the lines about his mouth only exaggerating his permanent frown. There's something about the dark-haired gentleman in particular that resonates with Rupert. He senses a peculiar kind of sadness taking root in the gentleman and spreading wherever he stands, almost like he is planting bits of sorrow wherever he goes. Rupert cowers a little when he recognizes this, wondering if the man might infect him with even more misery, more grief.

"There you are, dear boy," Mr. Esherwood says. "We had thought we lost you forever to your dreams."

"Feeling better?" Mrs. Esherwood asks with a genuineness that Rupert recognizes at once.

Rupert merely nods, still distrustful.

"Here," Mr. Esherwood says, motioning to him. "Come and join us."

Rupert hesitates. But something about Mr. Esherwood —something about his presence, his commanding nature— pulls Rupert along on an invisible wire until he is moving down the steps and arriving at Mr. Esherwood's side like some obedient pet.

"Gentlemen, the young lad will be joining us for today's demonstration," Mr. Esherwood says to the elders.

The group of elderly men look at one another, a little bewildered by the statement. Whispers filter throughout the small crowd of guests.

"Do you think it will be appropriate to have the boy

present?" Mr. Patefield asks, stepping forward and acting as a sort of spokesperson for the group.

"Why not?" Mr. Esherwood says. "You haven't told me exactly why you're here today."

Mr. Patefield nods, circling the dark-haired gentleman standing at the front of the crowd. The somber-looking man keeps his eyes lowered and fixed on the marble floor, as though fearful that a sudden glance at Mr. Esherwood might somehow turn him to a pillar of salt.

"Mr. Esherwood, this is Arthur Pemberton," Mr. Patefield explains. "His daughter was one of the many young children caught in the misfortune that occurred on Christmas Day."

Rupert notices how, when Mr. Patefield speaks, Mr. Pemberton's lips start to quiver, and he blinks as though his eyes were suddenly wet. Rupert thinks. He knows the name "Pemberton." There was a little girl who lived a few houses down from where he lived with his parents—her name was Violet Pemberton. She had starred in many of the school productions. She played Marian Paroo in *The Music Man*. The following year, she played Mabel Stanley in *The Pirates of Penzance*. Rupert had always enjoyed listening to her sing— the way in which she had commanded the stage with her larger-than-life presence, the softness and the tenderness she had brought to every single role.

He feels a sudden pang of guilt vibrating deep inside his chest for not realizing Violet had perished in the massacre a few weeks ago. But so many people had died; how was he expected to keep track and mourn every single slaughtered soul? Still, Rupert feels a tremor of anxiety for not realizing she had lost her life and for not honoring her the way he perhaps should have. *What a waste*, he thinks to himself. *She'll never perform again. She'll never enchant crowds of theatergoers with her infectious and alluring persona.* For someone so young, she had certainly made her mark on Rupert. He feels so much pity for Mr. Pemberton as he stands there in such discomfort, such visible pain.

"I take it that Mr. Pemberton would like to see the family downstairs," Mr. Esherwood says.

Mr. Patefield pulls Mr. Esherwood to the side of the foyer but remains in earshot, so that Rupert can lean in and hear what's being said.

"We've assured Mr. Pemberton that he will have fifteen uninterrupted minutes alone with the family," Mr. Patefield explains.

Mr. Esherwood stifles a hearty laugh. "I expect every mourning mother and father in Burnt Sparrow would want the same thing. But why are we giving him such preference?"

Mr. Patefield glances over his shoulder at Mr. Pemberton and then looks at Mr. Esherwood. "He's made a very sizeable donation to our organization which has guaranteed him certain rights, certain privileges. I know you'll understand. Especially since the guilty party still resides under our jurisdiction. You're merely housing them."

Rupert notices how Mr. Esherwood seems to deflate slightly, almost as if he has been challenged by someone, something he hadn't expected.

"Yes, I suppose I understand," Mr. Esherwood says, moving away from Mr. Patefield and back toward the small group of gentlemen swarming in the house's entryway.

Mr. Esherwood approaches Mr. Pemberton and comes upon him with such force, such closeness, that Mr. Pemberton recoils slightly and seems to look around for direction from one of the elders. The poor man looks frightened, like he had insulted Mr. Esherwood. His eyes widen and he nervously clasps his hands together.

"I'm very sorry for your loss, Mr. Pemberton," Mr. Esherwood says, offering his hand. "I'm sorry we're meeting under such tragic circumstances."

Mr. Pemberton hesitates and then takes Mr. Esherwood's hand. They shake.

Mr. Esherwood glances at the crowd of elders waiting for a sign of approval. "I suppose there's no point in delaying the unpleasantness. We'll begin the demonstration at once."

After motioning for Rupert to follow him, Mr. Patefield pulls Mr. Esherwood to one side once more.

"You're still certain you'd like the boy to be present for this?" he asks. "I expect Mr. Pemberton will prefer some privacy during his visit."

Mr. Esherwood shakes his head and then moves along, unlocking the cellar door. "The boy has already seen far worse."

Indeed. That's very true. Rupert knows this. There's a part of him that's curious what other monstrosities, what other godless horrors he will bear witness to when the unfortunate time comes.

Diary Entry Written By
RUPERT CROMWELL

April 2, 2004

All living things ache to possess someone, something. We yearn to destroy. Unfortunately, I have already been carved out from the inside by those who wished to take more from me than I was willing to offer. I have already been used and am well-worn by others. I resemble something tattered, almost threadbare, but not quite completely broken yet. Perhaps still salvageable. Perhaps still redeemable. That's why I'm used again and again—a reliable piece of property, an unfailing addition to their collection of lost souls. Yes, that's exactly what I am. A soul without purpose, without aim. A wanderer confined to an empty room without light. When people realize that they cannot use you as they had intended, they want nothing to do with you. It's almost like your very existence is an insult to their invention, their grand design. "If only I had met you sooner," they might say. "I would have delighted in being the owner of your destruction; in the carnage I could charm from you." Eventually, something that's been used over and over again will dissolve, break down until it's nothingness. Such things are unfairly inevitable. Perhaps it's revolting to admit, but part of me yearns to disintegrate. I ache to rot, to show them how they've taken penance after penance from me for the sake of a few fleeting moments of pleasure. But I doubt my destruction will have any meaning to the elders of Burnt Sparrow. They'll study the trails of my blood flow, the passageways of my innards. They'll make predictions upon my corpse based on how my body slumped when I was finally executed, when the blade cleaved the final petal of thought from the stem of my soul, and I was christened in a current of livid red. I suppose only then will I have a worthwhile offering for them to hold in their sad, trembling hands.

GLADYS
ESHERWOOD

Gladys finds herself all out of sorts after her husband takes Rupert and the other men downstairs to the cellar where the faceless family members are shackled, waiting to be tortured. Although she cannot pinpoint exactly why she feels this way, Gladys recognizes that she's begun to feel heartfelt pity for the peculiar family locked in the cellar. She would most likely never reveal this truth to her husband, or even to poor Rupert; however, she senses parts of herself thawing since they were first brought to End House.

She wonders why she should feel this way. There was once a time when she delighted in the idea of their suffering, their exquisite agony, their unbridled anguish. Her mind often turns to the horrible image that's been burned into her mind—the sight of her pathetic husband, pants around his ankles, forcefully mounting the poor woman like she was a toy designed for his amusement, his fulfillment. That's exactly how Cyril views those who live at End House—as though they are pieces of property to be bought or traded away to the highest bidder. How long will it be before something occurs and Cyril realizes he no longer needs her the way he had originally thought?

Gladys eventually moves from the empty entryway into the nearby parlor. She sits on the sofa and feels herself sinking further and further into the velvet cushions. She presses her feet against the floor and notices the space between her breaths—fleeting little moments when she can rest, when she doesn't have to remain so strained or so forced. She toils daily to remain calm and collected while residing at End House. For her, the very prospect of existence is nearly exhausting. She doesn't enjoy the idea of existence being so unbearable, so shattering. But how else can she view her prospects, with Cyril peering over her shoulder and grading her every movement?

While she idles there on the sofa, Veronica creeps into the room. Veronica's eyes are swollen red and puffy. It's obvious that she's been crying.

"Close the door behind you, won't you?" Gladys asks her.

Veronica does so and Gladys quietly thanks God that Veronica has remained obedient despite her unhappiness here.

Gladys's eyes follow Veronica as she moves further into the parlor, wandering over to the windows looking out over the ribbon of gravel stretching toward the house.

"Where have they gone?" Veronica asks Gladys.

"Downstairs for another demonstration."

"He brought the boy down there, I imagine?" Veronica asks, wiping some of the tears from her eyes.

Gladys nods.

"That boy's soul is going to be split apart by the time he's through at End House," Veronica says.

But Veronica doesn't need to tell Gladys that. It's one thing to care for a young person and mold them in such a way so that they're confident and caring. However, it's a totally separate endeavor to conjure horror upon horror for them and make them suffer in some pitiful attempt to annihilate their spirit. That's exactly what Cyril's doing to Rupert. He hasn't come out and explicitly said this; however, she's intelligent enough to realize his true motivations.

"Part of me wonders if he'll ever leave this place," Gladys says, surprised at herself for saying something that terrifies her. "I'm sure Cyril would like to keep him here for all eternity. To make him play spectator to cruelty after cruelty. To follow in his stride."

Veronica's voice firms a little. "He wants that for all of us."

"You've been crying," Gladys says, looking away.

Veronica laughs, her eyes sparkling dewy and wet in the parlor light. "Yes."

"Why?"

"Because I've decided I'm going to leave tomorrow," she tells her.

Gladys's attention snaps to Veronica all at once. If Gladys was dismissive of Veronica earlier, those attempts to play coy are now quite different. Gladys looks at Veronica with a wordless question, desperately trying to comprehend her. She's hopeful Veronica might understand her bewilderment, her confusion. But Veronica seems so incredulous as she stands there with arms folded.

Gladys can hardly speak.

"You're… leaving?" she asks her.

"I wanted to tell you before I left…"

Gladys deflates immediately. She expected this. Certainly, she wasn't foolish enough to think that Veronica would stay under her employ at End House. That would have been a ridiculously foolish pipe dream. Still, Gladys finds herself completely and utterly shocked by Veronica's confession. *How could she possibly leave me?* Especially after all they have been through, the love they have invented together.

"I take it that you can't be convinced to stay?" Gladys asks her.

Veronica shakes her head, almost looking disappointed that Gladys would say such a senseless thing.

"You're so determined to stay here?" Veronica asks her. "I thought you might ask to join."

Gladys is quiet, thinking for a moment. She has entertained the thought. But how would she and Veronica get by? With what money? After a while, they'd become broke. More to the point, for Gladys, the world began and ended in the town of Burnt Sparrow. Even though she is loath to admit it, everything outside the town's borders seemed so impossible, so indisputably alien. Gladys isn't even entirely certain if life exists outside of Burnt Sparrow. She knows she might sound silly if she ever confesses this, but it's the horrible, awful truth.

"Where are you headed?" Gladys asks.

Veronica shrugs. Her unconcern immediately vexes Gladys. How can she be so careless, so thoughtless and rash?

"It's so easy for you?" Gladys asks, trying to quiet some of the pain quivering in her voice.

Veronica squints at her. "You think this is easy for me? I offered so much of myself to you. I gave willingly…"

"We both gave," Gladys says.

Veronica softens a little, approaching Gladys. "Yes. We did… Why don't you come with me? Things will be different… This place is poisonous… It's suffocating us."

Gladys already knows this. She certainly doesn't need a reminder now from Veronica.

"It doesn't make it any easier to leave," Gladys tells her, eyes lowering. "I wish it did."

Veronica kneels beside Gladys, pushing her hand into hers and squeezing tight. "The only person standing in your way is you. All you have to do is collect your things and walk out that door with me."

Veronica makes it sound so simple. Perhaps it is. But in Gladys's heart, she knows it's not as easy as packing a suitcase and then traipsing out the front door. There are other matters to consider—especially poor, young Rupert. A few days ago, when things were different, she might have more earnestly considered the thought of abandoning everything and shadowing Veronica on her journey of liberation, of total freedom. But now that Rupert has become a guest in their home, she feels a level of protection for the boy she hadn't considered before. It seems inappropriate for Gladys to contemplate the idea of leaving End House forever. How could she?

Still, there's a part of Gladys that considers Veronica's offer. Why shouldn't she go with her? Veronica is her beloved, her beacon of light in such unrelenting, such unforgiving darkness.

Gladys starts to feel queasy, doubling over, and wondering

if she might be sick all over the newly imported carpet. For the first time in her life, she thinks of leaving End House, and of the infinite world outside the small enclosure where she's been trapped since her life began. *Does she dare?* Gazing at Veronica, she wonders…

RUPERT
CROMWELL

Rupert can hardly imagine what horrors—what indescribable catastrophes—Mr. Pemberton and his clan have prepared for the faceless family in the cellar. Even though Mr. Pemberton looks like a reasonable gentleman—mild-mannered, a steely glare, a mouth that effortlessly frowns—Rupert thinks there's the vaguest glimmer of hatefulness and severity lurking behind his even composure. Mr. Esherwood doesn't necessarily resemble the monster that he's proven himself to be.

Rupert wonders if Mr. Esherwood behaves in such a way to put on a show for Rupert's benefit, almost like he is delighting in the poor boy's bewilderment, his confusion. Rupert can't be bothered with such thoughts now. Not while they're inching down the cellar steps and wading into the seemingly infinite pool of darkness awaiting them at the foot of the stairs.

Mr. Esherwood guides the group further into the cellar, lanterns splitting open bright halos in the windowless dark. It isn't long before they come upon the group of prisoners milling about in the corner of the cellar. Right where Rupert had left them last night. Each family member starts to shift slightly, the way blind animals might react to the sounds of an approaching predator. Rupert's attention turns to Mr. Pemberton, who looks as though he's completely at a loss for words. He regards the family members with such confusion, such puzzlement. Rupert wonders if the poor man might collapse to his knees and start sobbing right there on the spot.

He doesn't.

Instead, he seems to recoil, a little suspicious.

"Can they be hurt?" Mr. Pemberton asks.

Mr. Esherwood glares at his prisoners, looking as though he wishes they could witness his loathing, his abhorrence.

"We're still uncertain if they feel pain," he explains to him. "But it definitely feels good for us to try…"

Mr. Esherwood plucks a small knife from the table beside one of the cots and passes it to Mr. Pemberton.

"Here," he says. "See for yourself."

Mr. Pemberton takes hold of the small knife's handle and then stares at the blade. Mr. Esherwood pats him so forcefully on the shoulder that Mr. Pemberton lurches forward, surprised, and approaches the faceless mother. He brandishes the knife in front of her and then deflates quite suddenly, looking as though he might feel foolish for trying to exhibit so much confidence, so much cruelty. He's about to make the first incision—about to press the edge of the blade against the woman's skin—when he stops himself. He stands there, his head lowering like he's deep in thought. Eventually, he turns and faces Mr. Esherwood.

"None of this will ever bring back my daughter," he says, tossing the knife on the floor, where it clatters. "All of this is so fucking *pointless*. You know it's true…"

Mr. Pemberton turns to address the small crowd of elders who have gathered in the dimly lit cellar.

"All this torture… All these cruelties… Nothing will bring back our loved ones," he says. "So, why bother? Either destroy them and get it over with, or simply let them be… Enough of these senseless brutalities…"

Mr. Pemberton then elbows his way through the crowd and makes his way up the cellar steps, until he disappears from sight. Whispers begin to filter throughout the crowd of elders milling about in the cellar. For the first time in a while, Mr. Esherwood looks as though he doesn't know what to do. He's unsettled, his eyes wide and fearful. Perhaps he knows in his heart that Mr. Pemberton is correct. What's the true purpose of all these brutalities?

Mr. Patefield shoves his way toward the front of the guests, pulling Mr. Esherwood's ear close to his mouth.

"We must speak in private," the older gentleman says to Mr. Esherwood. "The committee thinks other action needs to be taken…"

"So suddenly?" Mr. Esherwood asks.

"Would you care to settle it personally with them?" Mr. Patefield asks, his voice thickening with an unspoken command—an unmistakable directive for Mr. Esherwood to relent. "We can arrange that."

Mr. Esherwood pales a little, his mouth sagging with a look of surprise. Perhaps he's never been questioned before. Perhaps he doesn't take kindly to orders. Regardless, he looks like someone who's been trapped, and who understands his well-being is at stake if he chooses not to follow suit.

He motions for Mr. Patefield to shadow him upstairs.

"We can speak privately in the library," he tells him.

"Some of the committee members will join us," Mr. Patefield announces, turning and heading toward the stairwell.

Mr. Esherwood grits his teeth, obviously incensed by the idea of others joining their private dialogue. But what can he do? He knows he must submit to their orders, or else.

With a look of reluctance, he begins to make his way up the stairwell and out of the cellar. Rupert follows him.

When they reach the doors to the library, Rupert gazes at him with a soundless question. The boy wonders if he'll be invited inside for their private conversation. For the first time, Rupert yearns for an invitation. He hopes to be included in their discussion. But Mr. Esherwood immediately snuffs out any sort of hope in Rupert's heart when he tells him that he's to wait outside until they're finished speaking.

Mr. Esherwood and the other elderly gentlemen file into the library, shutting and locking the doors behind them.

Rupert shoves his hands in his pockets, pacing the floor and wondering what they could possibly be discussing. He twists the small pendant dangling around his neck between his thumb and index finger. Thinking of the faceless boy in the basement, he ponders absolution. He thinks of liberation. Most importantly, he thinks of monsters—all kinds of strange, wondrous creatures he had never realized truly existed. He smiles, figuring that if such fabled monstrosities exist, then magic must exist as well…

———

A few hours pass and it's nighttime. The library doors finally open, various elderly gentlemen spilling out into the entryway and shuffling past Rupert as they make their way out of the house. Rupert looks for a sign of what's to come, but they elbow past him as though he were a nuisance, a soulless commodity that has worn out its welcome. Finally, Mr. Esherwood appears in the doorway. His mouth droops obscenely. His eyelids appear heavy.

Rupert gazes at him with such puzzlement, his mouth opening with the start of a question. But Mr. Esherwood beats him to it:

"We've been going about this all wrong," he tells him. "Things are going to change."

Just then, Mrs. Esherwood appears at the top of the stairwell, peering down at them.

"Darling," she says to her husband. "Something's happened?"

"Yes," he says, sighing deeply. "Come down here, won't you?"

Mrs. Esherwood glides down the staircase until she's in front of her husband and Rupert. Mr. Esherwood looks obviously distraught, his mouth opening and closing with the beginning of a sentence many times before he eventually pushes out what he wants so desperately to say.

"The committee has decided to change their plan concerning what's to be done with the accused," Mr. Esherwood tells them.

Mrs. Esherwood inhales sharply. "They've decided—?"

"They think it's useless to keep them here in such a way," Mr. Esherwood explains. "They would like us to abandon all further demonstrations with the prisoners."

"And do what instead?" Mrs. Esherwood asks.

"To let them be," Mr. Esherwood says. "To leave them down there. Completely unattended. Until they finally die…"

Mrs. Esherwood's mouth hangs open, trying to comprehend. "They want us to—?"

"Bury them alive," Rupert says, finishing the grim sentence.

Mr. Esherwood nods, patting Rupert on the head.

"They think that's for the best?" Mrs. Esherwood asks.

But Mr. Esherwood won't answer. His thoughts very obviously elsewhere as he looks off, his eyes seeming to cloud over the way all daydreamers seem to become enchanted. However, it doesn't look as though Mr. Esherwood is enjoying his momentary fantasy. Instead, the man looks horrified, as though his worst nightmare has finally come true.

—

It's nearly three o'clock in the morning when Rupert makes the decision to head into the cellar and free the faceless family, before Mr. Esherwood has the opportunity to bury them alive. He has wrestled with the idea for hours, before eventually sneaking out of his bedroom and creeping down the stairs until he's standing in front of the locked cellar door. He pulls the set of keys from their handle and starts unlocking the various locks until the door eventually swings open. It makes a loud creaking noise and Rupert holds his breath, hoping the awful sound doesn't wake the others in the house.

He swipes a nearby flashlight and heads down into the dark cellar. He can hardly believe what he's doing. A few months ago, he would never have considered himself capable of such a thing. He's not even quite sure why he's doing this. Obviously, he feels a bit of affection for the faceless boy and he's curious about him, but he's still surprised at himself for overlooking the sad fact of all the devastation they've caused. He's not sure why, but he knows they don't deserve to meet such an agonizing end. Even if they are murderers, even if they are monsters capable of the most heinous corruption, Rupert truly believes that they do not deserve such a cruel and careless fate.

Peering into the cellar from the bottom of the stairwell, Rupert sees them dozing in their beds. He approaches them cautiously, his hands nervously fumbling with the set of keys. One of the figures darts up from sleep. It's the faceless father. He stirs, obviously uncomfortable, making soft, mewling noises at the slightest sound of a possible threat. Rupert tells him to be quiet and assures him that he's here to help.

Soon the mother as well as the teenager are roused from their sleep, straightening in their beds and trying to comprehend what's happening, like small children being awakened from a deep sleep. Rupert grabs hold of the shackle securing the father's wrist and pushes the black key into the lock, unfastening the bolt. The shackle clatters on the floor. He does this again for the mother. And then, finally, the teenager. Rupert recoils a little when he brushes against the teenager, surprised at the touch and perhaps even a little embarrassed. When all three family members are freed from their chains, Rupert leaps to his feet and orders them to follow him.

For a moment, the family members idle there, clearly bewildered. They don't seem to respond to him, perhaps a little unsure of his motivations.

Without hesitation, Rupert grabs the teenager's arm and pulls him out of bed until he's on his feet. He does this with the father and with the mother, until the entire family is standing and prepared to move. Luring them the way a shepherd might tend to his flock, Rupert guides each of the faceless people up the stairwell and into the foyer. He half expects Mr. Esherwood to be waiting there with a rifle pointed at him, charging him with questions, screaming at him until hoarse. But no such thing occurs. Rupert is certain someone in the house must have heard the door to the cellar creaking open. But perhaps they're still sleeping.

Once they have emerged from the cellar, Rupert guides them across the entryway and toward the front door. He opens the door and steps outside, waiting for them to follow. But something weird happens. They stop short at the threshold, seeming to become unsettled—almost frightened—at the very prospect of stepping outside the house. Rupert motions for them to follow him, but then feels quite foolish because he knows that they can't see him. *Or can they?* They executed the carnage on Christmas Day with flawless precision. Perhaps they see in other ways that normal human beings are not capable of.

Rupert watches as the faceless people mill about the threshold, hesitant to cross over and making horrible little noises of loathing and disgust. Worried that someone in the house might hear them, Rupert grabs hold of the father and drags him across the precipice until he's outside. He does this again with the mother. And then finally with the teenager. Closing the door behind them, Rupert moves in front of them and makes his way down the front steps until he's standing in the driveway. He looks at the faceless people, bewildered by their caution. They seem to be unnerved by the fact that they're standing on the outside of End House.

Rupert laughs a little to himself. *Why aren't they celebrating? Why aren't they running away from this place? Why aren't they doing everything they can to get away from here, to revel in the fact that they've been set free?*

It makes little sense to Rupert. Still, he encourages them to leave as he waves them off.

"Go," he says. "You're free now. You don't have to stay here…"

He turns and looks up at the starless night sky—dark and infinite.

"You don't know how much I envy you," he tells them. "I wish I could leave, too…"

When he turns back to face them, he finds that they've already vanished. The place where they were standing on the front steps of End House is now completely empty. A wind whispers past Rupert and chills him, so he turns up his collar to warm himself. He looks around, wondering if they've perhaps moved off in another direction. But he sees nothing.

For a moment, he's touched with a feeling of sadness, of unspeakable sorrow. He wishes he could have said one more thing to the teenager he had become so smitten with. He doesn't know exactly what he might have said; however, he would have preferred the chance to say something, no matter what. Even if what he had said was so pointless, so embarrassing, he knows he deserved that moment with him. He lowers his head, realizing that such a time with the boy will never exist now. It hurts him.

Just then, as he's about to step back inside, he notices how he's begun to feel queer. Queasy, almost. He looks down and notices the skin on his wrist is spiderwebbing with cracks, like a marble statue that's been chipped or broken. Parts of his skin begin to harden and then break off like bits of baked clay. Rupert's eyes widen, trying to comprehend what's happening to him. More cracks begin to work their way up the length of his arm, his skin starting to split open as though a seam has been undone somewhere deep inside him. He pushes himself inside the house, flinging himself on the floor of the entryway and catching his breath.

He swallows hard, panting violently. It's then that the queasiness starts to settle. The cracks that were running along the length of his arm have begun to dissipate, disappearing entirely. Rupert shakes his head in disbelief. He can't quite appreciate what just happened. *Could it really be? Or am I dreaming?*

Looking up and glancing out the open doorway, Rupert slowly approaches the threshold and whistles. He stretches his arm out until his fingers are past the doorway and outside. His fingers start to crackle and crisp almost instantly, dark lines zigzagging across his skin and small bits cracking off. Immediately, he pulls his arm back inside the house. Once more, the broken and blighted parts of his skin start to heal and he's complete again.

Rupert collapses to the floor. His breathing becomes shallower and shallower, dreading the moment when the Esherwoods awaken and realize what's happened—the misfortune that's come to settle over the property at End House.

"*What have you done?*" they'll scream. "*How could you do this?*"

They'll chastise him and lock him in his bedroom for weeks. They'll scream at him through the walls until their voices are raw—bleeding, aching. Secretly, Rupert wanted them to feel those things. However, he wanted to be far away when those horrible effects finally came to take possession of End House.

Rupert knows the awful truth while he lies there on the marble-floored entryway, the ground feeling like it could give way beneath him at any moment. They'll never be able to leave this place no matter how hard they try. Instead, they'll have to dwell here day in and day out, suffering the cruelty of one another's company and the sorrow they had unfairly invented when they chose to imprison the faceless family of murderers.

Rupert does nothing. He cannot move.

He sits in the corner of the hallway, knees pulled tight against his chest—feeling as though the slightest movement will cause him to come apart. He listens to the shallow sound of his breathing, his heart ticking away like a tired clock inside his chest, and he waits for the dawn to finally break, for an absolution he knows he will never deserve.

—

It's early in the morning when both Mr. Esherwood and his wife startle Rupert awake. He has been dozing for the past few hours, slumped against the credenza in the entryway. They're shocked when he informs them of what he has done—the monsters he has unleashed upon the world, how he has set them free. Mr. Esherwood doesn't believe him at first. He's completely incredulous, forcing a hearty laugh that eventually softens and sours when he tiptoes downstairs into the cellar and finds the room empty.

It isn't long before he reemerges, standing there in the cellar doorway like some forlorn specter. He can't seem to form words properly, his mouth flopping open and speech suddenly quite impossible. Rupert then informs his captors how his skin began to break apart and crack like expensive porcelain when he set foot outside End House. But Mr. Esherwood can't be bothered with something so seemingly trivial. He's far too distraught.

"Dear, please be calm," Mrs. Esherwood begs her husband.

He pushes her aside, elbowing his way past her and Rupert until he's at the front door. He swipes his coat from the nearby rack, sliding arms into the sleeves.

"I'll see to it that you pay for this," he says.

The way he looks at Rupert seems to promise such cruelty, such unmitigated horrors.

Rupert curls inward, afraid of what Mr. Esherwood is capable of doing. *But will he be able to follow through?* Rupert could beg him to stay, could try to prevent him from going outside and following wherever he thinks the family has run off to. But Rupert doesn't.

If he walks out there, he'll die, Rupert thinks to himself. He knows this. Once again, he stands at an imaginary threshold— shackled in place and begging for a sign to follow. *Do I let Mr. Esherwood know of the danger? Or do I send the man to his untimely demise?* Rupert stirs there, uncomfortable. He can't quite imagine how he might feel if Mr. Esherwood perished because of him, because of his scheming. Rupert's stomach feels like it's smoldering. Is he capable of hurting another person, of undoing them and sending them to their execution? He cannot be certain. Then again, if Mr. Esherwood remains here with him at End House, Rupert knows that his days are numbered. Mr. Esherwood probably harbors a calculated plan for Rupert's destruction, filing away at him bit by bit each day. Rupert realizes that Mr. Esherwood's demise could be considered an act of self-defense. If he doesn't dispatch the man, Mr. Esherwood will surely come for him next, will surely do everything in his power to annihilate Rupert.

Daylight floods the entryway as soon as Mr. Esherwood eases the doors open, wandering outside and down the front steps. Rupert observes quietly while Mr. Esherwood starts to make his way across the snow-covered apron in front of the house. Both he and Mrs. Esherwood watch him carefully as he makes his way through the snow. But something appears off. He looks as though he's slowing down—as if something pains him, as though he's been besieged by some kind of invisible malaise.

"Darling?" Mrs. Esherwood calls out to him from the threshold. "Is something wrong—?"

But Mr. Esherwood cannot answer.

He twitches. Tiny white specks begin to swirl all around him, like he is caught inside a squall of snow.

Mrs. Esherwood calls out to him again, about to step across the threshold and move outside. But Rupert stops her.

"No," he says. "Don't."

Mrs. Esherwood's eyes widen with fear when her husband turns slightly to face them. A gaping black hole has collapsed open where his face once was, the edges of the dark crater breaking apart and then floating away like small petals of sun-bleached paper. Mrs. Esherwood covers her mouth, stifling a scream, as her husband seems to come undone—threads of his skin rising in the air like little wisps of smoke from a candle and then fluttering away, dissolving before their very eyes.

Both Rupert and Mrs. Esherwood watch in silence as Mr. Esherwood breaks apart in the distance. Eventually, he sinks to his knees and topples headfirst into a tall pile of snow. There's a vulgar cracking sound that follows, presumably more parts of him coming undone and then drifting away. Downy white specks—as fine and thick as ash from a bonfire—circle in the air and then spiral away, carried off on a gust of wind. His secrets, his perversions, his monstrosities—now gone forever.

Mrs. Esherwood sinks to her knees and sobs. Rupert had thought it was impossible for the woman to feel a pittance of emotion for the man who so callously and cruelly controlled her life, her very existence. Mr. Esherwood was so monstrous to her. He was an uncaring brute who delighted in the misfortune of others. Surely, Mrs. Esherwood should know this. *So then why does she mourn for him?* But perhaps he shouldn't be so surprised. He had felt the same feelings for that faceless boy who had so abruptly entered his life and then vanished. He had felt that very familiar pang of unexplainable affection for a person he hardly knew anything about. Rupert concedes it's ridiculous that both he and Mrs. Esherwood should mourn these souls so undeserving of their care, their attention. He wonders if he's mistaken. Perhaps they *should* mourn their trespassers. All kinds of transgressions form and remake a person. Abuse and violence shape all human identity. But does such a meaningful act deserve grief? Rupert isn't sure as he stands there at the threshold of End House, staring out at the morning light winking at him and summoning him with a quiet invitation he knows he can never accept again.

—

An hour or so passes.

Rupert and Mrs. Esherwood remain at the threshold, gazing out on the lawn—the world, the endless possibilities they will never savor again.

"I suppose I should go tell Veronica what's happened," she says to Rupert.

Rupert's eyes lower. He's afraid to be alone now. Once, he might have enjoyed the solitude. He might have basked in the warm comfort of nothingness. But certainly not now.

Recognizing his sudden uneasiness, Mrs. Esherwood softens a little.

"That can wait," she tells him, wiping tears from her eyes. "There's no rush to tell her."

Indeed, she's right. They have all the time in the world.

Rupert kneels on the floor, positioning himself so that he's right against the doorway. Mrs. Esherwood kneels beside him, wrapping an arm around him and pulling him close.

"Wasn't it Goethe who said that 'the threshold is the place to pause'?" Mrs. Esherwood asks him.

Rupert looks at her, bewildered by the question. He feels foolish for not being able to answer right away.

"I've been standing at a threshold with that man for many years now," she says. "A threshold he's finally crossed... Life is nothing more than a series of thresholds."

Mrs. Esherwood turns and seems to recognize Rupert's incomprehension.

"He's gone now," Rupert assures her.

"Yes," she says, her voice trembling with such worry, such apprehension. "But we're still here. We're always going to be here."

Rupert's shoulders drop. His stomach crimps again. She's right. The time to cross the threshold has now forever passed. They are true prisoners in every definition of the word—pathetic captives, unfit to be rescued.

"Will you tell me a story?" she asks him. "Something to distract me?"

Rupert shakes his head in disbelief. He hadn't expected her to ask for something so unusual. Rupert feels a dull pain spreading deep inside his bowels, wondering if she perhaps knows he is a failed storyteller.

He thinks of his angelic mother—all the wonderful, captivating tales she once told him before bedtime every night. He'd give anything to be able to tell her a story—to soothe her, to calm her, to send her off to sleep. Then he thinks of some of the stories he's invented over the years—stories that he's never been brave enough to put pen to paper. He feels foolish for never writing them down, wondering if he can remember what he had once envisioned.

Rupert clears his throat and straightens a little, preparing himself.

"I fall in love with Finn Kitrick the day after my seventeenth birthday, and I tell him that I would gleefully undo my vertebrae for him if he ever asked," Rupert tells Mrs. Esherwood. *"He looks at me queerly and I assure him that I'm capable of performing such miracles, such otherworldly wonders—a desperate attempt to attract him, to undo all the resistance I can taste when he's near me. When his eyebrows raise with the visible sign of interest I had been searching for all evening, I tell him how I'd gladly unspool the secrets of ageless constellations from my hair. I tell him how I'd pluck the fetid remnants of a decaying universe from my mouth like baby teeth. I'd pry myself open like a carcass, singing a soft hymn, and I'd let him nestle there the same way an orphaned fawn might seek comfort during the cruelty of a summer storm. If the two of us were truly trapped in a storm, it's unmistakably the very same storm that seems to follow all men who routinely couple with other men—an unhappiness that claims all of us and is expected to be endured for the sake of our sacrilege, our abomination. I know that Finn is vile and monstrous when I first fall in love with him. I love him with the same ferocity, the same unrelenting passion even if he weren't so cruel, so loathsome. I continue to undo my vertebrae for him—night after night—in a feeble attempt to satisfy his desires. I sing to him night after night, lyrics parched for*

affection and music livid for warmth. But I soon realize that he asks for my discomfort and my suffering far too frequently. Things change between the two of us the way all love seems to eventually spoil and rot."

Rupert glances at Mrs. Esherwood, wondering if she's still enraptured, still captivated by his tale. Thankfully, she is. She gazes at him with eyes wide and filled with such amazement.

"I dwell comfortably in the peaceful moments between thrashings—the tenderness to be found only in the fleeting instances between the nightly beatings, the cruel transgressions we craft against one another. Perhaps once I might have opposed such violence, such poisonous venom directed at a loved one, but like all peculiar rituals that eventually soften to routine, these atrocities become a habit that I could never bear to free myself from. I enjoy hurting him. I know for certain that he finds such divine pleasure in hurting me.

"I delight in the way it feels when my hand smashes into the crook of his nose, red and wet spraying my face all at once. I find such pleasure in the moments when I'm pinned underneath him, the firmness of our bodies rubbing together when his fist heats my cheek red with a new welt—another souvenir to be displayed in the museum of affection, our private gallery of living carnage.

"I sometimes wonder what he thinks about while he's straddling me, his curled fists pummeling my face and chest again and again until bones crack with vulgar crunches and blood begins to flow like a secret fountain.

"We are tethered—our agony, our blood webbing together until it forms a gentle current. Sometimes it feels as though a thin rope has been fastened between our ribcages. Every punch, every stroke—a way of knitting us together more and more.

"Perhaps one day we will come apart from one another—our spines disentangling until we're loose and unbound, the communion of our blood softening to a mere murmur.

"Yes, perhaps all those freedoms will occur. But not today. Hopefully, not today."

Rupert swallows nervously, wondering if he should stop telling the story. But when he pauses, Mrs. Esherwood seems to gasp a little—almost like she's frightened at the prospect of the tale coming to an end.

Rupert continues:

"I dream of telling Finn how I often imagine the two of us dying. I tell him how I revel in the thought of him bursting apart like confetti exploding from a cannon. In my dream, I tell him how I pull him close to me until I can hear the drum of our heartbeats hammering together like we shared the same vital organ. We're locked together for a moment, the warmth of his naked skin heating mine. Then, when we soften and our guards have been lowered completely, we explode together—shining bits of gore raining down on the recollection of our silhouettes like a hailstorm at sunset.

"We curl ourselves in the furthest corners of our bedroom like wild beasts after a brawl to the death, far away from one another so that we can heal and properly repair ourselves—a preventive measure that we've learned to accommodate after the violence of every ritual. It's a threshold we cross time and time again.

"Sometimes, I imagine that I can hear threads of our skin gently knitting together, bones stirring and fastening in the hollow crypts where sockets meet, blood drying and whispering away until vanishing entirely like water on a highway in the desert.

"'How's your nose?' Finn asks me, probably realizing he was a little more forceful than usual this time. 'Does it hurt?'

"I respond by merely shaking my head 'no,' my throat clogged with the blood still pooling there.

"'Trent, would you undo your vertebrae for me again?' he asks, his voice brittle thin and pathetic sounding—as if he already knows that he's asking too much.

"But how could I possibly reject him? How could I ever deny him what he lusts after, what he so desperately craves?

"I reach behind my back, across my shoulder, peeling back curtains of flesh, and before I'm fully healed, I pluck the ivory jewel from my spine and present it to him with such care, such reverence—a holy relic that I know he will worship.

"In that sacred moment, I am his God, his Creator. He answers only to me.

"Finn looks ugly to me when he heals after our nightly ritual. I'm afraid it has always been this way. He resembles a Godless absurdity conjured by some careless dilettante—his skin pooling there like liquid metal, his blood viscous and almost rubbery-looking, his bloodshot eyes rust-eaten and loose, dangling by pink threads from both of the sockets I have pried open there. I, of course, don't presume to think I resemble some God-like athlete—a perfect specimen of manliness and brawn—during the moments when I'm most defenseless, the moments when I need to repair what he's broken and shattered. It's easier to find fault in someone else than in your own reflection. That said, I recognize so much disgust in him while he's curled, tucked away in the far corner of the room where I cannot reach him, where the light cannot follow him. I imagine I must look ugly to him as well—my wounds probably resembling grotesque, pus-filled sores. I wonder if he would ever tell me how loathsome, how disgusting I look to him. I've certainly entertained the horrible thought of telling him what I see when he's at his lowest, his most unseemly and pathetic. I think of smearing him across the tread of my boot, hurting him when he can't defend himself. I'm shocked I would think of something so cruel. I wonder if he thinks the same awful things about me. Oh, to peel open his mind and stare unblinking into the consecrated viscera of his every thought—the innards of his most private and most destructive confessions. I would give anything to see that, to truly know what kind of horrible monster he is.

"It seems so impossible to me that humans do not explode after intercourse. Perhaps it doesn't necessarily astonish me as much as it vexes me. There's a cruel, vindictive part of me that wishes we were somehow endowed with vital organs that detonated upon the slightest arousal, the most inconsequential of sexual awakenings. If that were the case, Finn and I would have perished long ago— martyrs of our lust for one another. It would make sense for humans to procreate once and then perish. It certainly would curtail any issues of overpopulation. Children would be raised without a mother's love, without a father's guidance. But public servants who are forced to abstain from sex could easily be implemented to care for the young ones. Then again, what about intercourse between two men or two women? Is it necessarily fair to perish for the good of longing, the sake of desire? It's impossible for two men or two women to create life when they couple the way heterosexual couples do. So, what is the purpose of their arousal? The purpose of their obliteration? I've been told that sex without the creation of life is meaningless—a mockery of the *coveted bond of flesh between two people. There are types of insects that explode after intercourse, so-called 'kamikazes of pleasure.' Since when are we any better than mere insects?*

"While we heal from our massacre, we sing to one another. It's the only way our bodies will properly repair themselves. It doesn't have to be a popular song. Or even a song with lyrics, for that matter. It can be any melody we invent, any tune we conjure for the moment. Sometimes, I'll hum a melody by Gershwin or Berlin. Finn always prefers Cole Porter. 'You're the Top' or 'Anything Goes.' Very often, I find my thoughts drifting away—the music dimming to a whisper—and I think of the heartache, the despair we invent for one another. Night after night. I think of our souls—the invisible bruises we've left there. But just as I'm about to surrender to the unpleasantness, the sound of Finn's humming always soothes me. I think of the sweet music our bodies create when we're bound together in our fight to the death—our symphony of utter cruelty.

"After he's done healing, Finn peels himself out of the corner of the room, and I watch him as he slowly drifts further into the glow of the nearby firelight. He regards me with so much pity, so much unreserved sympathy, while my bruises vanish from my skin and the blood dripping from beneath my nose begins to clot and dry away.

"It's always amusing to me how we conclude the ritual like we've just finished making love—a few pleasantries exchanged about how perfect everything had felt, a kiss on the cheek to prove that we still care for one another despite the hours we had spent enduring each other's cruelties.

"However, this time, when Finn draws near to peck me on the cheek, I lean away from him. He glances at me, bewildered—a

soundless question dangling there on the tip of his tongue. I've never denied him something before. Why should I be so brazen to start now?

"'I have to ask you something,' I say to him, my voice so deep that I surprise myself.

"Finn seems to realize the grimness lingering in the corners of my mouth—the soft places where he had once split my lip open now weaving together until the wounds are closed. He sits on the edge of the bed, wrapping a towel around his waist to cover himself.

"I shift in the corner where I've separated myself—the place where I'm free to heal, to mend the broken parts of my body from our ritual. I think of all the moments that Finn and I have wasted hurting one another—the promises we've made to each other that 'tonight will be the last night.' Unfortunately, those promises—though noble—were hollow and insincere.

"'Would you stay even if we couldn't hurt each other?' I ask him. 'Would you stay with me even if you couldn't use me as your personal punching bag?'

"Finn looks confused once more, almost like he doesn't quite comprehend what I'm asking. He tilts his head at me, his lips parting and mouth hanging open.

"I ask him again: 'Well, would you?'

"Finn seems to realize all at once. His face thaws with a smile, his lips curling as if he had been hooked there by some invisible, cosmic fisherman. He shakes his head with a look of disappointment.

"'What's gotten into your mind?' he asks me. 'What are you thinking about?'

"I crawl from the corner of the room, further into the light, when I feel comfortable. I can sense my body has healed and I'm fit once again.

"'We always promise ourselves we'll stop,' I tell him.

"'What's the point?' he says. 'We can't hurt each other. We might as well take advantage of that fact.'

"I shake my head. 'Don't you want to be normal for a day? Don't you want to forget what each other's blood tastes like?'

"Finn looks at me with such astonishment, a look of worry slowly crawling its way across his mouth like a fat caterpillar when he frowns.

"'You want to change everything—?'

"'Just to see what it's like,' I tell him. 'We'll go back to our routine if we don't care for it. But can't we at least try it for one night?'

"I watch Finn as he folds his arms across his chest. He pouts a little like I imagine he did when he was a small child.

"'It won't be for long,' I promise him. 'Just to be normal for a day.'

"But Finn doesn't look convinced. He looks at me with such spitefulness—as if to finally say, 'Darling, you and I will never be normal.'

"It's early in the morning when I crawl out of bed and make my way into the kitchenette. I find Finn already there. He's bent over the stovetop, eggs and bits of bacon sizzling hot in the center of a pan.

"'I didn't hear you wake up,' I tell him, swiping a cup from the counter and pouring some lukewarm coffee. 'I thought you had already gone to work.'

"Finn ladles the eggs and bacon onto two nearby plates, dumping the pan into the kitchen sink.

"'I took today off,' he tells me. 'I wasn't feeling well.'

"I think it's odd that he's been so flippant about calling out of work lately. I don't mind that he's here more often. But it makes me wonder if his employers are delighted with his absences.

"I pull a chair out from under the table and ease myself into the seat. 'I suppose we could try to meet with the wedding planner earlier if you're off today.'

"Finn approaches, sliding the plate piled with scrambled eggs in front of me. It feels unfamiliar to be served by him. He's never done this before. It makes me wonder if he's actually trying, if he's actually dedicated to the idea of being more conventional, more normal.

"When he sits beside me at the table, I steal a second to observe him—the dimples in his cheeks when he grins, the way he pushes his hair to one side, the lines around his eyes when he squints at me. It seems so extraordinary to regard him without the bruises, the welts I inflict upon him nightly. He almost looks like a completely different person when he's dressed and sitting at the table in our kitchenette. When the two of us are locked in our ritual, we are ferocious, remorseless beasts. But in daylight, we are something else entirely. We are disturbingly human.

"'Can I ask you something?' Finn says, forking a piece of bacon on his plate.

"I nod.

"'Do you remember the first time you thought of something truly violent?' he asks. 'Something that shocked you. Something that made you wonder if you were a terrible person for thinking such a thing.'

269

"'I don't know if I care for that question,' I tell him, lowering my head and spearing some eggs with my fork. 'We already promised we wouldn't do anything wild or cruel to each other today.'

"'For Christ's sake, we can't even talk about it?'

"Finn's voice sounds brittle, like it's on the verge of almost splintering apart. He sounds hurt. I can tell he's trying to connect with me on some crude, baseless level.

"'Why do you want to know that?' I ask him, throwing a glance his way. 'You're curious?'

"'I think you can tell a lot about a person by what they think about,' he says, taking a bite.

"It's a question that I've known the answer to for quite some time. The moment he's talking about lives with me permanently, almost like a spirit that's been tethered to my shoulder.

"'I suppose if you can't think of anything, that's okay, too,' he tells me.

"'No. I know what I thought about,' I say to him, inhaling deeply.

"I tell him about how when I was younger, I would often disable the child filter on our family's computer and search for the obscenest phrases. Eventually, I came across a blurry video of a busy market in Baghdad—a kind of rare security-camera-type footage. The video's title was: 'Some Like it Hot.' I recall how the shot remained fixed on the small marketplace, people milling about the open gallery and shopping. It wasn't long before a young man in dark clothing entered the frame and started barking obscenities. Just as people were closing in on the man, he opened his jacket and revealed something dark and small: a grenade. He pulled the pin and then held the device close to his heart. There was a bright flash and the camera shook, the entire screen filling with smoke

before cutting to black. Finn shakes his head when I finish telling the story.

"'I asked you about the first time you thought of something terrible and violent,' he says.

"'You didn't let me finish,' I tell him. 'When I finished watching that awful video, I thought of how I wanted to do the very same thing—to step into a crowded place with one of those things and gently pull the pin.'

"Finn recoils. Perhaps he's a little shocked by my confession.

"I stir in my seat, pleased with myself for appalling him.

"'What about you?' I ask him. 'Surely, there's a reason you asked me that. Something you want to tell me?'

"Finn's eyes lower. He avoids looking at me for a few seconds.

"'I can't,' he says.

"'Why not?'

"Finn inhales sharply and then pushes all the words out at once. 'Because I didn't start thinking violent things—truly violent things—until we first met.'

"Normally, I would have been frightened by his confession. But for some inexplicable reason, I'm not. A part of me had expected it. We've brought out the worst in one another, and I know in my heart that we'll continue to undo each other until both our bodies are withered and bloodless.

"I think we've perhaps survived a day of normalcy when everything is suddenly upturned, Finn asking me if I will once again undo my vertebrae for him. I remind him of what we decided. I tell him how we can't go on hurting one another night after night, singing softly to our wounds as our only means of survival. But he's adamant. He begs me. He tells me he cannot

go another moment without partaking in my ferociousness, my savagery. Finn knows exactly what to say to please me, to entice me, to indulge me. Even though I know better, and even though I promised myself I wouldn't be persuaded by him, I agree to his heartless whims. I reach over my shoulder, lift my flesh like it were a jacket and then remove another inch—a bleached gemstone as small as a pebble—from my spine. I present it to him with all the care and fondness of a mother handing over a newborn to another caregiver. He takes it and seems pleased for the moment. It's then we start to hurt one another. I had expected this. I had anticipated that a piece of my vertebrae wouldn't be enough for him and that he'd crave more from me. We pummel one another with our fists, our blood hosing the walls and dyeing the bedsheets dark. We curl into one another like cottonmouths in a nest, each horrible stroke against each other starting to undo all the love and compassion we had invented for the day. When we're finished beating against one another, we shuffle into our private corners of the bedroom to heal and repair the damage we've done. I'm crumpled, torn, and leaking everywhere. I wonder if I even have the strength to sing a song tonight, to help Finn regenerate. Somehow, I find the strength deep inside me and I start to hum a melody composed by Franz Liszt. My humming sounds watery and almost rotted. I cough on blood. My throat burns scalding hot. I gaze across the room at Finn, where he sits tucked away in the corner—his skin webbing together, his blood drying up. But he's not singing to me. He's not making any movement, any sound. Instead, he sits there, staring at me. I beg him with a look, hoping he might take pity on me, hoping he might start to hum so that I won't perish from my injuries. But he does nothing. He simply idles there, observing me with an undeniable look of hatred, waiting for my body to crumple up and drain out like a punctured carton of tomato juice. My vision blurs and becomes thinner. It hurts to breathe. I turn away from him, agony claiming me, and I know that Finn will never sing for me ever again. I feel myself loosen, the ivory ladder of my vertebrae finally and completely coming apart until I'm pallid and impossibly soft."

After he finishes telling the story, the weight of the last sentence hangs heavy in the air between them like a damp curtain of fine mist. Rupert wonders if Mrs. Esherwood might compliment him for his imagination, might congratulate him on inventing something so bold, so exciting and new.

She doesn't.

She says nothing.

Instead, she curls herself into a corner and tucks herself away like she is attempting to hide from everything—from the outside world, from the darkness, even from poor, defenseless Rupert.

There's a stillness after every story told—a queer kind of silence that takes hold of those who were subjected to the tale and forces them to come to terms with what they've been told, what's true, what's false, what remains to be seen. Thoughts are permitted, feelings are welcomed, while the single note of the story in question lingers over the space like some kind of vicious haunting, some incurable wraith desperate to possess, fervent to beguile and mystify. For poor Rupert, he feels spent, like he has hollowed out so much of himself and offered it to Mrs. Esherwood for her approval, her blessed sanction.

Rupert sits still. For a moment, he's impressed with himself and how he articulated the story he has been writing in his mind for several years now. Once again, it's a tale about thresholds—a legend about crossing a line and testing one's limits. Rupert is hardly surprised at himself for conjuring such a story at such an appropriate time. He wonders if he'll ever finish writing it down. If, perhaps, he'll take to writing now. He has all the time in the world stretching in front of him—an immeasurable length of time staring back at him and quietly mocking him, the way a small bird might mimic the sound of trespassers in their woodland kingdom.

Glancing at Mrs. Esherwood, he's met with a frightening look of apathy from her—a horrible kind of indifference at what's to happen to them, how they're to survive, how they're to carry on. Perhaps none of those things matter to her any longer. Do they matter to Rupert still? He's not certain.

"It's going to be dark again soon," Rupert says quietly, twisting the emerald pendant dangling from around his neck and praying for protection.

"Yes," Mrs. Esherwood tells him, her voice faint and thin. "It's going to be dark soon…"

Darkness, at a time like this, seems like something that Rupert's father might have once called "a backwards miracle." In the agonizing stillness, Rupert tilts his head and wonders if he hears someone—*something*—whistling. It sounds like a pathetic lament—a mournful dirge for all the thresholds he will never cross again, a somber poem to welcome him to his now eternal tomb.

Rupert reaches to turn on the small lamp arranged on the nearby credenza.

"No. Don't," Mrs. Esherwood orders him, the brittle sound of her voice suddenly very unfamiliar to Rupert, as though she were shrugging out of herself and exposing all the true horrific wonders of her being, her monstrousness.

"Let it be dark," she says.

End Of Book I

ACKNOWLEDGMENTS

There are two people to whom I'm forever indebted for assisting me with the creation of what would eventually become *We Are Always Tender with Our Dead (Burnt Sparrow Book 1)*. Those two people are Cath Trechman and George Sandison. Cath championed the book early on in proposal form and heartily encouraged Titan to purchase the trilogy of novels. Both Cath and George were hugely influential and helpful during the editorial development process of crafting the several drafts of this novel.

To that end, I am eternally grateful for the entire Titan Books team for their kindness and thoughtfulness throughout the publishing process. I send my sincerest gratitude to Katharine Carroll, Kabriya Coghlan, Hannah Scudamore, and Charlotte Kelly.

I must extend my heartfelt thanks to my dear friends Clay McLeod Chapman and Rachel Harrison for reading an early draft of the novel and encouraging me to be bolder, fiercer, more feral. I also owe so much gratitude to my literary agent, Priya Doraswamy, for her guidance and friendship as well as my Film/TV manager, Ryan Lewis, for his unwavering support.

Finally, I send all my love and appreciation to my boyfriend, Ali, for his everlasting joy and affection.

ABOUT
THE AUTHOR

Eric LaRocca (he/they) is a three-time Bram Stoker Award® finalist and Splatterpunk Award winner. Named by *Esquire* as one of the "Writers Shaping Horror's Next Golden Age" and praised by *Locus* as "one of the strongest and most unique voices in contemporary horror fiction," LaRocca's notable works include *Things Have Gotten Worse Since We Last Spoke*, *Everything the Darkness Eats*, *The Trees Grew Because I Bled There: Collected Stories*, and *This Skin Was Once Mine and Other Disturbances*. His novel, *At Dark, I Become Loathsome*, has already been optioned for film by *The Walking Dead* star Norman Reedus. He currently resides in Boston, MA with his partner. For more information, please visit *ericlarocca.com*.

For more fantastic fiction, author events,
exclusive excerpts, competitions, limited editions and more

VISIT OUR WEBSITE
titanbooks.com

LIKE US ON FACEBOOK
facebook.com/titanbooks

FOLLOW US ON TWITTER AND INSTAGRAM
@TitanBooks

EMAIL US
readerfeedback@titanemail.com